COLD CLEAR MORNING

COLD CLEAR MORNING

LESLEY CHOYCE

Porcepic Books
an imprint of

Beach Holme Publishing
Vancouver

This book is published by Beach Holme Publishing, 226-2040 West 12th Avenue, Vancouver, B.C. V6J 2G2. This is a Porcepic Book.

The publisher gratefully acknowledges the financial support of the Canada Council for the Arts and of the British Columbia Arts Council. The publisher also acknowledges the financial assistance received from the Government of Canada through the Book Publishing Industry Development Program (BPIDP) for its publishing activities.

The Canada Council | Le Conseil des Arts
for the Arts | du Canada

BRITISH
COLUMBIA
ARTS COUNCIL
Supported by the Province of British Columbia

Editor: Michael Carroll
Production and Design: Jen Hamilton
Cover Art: *Childhood Memories* by Joanne Chilton. Used with the permission of the artist.
Author Photograph: Larry Battle

Printed and bound in Canada by Houghton Boston, Saskatoon.

This book is printed on Eco Book stock from New Leaf Paper using vegetable based inks. The stock is 100% ancient-forest-free paper and 100% post-consumer recycled.

A special thanks to Julie Swan for her editorial advice and assistance.

National Library of Canada Cataloguing in Publication Data

Choyce, Lesley, 1951-
  Cold clear morning

  "A Porcepic book."
  ISBN 0-88878-416-3

  I. Title.
PS8555.H668C64 2002   C813'.54   C2001-910120-1
PR9199.3.C497C64 2002

ONE

I saw the boat before I even saw the house. It was there in the front yard with a FOR SALE sign on it. My old man's latest creation was about thirty feet long. I knew she was made of good wood, every inch of her. The cabin was painted glossy red. The boat sat on a cradle of logs, propped on all sides by sturdy spruce poles as if waiting for a really high tide, a Noah's ark of a flood to come and lift her off her resting place. There was a name painted on the side, my mother's name—HELEN. I knew what that meant. My father hadn't gotten over her yet.

I pulled the car to a stop in the driveway and got out. I heard the sound of old clamshells cracking underfoot. It was a white driveway, calcium-pure from years of dumping shells on it. It didn't look any different from when I was a kid. I tried to focus clearly on where I was and closed my eyes. Gull shrieks in the distance. Wind in the tops of the spruce trees. Smells. The forest out back of the house. A billion spruce trees, a carpet of moss, bogs, lichen, bugs everywhere. Saltwater sea someplace in the backdrop of it all. Home, Nickerson Harbour. Crunch of clamshells as I took the first few steps and my legs almost gave out.

The only way I could get those legs moving to get around the house toward the back door was to put one foot after the other, give them directions like a Hollywood director, remove myself to some other safer plane of existence and tell the actor who was inside this body to move it mechanically from point A to point B. Camera pulling away to a safe distance—above and back, a dolly shot. Things were going better than I'd thought possible.

Then the door opened. My father. So many years it had been without a face-to-face. Looked like seventy on his face. Add to it shock, surprise, some kind of hopeful excitement. He took a step forward, then had to steady himself on the railing. I knew there were rules to this game of return. I knew what I wanted to do. I wanted to throw myself in his arms and pretend I was a little boy, I wanted to say, "I'm sorry, I'm sorry, I'm sorry," but I knew it wouldn't be what he wanted. Or at least I was afraid to gamble. I'd seen him crack only once. Didn't want to see it again.

I nodded toward the boat in the front yard, put on the voice of an up-the-road Halfway Harbour fisherman. "What do you want for 'er?"

He was smiling now. "Give her away free to a good home. Only a fool would buy a boat to ride around in on an ocean with no fish."

"Good-looking boat, though. How many hours went into her?"

"I gave up counting."

Then I dropped the script. "You're still a damn fine builder, Dad."

He stepped forward, put his big bear arms around me, and squeezed hard. "Taylor Colby. I can't believe you're finally home."

I hugged the old man as tightly as I could. "I can't quite believe it, either. I guess I had to come back sooner or later."

I pulled off and he held me at arm's length, looking me straight in the eyes. "Sooner would have been better. But later is just fine if that's what I have to settle for. Gets pretty lonely around here."

"Nothing's changed much."

"Not on this shore. People have kids, the kids move away. Old guys like me stay here and do the only things we know how to do."

"Build boats."

"Build boats that no one needs and then we sit inside watching *Oprah* just to see how screwed up the rest of the world is. Don't know who's in sadder shape, us or them."

"I believe it's them. But just be sure to include *me* along with *them*."

"Come in, come in. I'll get you tea or rum or both if you like."

"Both would be just fine." I couldn't believe how small the back porch had grown over the years. Once it had been the size of a football field. Now it took two steps to cross. The back door was low and the house itself had diminished in stature during the years of my absence. But in the kitchen an old oil stove still sang its sombre little tune, the kitchen table was still a solid slab of forest oak, and a picture of my mother at twenty years old still hung over the sink. I looked at it and shook my head. "Jesus, Dad, you're some case."

He waved his hand in the air. "Your mother was a good-looking woman. No harm keeping her picture around."

"So you stare at it every time you wash the goddamn dishes?"

"Makes me wish she was still here to do them herself."

"She was never partial to housework."

"But she had her good points."

There we were already into the conversation. I had to ask. "You ever hear from her? She still in Ontario?"

My father sat at the kitchen table and looked at his hands. He put his right thumb in the palm of his left hand and seemed to trace the crease of his lifeline with his nail. "She's been gone a long while. Must be me or something. First she goes and then you."

"That's not the same at all." I suddenly found myself sounding overzealously defensive. My mother had left him—just walked out. Left us, that is, a long time ago when I was a kid. I had to watch my father fall apart and pull himself back together. I had to try not to show how hurt I felt that she had abandoned me, too. So I pretended for a long time that it didn't matter. But it mattered, all right.

"Sorry. I know it was different." He filled a kettle with water and placed it on the stove, then went to the fridge. "I forgot. Not a drop of rum in the house. Keeps me from doing something stupid. But I got a couple of beers here somewhere." Two bottles appeared in his hands and he smacked them down on the table. He twisted off the caps and offered me one. "Cheers."

"Cheers." The beer slid down my throat smooth as silk. "You never got over her."

"Never did. Some men are like that."

One swallow of beer and suddenly I was being escorted into the darkest of dreams. Not his dark dream, however, not the sad melodrama of my old man enduring the near-ancient loss of a wife who ran away on him.

"I guess the Colby men never get over their women," I said. "A sad pair, the two of us."

He studied the look of anguish on my face. "This town has never been able to accept what happened to Laura."

"Neither can I. I was afraid to come back here. Afraid her parents would blame me. Afraid they'd all blame me. After all the years of blaming myself, I still can't accept it. I loved her, Dad."

"I know you did, son." Over four years had passed before we had finally arrived at this conversation. My eyes welled up again, and I slugged back some more beer. *Laura, Laura, Laura.* Recently my memory had begun to erase the Laura I knew here when we were kids, growing up on the shorelines of Nickerson Harbour. The sun in the trees, the deep dark clear water. The love. All I'd been able to hang on to was the Laura I knew toward the end. The party freak, the wild one, the daredevil woman she had become in California. The one who overdosed and died. Now that I was back in Nova Scotia, I would have to reacquaint myself with the girl I had fallen in love with a long time ago. And it was going to hurt like hell.

"I don't know if I can stay long," I said. My head was about to explode.

"That's your decision. Stay as long as you can. You're always welcome here. And it's bloody good to have you back."

"Yeah. It's been a long time. But I guess we both said that already. Have you really heard from her? From Helen?" I didn't want to use the word *Mom.* Afraid to. *Helen* gave it some distance.

My father had drained his beer and got up for another pair of Mooseheads, which he set down with a thunk on the table. "There wasn't a word from her for a long time. Then a couple of Christmas cards. Then a couple of mimeographed newsletters from her and that guy Frank. Then some short letters and a phone call. It got quite regular there for a while—weird as all get out. We'd have these polite, meaningless conversations about the weather here and the weather in Toronto—Scarborough or wherever the hell it is she lives. And then nothing again for a while. About a month ago she called and started talking about taking tests."

"What do you mean, tests?"

"I don't know. She had some health problems, I guess. Doctors had her taking some sort of tests. I haven't found out anything yet. She thinks they just do it so they can collect their fees."

"Probably nothing." I refused to let myself feel any genuine concern for a mother who had messed up my life so much. Tests? Big deal. She always wanted so much attention, had to be the centre of attraction. Always wanted too much of everything. And she had left because she felt my old man wasn't giving enough to her, or that he wasn't good enough for her. After that the town pitied Horace Colby. And so did I.

"Probably. Still, she and I aren't young anymore. Anything could go on you at any time."

"Something screws up, they got replacement parts for it now. New pump this or that, new ticker. Out in California women get tired of the way they look, they get a new face and new set of boobs. When they wear out, they go in for a thirty-thousand-mile special and get another set."

"Yeah, I heard about that on *Ricki Lake* or somewhere."

"Christ, Dad, you watch *Ricki Lake*?"

"I still think about you out there by that Pacific Ocean, and sometimes when I watch TV from out your way, it makes me feel like I have some idea of what your life must be like." A little beer was trickling down from the corner of his mouth because of a smile that had cracked through. He was tuning me up to play a happier riff than the one we'd been playing.

"That's right, Dad. I've been meaning to tell you. In my spare time I'm a transvestite belly dancer going steady with a sumo wrestler."

"Just don't tell the kids around here. Some of them know about your music and think you're a legend. You leak news of this and pretty soon all the boys along the shore will be wearing dresses and high heels."

I shook my head and felt the warmth well up from deep inside. Staring at the intricate grain of tabletop wood beneath the shellac finish, I thought I saw a reflection of a little kid eating a breakfast bowl of cereal a long time ago in another lifetime, in another world where everything was safe and predictable. Where nothing ever went wrong because nothing ever could go wrong.

Two

Every time I lay down on my old bed, I felt myself shrinking back to being a kid again. Twelve years old, ten years old. A long backward trip in time. I felt myself slipping into some numb zone. What was it going to take to survive crashing head-on into my long-lost self on this, my shameless pilgrimage to my home? It was midnight. Zero ground. My private dark time of having to remember the perfect childhood abbreviated by my mother's leaving.

"She ran away," I used to tell Laura in my most angry, desperate moments. "I'll never forgive her."

Laura's voice was still in my head. Laura the brave one, the stronger one in so many ways. We shared an exclusive inner circle of close communion for so many years. Dreams, dreams, and more dreams.

I switched on the light and was surrounded by my old stuff. This had been my life. A good kid growing up in a little fishing community in some impossibly out-of-the-way part of the Nova Scotia coast. That was me in the mirror. Older now. Stupider. Doesn't know what to do next with his life. By the mirror, I saw an old game: Snakes and Ladders. Perfect. You rolled the dice or flicked the spinner, moved ahead two squares, or ten, or got a double and went again. You almost got to the top of the board, then you snagged the "snake" and slithered back down near the bottom. You were king. You were gloating and laughing with deep childish satisfaction at those beneath you. Next thing you knew you were back at the bottom where you belonged. Sucker.

I saw the spiders in the corner of the room now. Glad to have the company. Nova Scotian spiders never did any harm. My father could never kill one. "They eat the bugs that would chew up the wood," he'd say. "Nothing wrong with spiders."

It would be at that moment that I'd hear a loud *whack* as the rolled-up *Chronicle-Herald* whomped down hard on the spider and killed it. My mother's voice announcing, "Jesus, you'd think we were a pack of lunatic hillbillies." *Whack* again, and my father cringing. But he couldn't bring himself to raise his voice or an arm to stop her.

My father and mother were as different as night and day. He adored everything he had and everything that we were. She was never satisfied. In the end she took out her revenge on us in the cruellest of methods. She left. She ran away. Before she left she spit it out straight in our faces. My mother was no coward.

"You know I can't live like this forever. I don't want to blame you, Horace. It's just that nothing changes. You knew I was expecting more. I just can't live like this anymore."

Like this had something to do with spiders crawling through the living room, all of us sitting around an oil stove in a kitchen with an old TV that could barely pick up one station. It meant being married to a man who was *only* a boat builder—a simple soul who took so long to craft a twelve-foot dory that what he earned from it was below minimum wage.

Like this was not enough for my mother. Like me, I suppose, she had dreams. But I was twelve then. And by the time I reached thirteen she had walked out. Kids laughed at me. Laughed at my father. "Let 'em laugh," he said, a wood planer in one hand, his face stubbled grey, white, and pepper, the smell of sawdust and the feel of a wisp of shaved pine in my hand, curled up and delicate as something that might have fallen out of the sky. "Looks just like a wave, don't it?" my father would say.

The spider sat frozen in the corner, shocked by the light. This old room of mine had been dark in the nighttime for a couple of decades now. The room belonged to the spider, and here I was an intruder from the other side of the continent. On the wall just east of my mirror was an old pullout from *Surfer* magazine, a centrespread of a guy on a surfboard. He rode a long wall of blue-green Pacific Ocean at Malibu and the sun was out. The water was crowded, but everyone got out of his way. He had a look that said he was oblivious to all around him, just him and the wave. I think I wanted to be like that. I had become interested in surfing because I assumed it was a far-off, exotic California thing.

Soon after I'd fallen in love with the *idea* of surfing, however, music pushed it out of my imagination. Nobody surfed in Nova Scotia. I was sure it was possible; it was just that nobody was around to show me the way. I had watched the waves break on the rocks at Quoddy Point but could never imagine a surfer riding there. Couldn't imagine doing it myself and, of course, never had a board or a wetsuit.

And then music gobbled up my attention. Music and Laura were enough—or should have been. After Laura died, it was Larry, my drummer friend, who saved my life by teaching me how to surf.

I had closed myself up in the house where Laura had died. I surveyed over and over the catastrophe that was my life. I could never forgive myself for leading Laura to this. California. Music. Drink. Drugs. Happy. Happy. Happy. Then something went too far. I could see it going that way but couldn't stop it. Like my old man, in some ways. He saw that my mother wasn't happy. He could have tried to do something to keep her. Instead, he just kept on doing what he always did. He worked. Built his wooden boats. Came home to supper. Earned enough money to keep us. Was a good husband and good father. And that was what drove away my mother. Like Horace Colby, his son couldn't stop the life he was living, couldn't change directions. Play music, get stoned. Party. Have a good time. Play more music. Drive up and down Sunset or Santa Monica Boulevard from one event to the next. Nonstop. My life was a repeated trip down one freeway after the next, at dark, in the night, in the fast lane. Somewhere up ahead, in that endless loop, that elevated highway had cracked, collapsed, and crashed. Then it had all come to an end. Like that freeway in the earthquake. It was always hard to find a direction to point the car after that.

I pulled all the blankets off my old bed and spread them on the floor of my childhood bedroom. For some reason the feel of a hard floor felt good. Above me, the poster surfer remained aloof, back arched, toes planted firmly on the nose of his board. The wave, frozen into a magazine. I stared at the ceiling, at the dust, the two bare light bulbs, the cracks in the yellowing plaster, and I realized I had never properly thanked Larry for surfing and for saving my life.

Twelve days after Laura had been gone, Larry broke the lock on my door at 5:00 a.m. "God, this place smells awful" was the first thing he said.

I was awake but doing my best to imitate a man in a coma. Didn't care about anything, anybody. Larry could see that when he found me lying on the sofa, TV on but no sound. An old Japanese science-fiction movie with a sea creature about to swallow Tokyo.

"Taylor, man, what's up?" Larry knew what was consuming me more than anyone. He had gone completely berserk at the funeral, started screaming at her, then me, then at God, then at everyone. Finally he had fallen on the ground and cried his eyes out while the rest of us stood like zombies. I never cried at Laura's funeral. I was hiding behind my dark glasses, behind a thick curtain of dull fog. I never even acknowledged Laura's parents who had flown there to see their only daughter buried. And Larry had made the whole scene that much more bizarre as if he had been chosen to go insane for all of us. Larry, one of my few sane friends in the music business. A good professional drummer who was no Ginger Baker or Neil Peart, but he knew how to work with anyone.

While all around us the talented heroes were losing it to booze, coke, heroin, ego, or the occult, Larry had wired down a survival kit of his own: one joint, five beers per day, as many gigs as he could nab as a session player or stage drummer. He lived in Venice and sometimes Topanga and he surfed. "Don't knock my system," Larry told us all. "If it works, don't mess with it."

Why I had never surfed until Laura died was a bit of a mystery, but I had a handle on it now. I was this wicked guitar player with a hefty rep. I was *good* at this one thing and couldn't handle being a novice at anything else.

It was 5:00 a.m. in purgatory when Larry broke into my California house. I hadn't eaten for a long time. Wanted to die real bad but didn't really have the energy to do anything about it. "You need a bath, bro. Need to get you into some water. That's why I'm taking you surfing. Wind's offshore. Waves are five feet. Forty minutes from here and I'll have you back to life."

"Leave me alone, Larry," I begged him. But he carried me out of there, heaved me into the passenger side of the front seat of his big Ford station wagon.

"I got two longboards back there. One for you. One for me. Coffee's there in the thermos. Dunkin' Donuts in that bag there. Today is the day you make proper acquaintance with the Pacific Ocean on her terms."

I chewed, I swallowed, I felt a little caffeine kick in somewhere in my brain, sugar slip into my bloodstream. It was almost like being alive. By sunup we were at a beach, somewhere north of L.A., not Malibu. I could see oil rigs offshore. We weren't far from the highway, but there was no one else on the beach. Larry kept talking nonstop about waves, about surfing. "Once you tap into it, man, you'll dig it."

It was still easier to let someone just guide me around than try to make any form of protest. I carried the board to the water line. My feet found the ocean. Just as Larry told me, I lay down on the surfboard and paddled—straight out to sea. The sky was clear and the water was warm. We paddled without even getting our hair wet. I was amazed that my arms knew how to move. Then we paddled some more over to where waves were breaking on a sandbar beneath us. I watched as Larry did this thing I had dreamed about as a kid.

Smooth, easy strokes, then he had it. He stood, let out a loud yelp, dropped to the bottom of the wave, watched it feather at eyeball-level, turned, trimmed, walked to the front of the board, and scooted down the line as the wave broke in fine precision behind him. When he paddled back to me, I was shocked, almost angry at myself when he said, "Good to see you smiling, Taylor. Welcome back. Now it's your turn." I was shaking my head even as I followed Larry's instructions: "Face shore, lie down. Here comes one. Paddle hard."

Then I made my arms move. Suddenly I loved the feel of the warm water, the sensation of movement, of floatation. I loved the sky above me. I loved the feel of my lungs demanding oxygen. I actually felt the wave under me, matching my speed, picking me up. I leaned back, instinctively, so the front of the board wouldn't go under. The wave was beneath me. I knew I'd fall off if I tried to stand. I didn't need that. I felt a rush of speed, and it was as if someone was pumping the spirit of life back into me. I hadn't felt alive for days and had lost touch with everything except my own self-pity. I heard Larry yelling at me now. He had caught a wave behind and was following my first ride. "You got it, man! Keep going. Don't pearl."

I knew that pearling meant to slip too far forward so the nose of the board went under and you wiped out. Had I not heard him and considered the meaning, I probably would have done just fine. Instead I lost my instinctive concentration and pearled, holding on to my board, which was a mistake. The wave, once companion, now adversary, used its converging energy to flip me and the board, slamming down like a fist on the two of us. I didn't really care, because when I came up gulping for oxygen, Larry was right there grinning like a wild man, both arms in the air.

Climbing onto the board again, I paddled out and followed Larry outside to catch another wave. I was laughing at first, speechless, feeling good, feeling *real* good, and then out of the blue, as if I had been struck with emotional lightning, I started to cry. I cried like a baby for what must have been a half hour. Larry sat there saying, "It's okay, dude. It's okay. It's all salt water. Nothing but salt water out here." When a couple of young guys paddled out toward us, they quickly recognized a truly weird scene and caught waves that took them farther down the beach.

When the tears stopped, I screamed Laura's name to the sun. I screamed it long and hard twice. Then Larry had to look away; he was about to lose it. He splashed water on his face and, when he looked back at me, blinked more salt water out of his eyes. Then he dived off his board deep down under the clear blue sea and surfaced. I followed, and when I came up, I knew I would continue to live. I would move my arms and catch waves. I would learn to stand. I would learn whatever skills Larry had to teach about riding the wave, about avoiding the pitch of a collapsing wall of water, about survival.

I learned to surf that day by falling off dozens of times, by getting rolled, pummelled, and gulped by the power of the sea, by holding my breath, by relaxing in the face of disaster, by repeating mistakes until I figured out what I was doing wrong, by taking advice and by doing this thing over and over until it locked into my brain and I was standing poised, erect, balanced, perfectly in control across a five-foot wall of seawater arced in the most graceful, sensual curve ever seen on the planet. The world had colour again—blue and gold—and only in the distance could I see the L.A. smog that reminded me that nothing on earth was perfect.

THREE

When I woke up in the thin grey light of morning, I was still on the floor. Restless night, I guessed, because my face was stuffed against a wall in spider country. My first snack of the morning was lint and dust, but it was better than nothing at all. Neck stiff, brain cells trying to get organized into some kind of useful mode, I sat up and scanned the room of my youth. I'd gone so far, done all that stuff, thought I had it made and then, small bang, back in my old room feeling like a fooled and foolish little kid. I had to do what I did every other morning of my life as a lost soul: find a guitar and hit an A minor chord, wrestle with it until I could find a mate of a second chord and then start to finger-pick.

The only available guitar was the old black one with the stencilled cowboy picture on it hanging by the surfing poster. I picked it up and sat on my bed. The strings were rusty, but they were all still there. Tuning was like trying to persuade a politician he was wrong. It had a sound all its own. Something appropriate for a tin-cup cowboy who had grown up inside the music department at Sears and could never find the doorway out.

Nonetheless, the A minor chord did what it was supposed to do:

confirmed my feeling of being lost and lonely, which was what an A minor chord was designed for. So I hit it several times, worried over the high E string, feathered the low E with my thumb, brushed my callused fingertips across all the strings as if I were a lover of metal and rust. Thought of all the songs that had been written that began, "Woke up feeling like..." Fill in the blank. Country tunes, blues tunes, hard rockin', smoke coughin' electric guitar tunes. Thought about that one I'd been working on: "Woke up feeling like inventory day at the Lazy Boy warehouse/So I did a slow dance with the dark side of Chase and Sanborne..." Then where did it go?

Eventually I found an E minor and a couple of slightly more optimistic major chords and a seventh, finally arriving back in the world of the living. Sweet Jesus, what did it mean to be back on a foggy morning in early summer in Nickerson Harbour?

A tap at my door. It opened.

"Taylor. Son. Great to hear that thing still sings."

"It's a good guitar. My tenth birthday, right?"

"I think you were eleven. And you hated it, remember? Looked too much like a toy."

"Why Mr. Sears wanted to stencil a picture of some sad-ass cowboys onto the front of a black guitar is beyond me."

"Your mother thought it had something special. If it had been up to me, I'd have bought you one of Old Man McCully's rebuilt violins. But your mother thought the guitar was the instrument for this century."

"It was her idea?"

"Guess so. Sorry. Maybe I should have kept my mouth shut and taken credit for it."

"And you wanted me to be a another goddamn fiddle player? This province has always been infested with fiddle players." I knew I'd never have gotten along well with that puny little four-string whiner of an instrument. Guitar was in my soul. Part of me had been sitting around doing nothing inside my head for those ten or eleven years waiting to find a place to put three fingers on the neck of a cowboy guitar and strum my first A minor chord. The rest was history. And tragedy, of course. I shook my head. "Maybe if I had taken up the violin, my life would have turned out better than this."

I hit a fancy, somewhat dissonant jazz chord and set the instrument down. So the guitar had been my mother's idea.

My old man was zoned right in on my brain waves. "I called her last night."

"You what?" The thought of my father still having a civilized conversation with my mother in far-off Ontario sent a shock wave through me.

"Yeah, I called your mother. Told her you were here."

"Why'd you do that?"

"Dunno for sure. Felt like it, I guess. Remember she broke the ice a while back. I thought she'd want to know you were here. Just did it out of courtesy."

"Dad, she walked out on us when I was twelve. She scooped out a big hole in our lives and disappeared—the best I can figure it was because she wanted to live someplace where she could spend more time shopping in department stores. She shipwrecked this family, or what's left of it. And you felt the need to be courteous?"

"Just thought I should, I guess."

I was sitting in my underwear and a T-shirt with a ridiculous message: YOU MUST LOSE A FLY TO CATCH A TROUT. I pulled on my pants and threw on my only shirt. It smelled of airports and airplane seats and a man worried that he was spending twelve hours in an airplane flying in the wrong direction. I looked at my father—sixty-five years old, a stubble of grey and black on his face, shirt half tucked in, shoulders slouched. I tried to make myself look in his eyes, but I couldn't. "Don't you hate her guts?"

"Who?"

I made a fist but didn't hit the wall. I think I'd hit every wall of my house in the California hills until the plasterboard was dented and the paint cracked. It wouldn't work here on these walls of inch-thick, foot-wide planks of ancient spruce. "Who?" I snapped back. "Her—Helen. You're still naming your new boats after her. Like that one sitting out front. You can't forgive a person for doing what she did!"

My father refused to rise to my anger. "That was a long time ago. Not much point in digging up all that stuff." Then, as if the hurt of decades could now be swept out the door and forgotten, he asked, "Want some toast?"

"Yeah. Toast."

"Coffee?"

"What kind?"

He looked puzzled.

"Sorry. Where I come from, there's no such thing as a regular cup of coffee. You have options. It was a joke."

He smiled. Suddenly I saw the wrinkles, a lifetime of them, waves in the forehead, crow's-feet around the eyes. I saw myself thirty years from now, and desperately hoped I could be as sane as this man.

"I'll boil some water," he said, turning to go. "By the way, I told your mother you'd call her when you woke up. Phone's in my room. Number's right beside it. She said to call any time." He walked down the short hallway to the kitchen.

I was outraged. How could he do this? I couldn't call her. We hadn't talked in a long time. We didn't have anything to talk about. I stalked after my father. "You both must think I'm crazy. No way am I going to call her up."

My father was fussing with some dirty dishes in the sink, trying to get the kettle under the faucet. "I guess it's up to you. She just asked me to ask. Nobody can make you."

We'd played this one out before, as if in another life. My father, the diplomat. Why was it that other kids' parents would scream and shout at them, bash them over the head, threaten them with the most horrendous possibilities to get them to study? All my father ever used was the it's-up-to-you approach. It was powerful ammunition.

The oil stove was still singing the only song it ever knew. Same old stove, same old tune, but it was a good one. The room smelled slightly of stove oil, but for me it was what they would have called "aromatherapy" in L.A. Outside, the fog was waiting for me to come out to play just as it had done throughout my childhood. Fog never meant gloom to me; it meant a chance to enter into my private world where vision allowed short perimeters. Fog meant forest and fantasy life and dreams and falling in love with Laura.

I looked at the clock on the wall. Seven. "It's only six in the morning in Ontario."

"Your mother said any time was fine," he said nonchalantly as he plugged in the electric tea kettle.

Exasperated and confused, I wandered back down the hall to my father's room. I sat on the bed and stared at the old phone. Rotary dial. Put your finger in the hole and spin. There was the number. I picked up the slip of paper and stared at my father's immaculate numbers. Sloppy in his dress and personal appearance, a genuine Eastern Shore slob of a harbour boy, my father had learned order and precision in other areas of his life: numbers, tools, and the work he did with his hands, building boats of wood. "A thing well done" was the highest compliment he would pay anyone. I had heard it a few times, but I had craved to hear it more from him.

I dialled the number. It was too early there. I'd get an answering machine for sure. Then I'd feel free to vent my anger into it. Or I'd get the man she lived with, the man she married. There was a lot I could say to him.

A phone was ringing somewhere in the early-morning suburbs of Toronto. All too soon a voice answered. A woman's voice. Not fully awake. An unmistakable voice.

"It's you" was all I could think to say.

"Taylor, you called. I'm so glad." I was expecting hollow, meaningless language, expecting the strident, self-important voice I remembered. This was someone different. This was a warm human voice, not the voice of the witch I expected to hear.

"Dad said I should call."

"And you did. That's wonderful. You're back at the Harbour. We thought you'd never come back."

The words caught me off-guard. It was something I might have said to her. "I shouldn't have called so early. Sorry." And then I wondered why *I* was apologizing to her for anything.

"It doesn't matter. I told your father any time was all right. Frank and I were awake, anyway. We both have a hard time sleeping."

Yeah, right. Frank. Good God. My mother's *other* man. I reminded myself they'd been together for a long time. It wasn't exactly a flirtatious fling, a one-night stand. Still, I was speaking to my mother and she was lying in bed with this other man. This man I'd never met. This salesmen from Ontario, for Christ's sake. Silence on my end. I looked around my father's room. Big surprise. Pictures of boats. Photographs of her. And me. The way we were.

"I'm so sorry about Laura," she said. "Everyone said the two of you were made for each other."

"Now they say other things. But I don't want to talk about her. That's all over." Although it wasn't. Nothing was ever over. Nothing about Laura ever really got easier for me.

"How does Horace look?"

I guess I sort of snorted. "I'd say he looks okay," I said with venom. *Considering.* "He looks like the same old Horace—or what was it you used to call him, 'Horseface'?"

"I could be cruel at times. I hope he's learned to forgive me."

Nothing I was hearing was what I expected. I wanted to hate the woman who was going to answer the phone. I wanted her to hear rage and disgust and loathing from this end of the phone slamming into her ear at 6:00 a.m. in Ontario. Why was it I couldn't rally the hate I had been cultivating for so long?

Now I heard her say something to this other man, this Frank, with her hand over the phone. Then she was back on the line to me. "There. Frank's up. He's in the bathroom now. You know how men are. Always have to pee as soon as they get up." I detected a change in voice. She was holding back something. Sucking in air as she spoke.

"What is it?" I asked. I still couldn't bring myself to add the word *Mom* or *Mother* or anything endearing. This was the hag who had made me feel inadequate and insecure for so long.

"I had some tests done."

"Yeah, I know."

"It doesn't look good. They're not sure, but it's possible that it's already spread."

"Cancer?"

Now she was crying.

"Damn. I'm sorry. I'm sorry, Mom." My head was swirling again. "Maybe they made a mistake." I couldn't think of anything else to say. It was a bad line from a TV hospital show, but it was all I had.

"I need to come back to Nova Scotia. I need to see both of you."

I said nothing but discovered I was shaking my head. I felt as if I'd been blind-sided with a rock to the skull. What good would it do for her to come back here? What if she did have cancer? What would happen to my father? I didn't know what to say. What I really felt like doing was to get the hell out of this return-home nightmare, climb aboard another plane, and fly off to Tokyo or Bangkok.

"What about him?" I asked. "What about Frank?"

"Frank's a good man" was all she said. "He's a real good man."

"Yeah, so was your first husband."

"I know what you think of me. But I still want to see you both."

I had lived for so long without a mother. Now I had one again, and she wanted to come back into my life. I took a deep breath. "I'll be here. We'll both be here."

"You're a good boy, Taylor. You were always such a good son." I set the old black receiver gently back into the cradle, then walked down the hall and into the kitchen where my father was shuffling four eggs in an old black cast-iron frying pan.

"What'd she have to say?" he asked.

"She's coming home."

He put the frying pan back down on the cook stove. "Damn." Then a big goofy smile broke out on his face.

FOUR

I didn't tell my father anything about the test results. I didn't mention anything about Frank. As soon as we had eaten, my father started fussing around the house, cleaning. I didn't want to offer to help and I didn't want him to tell me why he was doing what he was doing. I needed a long, cool drink of morning fog, so I went for a walk.

Outside, my recently acquired rattletrap junk heap of an automobile quietly rusted away in the yard. It had been rash to buy the clunker outright from a buddy at the airport, but I felt good about it. I'd hang on to that car. Fix it up maybe. I didn't know why. It just felt right. The *Helen VI* looked grand and glistening propped up in the front yard. White below the water line, red and green above. I could see nothing but the reflection of spruce treetops in the glass of the wheelhouse. My father had started building these cabined fishing boats because that was what the local fishermen wanted. He preferred crafting dories and rowboats, but the demand for them was long gone. And now the days of any fishing boat seemed numbered. Maybe already dead and gone. The seas had been plundered, the cod stock decimated. Nova Scotia had shared the deed with nations from around the world. Dragged and hauled and scraped the bottom until it was like a desert out there on the sea floor. And nobody accepted any of the blame. I decided then and there that I'd buy my father's boat. The *Helen VI* would slip into the sea, fish or no fish.

The village of Nickerson Harbour hadn't changed much since I'd left—at least it looked the same as it ever did in the fog. Fog, blessed fog. It made everything seem like a dream, took the edge off reality, softened all the hard lines. A couple of pickup trucks went by, and the drivers waved a slow, almost unconscious hello. I didn't recognize the faces, but they were old men driving old pickups probably to nowhere, to the store to buy a pack of cigarettes, and a can of tinned milk for their tea. The men of Nickerson Harbour. Fishermen without a future, most of them.

The houses were a fifty/fifty mix of good and bad repair. I felt friendlier toward the ones with ragged greyish wood shingles for siding, several reincarnations of paint, all faded and worn, yellow lichen feasting on the roof shingles. That seemed about right.

Old Acadian-style sheds were slowly rotting into pulp. Moss grew up the sides of one as if the stuff were green fur and the overall impression was that of a large green cat trying to crawl onto the roof. A few junked cars sat in front yards with plants growing through the front grilles and spring flowers reaching out from the side windows. And in every third yard a fishing boat, some of them the handiwork of Horace Colby, was perched on a bed of old creosote railway ties, propped up like a cartoon character from a kids' TV show with talking boats.

This was home. This was where I was at and where I would be from here on—maybe. Hell, I didn't have a clue about what I was going to do with my life now. There was only this one street in town and it ended the same place it had always ended, at the wharf on the harbour. Gulls owned the place these days—old grey-backed birds, probably as bad off as the fishermen, dreaming of the glory days when fish guts flew into the air with wild abandon as men gutted and cleaned their morning haul. It was yet another minor-chord tune, nothing this songwriter could ever find the words or the tact to get right. I was standing there looking at the best of a Stan Rogers ballad or maybe something more ancient than that. Longing for all that was lost, Celtic sadness, Acadian sadness, a blend of fog and sea smells and dilapidated wooden boats and old men at their teapots in the kitchens on an early-summer day where once they'd have been at sea. Good God, how well we knew how to ruin what we loved and then stand back and mourn the loss, feeling sorry for ourselves as if we were the ruined heroes of the world.

At the end of the wharf a kid stared into the water. He wore a Philadelphia Phillies baseball cap, an odd allegiance in these parts. Suddenly I craved talk of any sort, and I didn't have the courage to return to my house and watch my father fussing over the cleanup of the homestead.

I picked up a flat stone and skimmed it into the water. It made a triple skip before it landed flat and sank to join the crabs and sea urchins below. The kid turned to see where it had come from.

I walked toward him and sat. "I used to hang out here when I was a kid. Caught fish right where we're sitting. Big ones sometimes."

He looked straight at me, eyes not blinking, with a look that asserted he hated all adults. And anything that happened before last week was deadly dull, boring, and of no value. "You think I care?"

"No, guess you don't. Sorry." I got up to go but just then something splashed in the water out in the harbour. I saw a head pop up and recognized it as that of a young harbour seal. He lay back in the water and swam on his side straight toward us until he was close and able to look directly at me and then the boy. The seal had deep, dark, beautiful eyes and a comical wire moustache. He was watching the boy intently and now I could see why. The kid had a tin of store-bought mackerel, but he was trying to keep it hidden so I couldn't see.

"He was probably born on Sable Island," I said. "I'd guess he's about a year old. Still young and curious. I think he likes you."

The kid looked at me again. He'd cashed in the hard look for a face that suggested whatever I had to offer wasn't of any importance but that he'd tolerate the sound of my voice.

"You been feeding him?" I asked.

It was as if I'd caught him at an act of vandalism. "No."

"Then I guess you really like mackerel in a can."

The seal was within five feet of us now, eyes eager, awaiting his snack. I had obviously arrived at the scheduled rendezvous time and was intruding on an intimate encounter.

"Got it. Guess I'm out of here."

The fog started to lift ever so slowly. There was a vague rumour of a sun above the clouds that sat upon the face of the earth. The sound of my footsteps on the loose boards of the fishing wharf sounded hauntingly familiar.

"Wait," the kid said. "C'mere." I turned and went back. The seal was in the water almost at the kid's feet now. As I approached, he dived straight down, flipped his tail, then reappeared a little farther out in the dark, clear waters of the harbour. "You won't tell anyone, will you?"

"Tell who?"

"My mother."

"Wouldn't know her if I tripped over her."

"Or any of the creeps who hang around here."

"Okay by me. But what's the big deal?"

"You know. They'll kill it. I've heard them talk. They say they killed two last month. This one used to have company. Now it's gone."

I almost protested. I wanted to tell him nobody around here was into killing seals. But I'd been away for a long time. It sank in deep and fast. "I get it. The fishermen blame the seals for the fact the fish are gone."

"Right. If they see this one, someone will shoot it."

I turned and looked back at the community I'd grown up in. It was true. Nickerson Harbour was no sanctuary for wildlife. In my part of California, seals were well protected. Actually wildlife was better protected than people were. An environment-friendly computer technician from El Segundo might volunteer his time to save pink-eye sparrows from extinction on the weekend, but he might blow the brains out of his neighbour with a semiautomatic weapon if the neighbour happened to cut him off on the freeway. It was that kind of a place.

I pulled out my wallet and handed the kid my Greenpeace membership card.

"You got to be kidding."

"No kidding. So I'm on your side. Now feed him. Your customer's getting restless."

The seal pup was splashing now. I had interrupted breakfast.

"What's your name?" I asked, sitting beside the boy.

"Wade."

"Wade, I'm Taylor Colby."

Wade opened the tin of mackerel with a tug on the little metal handle. The smell of strong fish exploded like a bomb. Aromatherapy.

The boy tossed in the first piece, and it floated on the water. The seal came straight up from the depths, nabbed it, and swam back under. "He got a name?" I asked.

"Cobain."

"You're kidding, right?"

"No."

"You named him for the dead guy from Nirvana?"

"Kurt Cobain was great. I got all the Nirvana CDs." Wade tossed piece after piece into the water, and we both relished watching Cobain snap his teeth over the fish and disappear beneath. "Everybody I knew in Philly thought Nirvana sucked. But I hate rap."

"There's a lot of different styles," I said, not committing myself to any side of the musical fence.

"This town sucks," the kid continued. He was working on one of those lists. I understood the list. I had given up on documenting the particulars.

"Life sucks," I said. "So what else is new?"

He laughed. Or at least I think it was a laugh. He took the can, tossed it off the wharf, and watched as it sank, leaving an oily swirl on the surface. I wanted to point out that, as a card-carrying Greenpeacer, what he had just done wasn't environmentally kind, but I decided to keep my yap shut on that one.

"Where'd you come from, anyway?"

"I grew up here, but I've been away. California."

"Why would you want to come back here?" He took off his cap, and I saw that he had a partial brush cut with hair shaved right off one side of his head.

"No place left to go, you go back home."

"I'd rather be back home in Philadelphia than here. Any place is better than here. It was my mother's idea—as far from my old man as she could get."

"They didn't get along?"

"Something like that."

I could tell he didn't want to talk about it.

Cobain had returned. "Sorry, dude," Wade said, "that was all I got."

"I might be able to find some more at my house."

"It's okay. My mom's going shopping today. I steal the stuff from the IGA. She'd be too cheap to buy it and, like I said, she doesn't know about Cobain, anyway."

"I sure won't tell her. But I got a bad feeling about you feeding Cobain here all the time. Somebody will see you and then, well, you know."

"Yeah, you're probably right."

"Safer to stop feeding him altogether so he won't be attracted to people. So he'll keep a safe distance."

Wade shook his head. He didn't like what I was saying. "You read that in the Greenpeace handbook?"

"Something like that."

"I get it. Cobain's the only thing I like about this suckhole town, and if I try to hang out with him, I'll probably get him killed."

"Life sucks," I repeated.

I wondered if I should have said nothing at all. I watched as the boy planted the baseball cap backward on his head and walked off the wharf. Cobain was left staring at me with those deep, dark eyes. I had a sudden craving to jump in the water with him and swim.

When I was a kid, I used to swim in the harbour with Laura. The water was icy cold but so clear you could see the urchins, starfish, and lobsters on the bottom, magnified twenty times larger than they really were. Farther down the harbour toward the sea, away from the fishermen, was where we swam in our underwear. After that we would sit in the warm sunlight on a large rock at the edge of the water. Nearby was a little pebbly beach at the mouth of a tiny brook known as Scarcity Run. We sat there together, the two of us, not much older than Wade was now. The sun was warm and golden in those days, and the air had the tantalizing salt smell of a clean sea. If one of us cut a finger or a toe on the razor-sharp barnacles, the other would kiss it and suck the blood off. We were kids and, at least in my memory, there was nothing sexual between us. Romance but not lust. That was how I remembered the early days of warm summer sun and Laura.

I lay back on the wharf and stared into the sky. Although everything seemed grey below, it was blue above. Fog was just low cloud, too lazy to lift its ass off the earth. I'd talk to the kid again if I could, convince him he should feed Cobain farther away in the harbour, out by the big rock—Grandfather Rock, Laura had labelled it—at the mouth of Scarcity Run. Maybe we couldn't teach Cobain to avoid humans altogether, but perhaps we could steer him clear of the most dangerous ones.

That was when I heard the car horn. I sat up and saw what looked like an RCMP car parked at the end of the wharf. Whoever was in it honked his horn and then laid on it hard. The car was blue and Mountie-looking, but had no bubblegum top. Although I couldn't see who was inside, I did notice an arm reach out of the window on the driver's side and wave a bottle of beer. The windows were tinted, so I couldn't get a good bead on who the hell it was, but as I watched the bottle sway erratically, sudsing beer and sloshing it on the side of the car, it wasn't hard to guess. The only really shocking thing was that Paul Mascarene was still capable of driving, or waving a bottle of beer in the air even, or blowing a car horn. I had assumed Paul would have been killed one way or the other a long time ago.

FIVE

Paul Mascarene was probably the biggest screwup I'd ever met. And he was certainly one of the most profound influences on me. He was a legend and a hero. Played guitar in a band called the Savages way back when. Played excellent guitar through a hundred-watt Fender amp on his old, beat-to-primal-pulp Stratocaster. Played with maxxed reverb everything from Duane Eddy to Sam and Dave to the Rolling Stones. Somehow he could slide Hank Snow or Waylon Jennings in there as if it matched and roar right on through to some distorted axe-whacking Pink Floyd if he wanted to. He had the only live band going where I grew up.

Paul was older than I was, braver, stupider, and more full of whatever it was that made life worth living and raging for. I learned guitar just by studying him as the Savages wailed away at the Royal Canadian Legion on Saturday nights. When I first saw Paul play, his band was still called the Shore Boys. I was only thirteen and it was a golden moment. I knew I had to play guitar like that and would pay any price to be able to do what Paul was doing up there onstage. Little did I know that it was Paul's influence that would lead me into a life of professional music and tear me away from the sanity of

Nova Scotia, send me scavenging for success and some kind of glittering ecstasy in California in the search that would lead to the death of Laura.

"Colby!" Paul was shouting at me now. "Damn it, Colby, get your sorry ass over here."

Just like Paul not to get out of the car but to wait for me to come to him. I took my time, felt every board bend beneath me on the old fishing wharf. What did I want to do? Greet him like an old friend or haul him out of the car, connect a fist with his face, and then try to drown the bastard in the harbour? I had been hungry to place blame for all my pain on someone for a long while now. Paul was a proven factor. If I could blame anybody, maybe he was close enough.

And then the mountain moved. The driver's door to the old Mountie car opened, and he started to get out. Or tried to. At first I thought he was just drunk. Nine o'clock in the morning and he was bloody pissed. Jerk. Observe the long decline of a legend who was nothing more than a couple of good licks on a Strat, a few well-placed high notes by a moron with a good smile and a great backup band.

The Moosehead beer bottle fell out of his hand and rolled down the gravel into the water. Paul laughed. "Jesus, Colby, you finally found your way back to visit the mortals."

The voice was his, but almost everything else had changed. He'd lost most of his long greasy blond locks, and had a protracted curving scar below his jaw, a red insignia that reminded me of what pirates did: they slashed your throat. There was something else beyond that. He wasn't just drunk. Paul was reaching behind his seat for a pair of wooden crutches. He fumbled to get a solid footing and could tell I didn't know what to say.

"Don't look so bloody shocked, Colby. Never see a cripple before?"

"Paul," I said, "good to see you."

He lurched forward, and the tip of his crutch caught on a round stone that slipped out from under it. As he started to tumble forward, I grabbed him and held him up. He smelled bad. It wasn't just the beer. It was something else. It was a smell I could only associate with death.

"Thanks, man," he said, trying to straighten. He was smiling now. His eyes still had the same blaze I had seen when he was up on the Legion stage. "I heard you were back. Couldn't believe it."

"I'm having a hard time believing it myself." Up above, the sun began to beat back the fog. Pure sunlight planted its first real morning kiss on the cold, deep waters of the harbour. Grey was bullied by blue, and I could see wisps of leftover fog dancing toward the sea. Paul backed up a step, leaned against his car in a classic James Dean pose, and pulled a pack of cigarettes out of his pants pocket.

"I got up early to come down here and look for you. I always felt we had a special relationship and wanted to be among the first to welcome you back." He tried to light his cigarette three times with different matches, but they kept blowing out in the gentle wind.

"You were the one, Paul, who played the tune that stuck in my head so solid I had to follow in your footsteps."

He pulled out a lighter and made it flare with a wicked blue flame, nearly torching half the cigarette before he got a drag. Bobbing his head, he sucked a lungful of smoke, then blew it straight into the clear sky. "Those were some times, eh?"

"I'll never forget the Savages."

Paul shook his head. "We had it *all*." It was a haunting thing to say, but true. Paul had it all back then. He had the girls after him. He had his music. Plenty of work for the Savages up and down the Shore. He had more money than most of us and a hot car. Partied nonstop. "Fun, fun, fun," he said.

"Till her daddy took the T-Bird away."

Paul laughed, coughed hard, laughed some more, then coughed until he could draw a wad of something deep from his throat and spit it on the ground. His crutches slid off the car and rattled onto the stones.

"What happened?" I asked.

"What do you mean?" he fired back innocently, making a game out of it.

"Well, you've changed."

"Hey, I'm not nineteen anymore," he said, brushing a hand over the peach fuzz on his skull. It was funny that he was more self-conscious about the vanished hair, then the scar or the crutches. "Don't worry. I lost my hair, but I haven't lost my pride or dignity." He belched loudly.

I picked up the crutches and handed them to him. "I didn't mean that."

"Oh, this. Little accident. Funny you didn't know about it. Happened five years or so after you left. Guess you were in your own little world by then. Didn't keep up with the news from back home."

"Own little world is right," I said. Five years out of Nick Harbour was the highest of times—a cold steel spike driving straight through my spine. That was what it felt like to think about all the wrong turns toward glory that had destroyed my life.

"It was amazing nobody got killed," Paul continued. "Smelt Stephens was coming up over the hill on Shore Road, passing a school bus in a no-pass zone. I was coming the other way. I knew Smelt wouldn't back down once he saw me. I was doing a hundred and twenty klicks. Smelt must have been close to the same. I figured I had three choices—run the school bus off the road, go head-to-head with Smelt, or dive for the ditch. Remember my bass player, King? He shouted out the stupidest thing he could think of. He screamed, 'Turn around!' He was a nice guy but dumb.

"I saw a handy little grove of crabapple trees to my right and decided to park there. Had no choice really. School bus and all that shit. Brakes didn't do much good. I caught on Smelt's bumper just as we left the road. It spun Smelt's car around and flipped it off the other side. School bus kept right on going down the road, slid right through clean as a whistle. It all happened in a matter of seconds, mind you. Kids had one hell of a show."

"Guess you didn't have a seat belt on," I surmised, but I don't think Paul heard me. He was lost in his story. This had been his forte. When I left town, the idiot had already logged at least twelve car accidents, totalled four cars, lost his licence long ago, but continued to drive, anyway.

"King got off with just brain damage, which I thought was pretty lucky. I went through the windshield." Paul traced the red line around his neck. "Lost most of the feeling in my right leg. That slowed me down some. But you want to know what the best part was?"

"What?"

"We went to court and my lawyer sued Smelt and his insurance company. We got a compensation package that means I never have to work a day again in my life. Talk about good luck."

I looked hard at Paul's face, hoping to see a dark hint of remorse or a devilish grin that would let me know he thought the accident was a cruel twist of fate. But there was nothing like that. "You always had lady luck on your side, Paul."

"Ain't it the truth. Come on. Hop in. Bootlegger's still down the road. I'll buy you a beer."

I shook my head. In truth, I wouldn't have minded. If I went numb for a day or two, maybe everything would be easier. But there were a lot of loose ends to work on. I didn't need Paul's idea of luck. I didn't need to be seen riding around with him, either.

"Come on, man," he said. "Tell me all about the music scene out there. I need to hear it. Couple of times I thought it should have been me out there playing in those recording sessions, not you."

I heard something in his voice. Jealousy. If Paul really knew what I'd been through, he wouldn't have felt envious

"Paul, you wouldn't have had your accident and been set for life if you'd left here. Out there you make the money, sure, but you piss it away pretty quick." I think I wanted to give him a hug. Fallen hero, tarnished legend, macho pig, and half-drunken crippled idiot. We were from the same tribe of victims. The only real difference was that he didn't know he was a victim because he believed he was golden— scarred necked, bum leg, and all. Everything was good luck to him. "I gotta do some stuff, Paul. I want to spend some time with my father. And my mother's coming back."

"Your mother?"

"Yeah. The Wicked Witch of the West is coming home from Ontario." I said it without malice. Paul knew enough about me to know exactly what I meant. Suddenly, I remembered that way back, in the days of the Savages, when I asked Paul to teach me some stuff on the guitar, when I showed him the geeky cowboy black box with six strings, he'd given me the brushoff twice before he found out I didn't have a mother, that she had deserted the family. Then he had changed. He showed me four chords, taught me how to play "Johnny B. Goode," then let me play his Stratocaster once. I even started hanging out at his house with Laura. I didn't learn until we graduated that he had tried to put the move on her a few times.

"Okay, okay. I get the picture. No sweat. I've got a few spare beers with me. Think I'll just hang here for a while and see if anything's gonna happen today." Paul hobbled around to the trunk of his car and unlocked it. From inside he took out another bottle of Moosehead Dry.

"You used to drink tequila with your Moosehead. We thought that was pretty exotic in those days."

He held aloft a brown bottle with a moose on it. "I had to ease up over the years. And I decided to give up on Mexico, stick with the local product, and support workers here."

"Smart move." I walked over to the trunk and saw a half case of beer, a box of tools, and a shotgun. "What's the gun for?"

Paul laughed. "Don't worry. I use it for entertainment, not anything criminal. When things get desperate, I shoot at a few gulls or crows. Maybe kill a few ducks and have a feed."

I squelched the lecture. Wrong time, wrong place. But I didn't like seeing guns at Nickerson Harbour. I associated guns with L.A., with crime. I'd forgotten that some people on this shore got their jollies from killing things. I'd read somewhere that killing anything human or animal for fun was truly a form of male sexual perversion. It had made sense to me, and I wondered if that was true with Paul. As he slammed the trunk shut, I immediately thought about Cobain and Wade. I knew Paul Mascarene well enough, or so I thought, that I wouldn't open my mouth and tell him *not* to shoot any seals. That would only put the thought in his head, and if I told him about Cobain, he'd end up lying in wait for him.

"You always did have all the toys," I told him.

"All the toys and all the luck," Paul shot back, hobbling to the front of his car and hoisting himself onto the hood. He leaned against the windshield and looked into the sun. "This is the life," he murmured, his eyes closed.

"See you later, man."
"Yeah. Let me know how it goes with the family reunion."
"I will if I survive it."

SIX

When we were children, Laura was just a friend, but we were very, very good friends. She had long golden brown hair and freckles. She had more enthusiasm for everyday life than anyone I ever knew. She was smart. She was thin and agile and she was better than I was at just about everything. Summers were warmer then, in my memory, but the sea was colder. Alone, the two of us in our underwear at Grandfather Rock at the place where Scarcity Brook ran into the harbour, we swam, soaked up the sun, talked endlessly. I had my dreams. I wanted to grow up and move somewhere else, be somebody famous. I don't know why. I think I just liked the idea of getting a lot of attention.

Laura never spoke of her dream except to say she wanted to be married and she wanted to be happy. We were twelve then. In retrospect I can't believe there was nothing sexual between us. All I had on was my jockey shorts. She had on her underwear and a sleeveless T-shirt. Once raging hormones took me over, I couldn't imagine any life, especially my own, as one without some sexual imperative. But there we were, two innocents sitting on Grandfather Rock at the edge of the harbour, speaking from our hearts.

"Adults try so hard at everything but learning how to be happy," Laura said. "I don't know how it happens to them."

"My mother's never satisfied."

"It's like a disease. My father has it, too. He hates his job but can't bring himself to quit because he says the money's good."

"At least he *has* a job."

"Yeah, but he hates it, and as a result, he hates himself. He yells and screams and then tells my mother and me he's sorry."

"He never hits you or your mom?" I could easily envision Jim Dan McGillivray losing his cool and taking it out on whoever was at hand.

"Never."

We went ashore and lay down on the shoreline. There was no sand but, instead, a beach of egg-size stones exquisitely heated by the sun. We thought nothing of flopping onto a rubble of rock as if it were the softest substance on earth. We nestled side by side, nothing touching but the saltwater-damp skin of our arms. I closed my eyes and felt at peace being here with such a good friend, doing nothing. But my serenity kept getting interrupted. Something inside me insisted this wasn't enough. I shouldn't just lounge here. I should be riding my bicycle, or handlining for fish, or reading a book.

"I wish I could be like you," I told Laura.

"Why?" she asked, giggling. We weren't looking at each other at all. We were lying on our backs now, eyes closed. I could see only the red of the inside of my eyelids with a full furnace of sunlight on my face.

"You know how to be happy. It's like some trick you can do that I can't do."

"I use my mind. I can do anything with my mind."

"It's because you're so smart."

"I don't think so," she said. "It's more like something else, something I was born with."

Later I would have words to define the difference between us. Laura *lived* life. Every minute of it. She became totally involved with whatever she did. If we dived into the water, she went deeper, stayed down longer. If she read a book, she lost herself in the words. If she studied for a spelling test, she absorbed every letter into herself. If she wanted to be happy, she was happy.

On the other hand, I was never fully *there*. I was always partly someplace else, or wanting to be someplace else, or thinking I should be doing something else. But Laura was my best friend, my only real friend. Often I wished she wasn't a girl. That confused things. I wanted to be more like her in so many ways, but there was an unyielding barrier between us because of our sex. Once again I couldn't be satisfied that my best friend was a girl. That was what I was worrying about as we lay on the smooth stones. If our eyes had been open, Laura would have seen me knit my brow. She always knew when I was worrying about something, and she would distract, entertain, or challenge me with some athletic feat.

"Tell me a story, okay?" I asked.

Laura had incorporated into her vast storehouse of twelve-year-old knowledge details about the history of Nova Scotia as well as information about more exotic portions of the world. She knew amazing things about hangings and sailing disasters and crimes at sea. Some she had learned from her father, a frustrated landlubber coal miner who had forgone a life at sea on big ships. Other stuff she had picked up from books.

"I don't think I've told you the story of the *Saladin* yet. My father told it to me but made me promise not to repeat it. He said my mother would be very upset."

"I promise not to tell a soul." I was still staring up at the sun. Side by side, our arms touching, I felt as if we had been welded together, joined not only in mere physical touch, but physical fact. And a pact of silence upon a secret made the cement that much stronger.

"It started out in South America," she began. "A captain named Sandy Mackenzie had a valuable cargo he was taking north."

"What was the valuable cargo?"

"Copper, bars of silver, a money chest. But, get this, most of the ship was filled with something else. You won't believe what it was."

"Gold statues? Jewels?"

"No. Guano."

"Guano?"

"Bird shit."

"No way. Bird shit?"

"Guano was considered very valuable for fertilizer in those days."

"Holy jumpin'!" I knew Laura wasn't lying. History was something sacred to her, and if her father had reported they were hauling bird shit from South America, it had to be true.

"Sandy Mackenzie offered a ride back home to a troublemaker named George Fielding who had been in prison in Peru for trying to smuggle illegal guano out of the country. Once they were out to sea, Fielding convinced the guys onboard to take over the ship."

"I never heard of a guy who wanted bird shit that bad." I was giggling now and my sides were shaking.

Laura slapped me gently on the stomach. "Shut up and let me finish."

"Sorry."

"I guess they were hungry for the silver and the money. Everybody got greedy and they killed the carpenter with a hammer, then they killed another sailor. Fielding himself killed Sandy Mackenzie with an axe."

"The bastard!"

"Don't worry. He got what he deserved. Everybody got drunk and then threw Fielding into the sea. They say it took him four minutes to drown."

"How would anybody know that?"

"I don't know. I guess somebody timed it. These were pretty nasty men. After Fielding went under, they tossed him his son. He drowned, too, but I don't know how long it took. After that things settled down, but they had a hard time sailing the ship in the right direction. Eventually they went aground by Country Harbour, down the Shore. A local captain thought he smelled a rat and had the men arrested. Four of them were hanged in Halifax. It was a big deal. People came to town from all over to watch."

"Wow." I was having a hard time believing now that the story was true. "I think you must be exaggerating. I don't think people can be that mean and rotten."

"I'm afraid it's true."

And I didn't have much option but to believe her. I sat up and tried to focus my eyes on the sparkling water of the harbour. Suddenly I wished she hadn't told me the story. As long as I was with Laura, the world as I knew it was a fairly simple place where little went wrong. The worst thing that had happened in my life up to that point was when Milt Boyle's Labrador retriever got run over by Vance Beaudreau's truck. I had liked that dog a lot. Vance felt bad and Milt said not to worry about it. Nobody's fault but the darned dog. It was always falling asleep in the middle of the road. Vance bought Milt a new puppy, anyway.

Laura saw the concern on my brow. She put a hand on each side of my face and squeezed my cheeks. "What's the matter, Taylor? It was just a story. People were like that in the old days, I guess."

I didn't want to let her know about what I was feeling, about the shadow that had come over the world. "I was just wondering what happened to all the bird shit."

She squeezed my cheeks harder. "You're cute, you know that? Stupid, but cute."

After that we waded into the water and climbed onto Grandfather Rock. I tried to push her into the water, but she was as strong as I was and fought back. I was amazed at how hot her skin was from the sunlight. Eventually she threw me into the water, which burned like icy knives. Then she flung herself in on top of me and I got an elbow in the eye. I swam down and away from her, and when I surfaced she was right there in front of me again.

The water was deep, and I could feel the insistent tug of the current that would send us straight out to sea if we let it. The story still haunted me, I guess, because it was about the sea, because the ship was found down the Shore not far from where we were, and because the men were hanged in Halifax. Even though it had happened over a hundred years ago, there was something about it that gnawed at me: the betrayal of an act of kindness with mutiny and murder.

I held Laura's hand as we floated on our backs until I signalled we should go ashore. The water was even colder now, and we swam sideways across the current to a rocky shoreline blanketed with tiny black mussels. They were razor-sharp, and we gingerly pulled ourselves up onto them. When Laura cut her toe, I watched a stream of red blood pour onto the obsidian black of the mussel shells.

"It's okay," she said.

Laura hobbled and I held her up as we walked barefoot back along the shoreline littered with sharp stones, shells, pieces of glass, and sharp sticks. We put on our clothes and shoes and started to walk toward the wharf, bumping into each other as we went. It was a thing kids did. You walked side by side, and since you were so close, you casually knocked into each other in an easy, friendly rhythm. Halfway back to the wharf, we stopped doing that for some reason. We didn't look at each other and we didn't say anything except "See ya" when I left her at her house and continued on.

Six months later my mother left her boat-building husband, her all-too-small kitchen, her gossipy friends, her church choir, her Thursday-morning shopping trips to the IGA, her childhood hometown, and her only son. She left all that and more and caught the once-a-week bus to Halifax, then a train that took her to Toronto. She'd warned my father and me that she needed more than what we could give her. She'd said it a thousand times, chanted it like a sad Gaelic dirge or cried it out like an angry anthem. But when she finally left, it paralyzed my father and took away my ability to talk. I sat in my room and played two chords on my cowboy guitar over and over. A minor followed by an F. I don't know why those two chords conveyed my feelings, but they did.

Years later I would hear a Neil Young song with the unlikely title "Cowgirl in the Sand." It was a song full of beauty and sadness, and it had something to do with disappointment, disillusionment, abandonment, and loss. The lyrics were surreal, but they made perfect sense to me, and the music pierced my chest like Fielding's bloody axe. Then I realized that the primary chords to the song were A minor and F. I was all alone at the time, driving back to Nickerson Harbour from Halifax when I heard it on the radio, and I began to cry. After four minutes of drowning in my tears, I stopped the car and screamed at my long-gone mother, facing up into the night sky and shouting loudly as if she had been taken from me aeons ago by the Greek gods and carried off to the dark heavens to become part of a constellation.

I turned thirteen a month after my mother left and received a birthday card from her in the mail. It arrived right on time, not a day too early or a day too late. There was a ten-dollar bill inside and a note that said she loved me very much. But there was no apology. I kept turning the Hallmark card over and over in my hands, expecting it to hold some kind of clue or explanation. It was obvious why she had left, but I still felt clueless when it came to figuring out *how* she could actually bring herself to do it.

Laura kissed me for the very first time on my thirteenth birthday, bringing a firm and final end to our "friendship." That first kiss, while sitting on the cold autumn back steps of my house, threw a switch inside my head, lighting up a big neon sign with FOREVER blazing in the shrouded confusion of my thoughts. I was still holding on to her and my mouth was glued to hers when she pulled away to get some air.

It was as if I had a whole compartment of my brain getting ready for falling in love with Laura, but I'd kept the door locked tight for six years or more waiting for the time I would be ready, waiting for the time I would need her most. My thirteenth birthday was that occasion.

Looking back, I think thirteen is the most difficult year of a boy's life. I don't know about girls, but I think thirteen is the year when boys suddenly realize they don't understand anything about life. What happens next is a seesaw between wonder and horror. If it hadn't been for Laura in my life, I think I would have been stuck high in the air, on the horror end of the teeter-totter with some invisible fat person holding down the other end of the board, taunting me until he made me scream. But Laura saved me from that, and so I went up and down in bliss and terror for at least a year, maybe more.

SEVEN

Laura had turned thirteen a month before me. That was a big deal to a kid. I would always think of her as older, wiser. She figured stuff out before I did. She also took bigger risks. Laura was an only child and her parents loved her deeply. Her mother, Sheila McGillivray, was a stay-at-home saint of a woman who had pity in her eyes when I showed up at her doorstep after my mother left. Her father was a large, fierce-looking Cape Bretoner who had once been a coal miner but had moved to Nickerson Harbour after the roof collapsed on him in a tunnel beneath the ocean somewhere near New Waterford. Both mother and father liked me and trusted me with their daughter.

"Don't let *her* do anything stupid," her father told me, this from a man who spent ten years underground in a cave beneath the Atlantic Ocean blowing up coal faces with sticks of dynamite. But I knew what he was talking about. Laura liked to push the limits of some things. She didn't always know when to stop.

By the time January rolled around, a painfully hard winter had set in on the Shore. Cold and snow ruled. Other winters had been mild with wet snow, quick melts, slush, rain and soft foggy nights, mornings of mist, and glistening frosty dew. But the winter of our thirteenth year on earth was something else for Laura and me.

My father stoked the wood stove in his shop and worked long into the night on a Cape Islander he would sell come spring. If spring ever came. The snow was up to the windowsills of our house and we had shovelled over and over a path from the door to the driveway and on to the boat shed. After each blinding snowstorm, it got colder as a bitter arctic wind raced through the village and forced everyone inside to huddle near oil stoves for warmth. Pipes froze in basements and in walls. Dogs who lived outside in doghouses died and froze solid overnight.

I began to imagine that my mother had seen this winter coming and got out while the warmth of the fall still lingered. Ontario might have been as cold, but I was sure the central heating in that province was working wherever my mother was at. I secretly prayed she'd hear how bad things were down home on the Shore and return to help us tough it out, like a good mother, like someone who knew the importance of keeping a family together. But she didn't return.

Laura and I watched as the harbour rimmed with white frosting and then soon began to glaze over with a thin, clear pane of ice. This harbour had never fully frozen across its width in over fifty years. One or two old-timers remembered the old days "when it was always cold in winter," but admitted the harbour had never "froze up solid." But that was what it did that year. Most fishermen had taken their boats from the water as a matter of good sense. A few had been handlining fish right up to the cold snap, and by the time the thin ice began to form, in a near panic, pulled their boats from the icy grasp of the sea and trundled them to someplace high and dry.

Vance Beaudreau was one of the few men who had let his boat, the *Casual Observer*, sit in the water. "A little ice ain't gonna make me sweat none," he told my father. But sweat he did, once the ice was three inches thick. By the time he was ready to admit he had a problem, the snow was too deep and everything around the edge of the harbour was too iced up to get any equipment near to help. Vance spent his nights on the boat keeping the stove going inside, hoping to ward off the demons of winter. His wife worried herself silly about Vance, who was probably inside his old boat mixing rum with his tea, which was why he overslept one morning until 10:30. When he went out on the ice-glazed deck to find his log pole for busting the harbour crusts from around the water line, he discovered the ice was too thick to hack through. He called my father to come down with an acetylene torch. My father tried to melt the ice in a neat outline around the boat, but almost as soon as he punched a hole through it with his blue flame, it began to skim over with crystal growth.

I was inside the *Casual Observer* trying to help my father and Vance brace extra timbers from side to side when we heard a godawful crack followed by a splintering of wood as the ice broke the heart and soul of what once was a good fishing boat. Water started to seep in from below. My father took my hand and led me up on deck, then had to go back to put out the stove and persuade Vance to abandon ship.

Anybody who wasn't scared to death of the bloody cold was down on the wharf watching the slow, painful crushing of Vance's boat that day. It was as if the force of harbour ice had Vance's boat in a vise and ever so slowly torqued her down. The *Casual Observer* didn't sink that day or the next. It grew more narrow and pinched as if on a crash course diet, and every now and again the sound of cracking timbers rang out like gunshots.

Everybody now had stopped calling Vance a fool and had moved to a more compassionate mode of offering sympathy. Within three days the ice had fully scissored right through the boat. Many thought this a spectacularly cruel feat of nature. What was left of the cabin, above the water line—or ice line in this case—sat there on the frozen surface. It was adopted as a serviceable shack for Paul Mascarene and his high-school cronies who drilled holes through the ice with an auger and fished for smelt and mackerel.

People were testing the ice more and more each day, walking, sliding, or skating on it, but never venturing out farther than the wharf, for the most distant reaches of the harbour were still open to salt water and no one could tell for sure what was safe and what wasn't.

Winter was making all of us a little foolish, but we were adjusting to it, if not loving it. The Monday the pipes froze at the school and set us free for the week, Laura arrived at my door and asked me to go for a hike.

"Where to?"

"Grandfather Rock," she said. "Just like in the summer."

"Sure. Just like summer." I didn't know what she had in mind, but she had a devilish look. She was bundled up beneath a parka hood, but her face was radiant and beautiful. I bundled myself up and we went out into the cold, bright day.

Kids were skating on the harbour near the remains of the *Causal Observer*. We were enchanted by the dance of sea wraiths in the distance—ghostlike swirls coming up off the salt water farther out toward the mouth of the harbour. Trees were coated with ice, and everything sparkled and glistened as if we were in a fantastic crystalline world. I didn't know why we were going to Grandfather Rock, but it brought back images of summer. Summer and Laura. In a few short months our friendship had been swallowed by love. I was in love with this crazy, beautiful, smart girl. I wasn't very good, however, at expressing the way I felt. I wasn't good at expressing anything in those days.

But I knew I was in love with her, I craved being near her, and I felt blessed every time she danced into my life. And dance she did. She had grown graceful and moved with a kind of liquid motion. She swirled as she walked sometimes like those sea ghosts in the distance; she drifted as if in a dream or ran with the grace of a swift, wild animal from the plains of Africa. And so she danced me through the snowdrifts until we fell together into the white fluff or crashed our heads into the bejewelled splendour of the trees laced with the weight of all that frozen beauty.

Despite the fact that it was the dead of winter, I convinced myself that what she had planned was something sexual. It was the way she looked, the way she moved, the way she held my hands, even though they were insulated with heavy gloves. I didn't think we were going to go all the way. I was still confused about too much of everything even to comprehend the possibilities of that. We kissed heavily, rolling our tongues about, breathing warm, sweet air into each other's lungs, lips crushing upon lips until they were sore. We sometimes sat tightly together, arms entwined, or we would even lie down and I would press myself tightly into her soft, yielding body. Maybe I thought we'd build ourselves a fort from spruce boughs and snow and we'd re-create summer as best we could with body heat instead of vernal sun. But that wasn't what she had in mind at all.

At Grandfather Rock, Scarcity Brook could be heard gurgling beneath a sheaf of white ice humped up over the rocks like galvanized mushrooms. All the rocks along the shore, including Grandfather, had big round hats of ice. It was hard to stand on anything along the shore without slipping, so we were on all fours by the time we made it out on top of the flat ice by the harbour edge. Laura began to walk farther out onto the harbour, but I didn't trust the ice this close to the sea. "Come back, Laura. What are you doing?"

"I want you to walk all the way across with me. Would you do that?"

I knew the salt water wasn't far off. I knew the other shore was nearly half a mile away. "No way. And neither are you. I'm not letting you go out there."

She stood and scowled at me now, folded her arms and remained mute. I was thinking about what her father had said to me. He had good reason to give me instructions to protect his daughter from doing foolish things. I walked to where she stood, but she started to run away from me, playfully as always, out toward the centre of the harbour. I grabbed her finally and we both lost our footing, then slammed onto the ice. That devilish look on her face again. She pulled her parka hood off and shook her brown hair in the sunlight, then puffed frosty air into my face.

"Let's go back onshore," I said. "Look!" I pointed south to the sea dancers. "It's not frozen out there. There are currents under the harbour. There's no telling where the ice might give way. What got this into your head?"

"I had a dream last summer. It was you and me and it was winter, just like this. And the harbour was frozen solid. And we walked from the east shore to the west shore, the two of us."

"It was just a dream. Doesn't mean you have to live it."

"No, it wasn't just a dream. It meant something. I wrote it down, but I didn't think it amounted to much until I woke up this morning and knew the dream was real. I saw into the future somehow. And now we *have* to live it."

"Why do we have to live it? I'm flattered I was in your dream, but we don't have to walk across a frozen harbour halfway out to sea. What would it prove?"

"It would prove you love me."

Jesus. There was no logic to this. Reason had gone on winter vacation. School wasn't the only thing that wasn't in session that day. "I do love you," I said awkwardly, the words catching like salt and vinegar in my throat.

"No one has ever done this before."

"So?"

"So we can do it. If you don't want to come along, I'll go by myself. I know it's safe. I made it to the other side in the dream."

"When did you start having to act out what you dream?"

"Now, I guess. I know it's okay. I saw myself on the other side in the dream. The ice was solid."

"And you saw me there with you on the other side?"

She seemed a little more unsure. "I think so. I remember starting out with you. Then I got all caught up in how beautiful everything was. And then I was on the other shore."

I was spooked. Was I supposed to believe this dream was a leap into the future? I knew Laura read books about dreams and psychic stuff and all kinds of hocus-pocus. I was the practical, down-to-earth one, or used to be. So did I make it to the other side in the dream? Did I chicken out halfway across and let her go on her own, or did I drown in the process of following her insane whim?

Laura got up and brushed the snow off. She held out her hand and I stood. The ice looked solid. The sun was still bright, the vision good. Maybe we could see if the ice was thin or if we were getting too close to the salt water. The sea dancers were bending our way now as a light breeze came up off the ocean; they were leaning toward us as if inviting us to a watery death. I could see clouds out to sea. A storm was there somewhere. If we delayed, conditions would be much worse. Damn, I hated this.

"Trust me," she said.

"You're crazy, you know."

"I love you" was all she said. And we began to walk hand in hand. The ice was opaque. It was hard to judge thickness or safety. I moved one foot after another. Farther down the shore I heard the ice groan and give out a low, dull thunk, a sound my father always called a "safety crack." I knew the ice was still rising and falling with the tides to some extent. Perhaps the most dangerous places would be where the tide had slipped out from under the ice, leaving air and making the ice weaker without the support of the water beneath. Was the tide coming in or going out? It was coming in. Both good and bad news. More water for support underneath, no air pockets, but soon it might also flood up over the ice we were on, the salt water helping to eat away at the floor where we walked.

"Taylor, I want you to know that whatever happens to us in our lives, that you and I will always be together in some way."

I wasn't in the mood for a heavy conversation right then. I was trying to be the brains of the outfit, attempting to hang on to some common sense in this nonsensical situation. "Laura, you know I'd do anything, anything at all for you. When I'm not with you, it hurts. When I'm with you, it sometimes hurts, too, because I can't hold on to you all the time. You know I need you. I think I need you in order to live even."

There was a crack then, not a final, fatal crack, but a crack nonetheless. A long, shattered line had appeared, running north and south, as we stood near dead centre in the harbour. Laura was slightly ahead of me. My own ponderous thoughts and halting words had made my feet drag. Laura was on the other side of the crack. Now it felt fully like a dream. Should I dare cross over the crack or simply stop and go back?

I hadn't asked the question, but Laura was reading my thoughts. "I think you should go back." There was real concern in her voice. The spell had been broken. I looked down and saw there was salt water seeping through the heavy crack in the ice. I registered an incoming tide, a further shift in the wind rising a notch higher. Fear was an appropriate emotion under the circumstances. I took a deep breath and saw that the sea dancers were gone now; they had merged forces to become a dull grey mist driven our way.

"No," I said, "I'm with you all the way." But instead of taking a bold leap I got down on all fours and crawled to where Laura was. My knees felt the sting of the icy water flowing up from below, I heard a sound that told me ice was rubbing against ice, but the sea was kind to me. I stood and we walked on, holding hands but keeping ourselves at double arm's length to distribute our weight. Within the next minute a grey roof filled in above us. The wind upped the gamble yet again, and the bone-chilling mist descended on us until we were surrounded.

"This wasn't supposed to happen," Laura said. "In my dream the sun was out. Everything was beautiful."

"So much for dreams."

"I'm scared, Taylor. Why did you let me do this?"

Why, why, why? "Because," was all I said. I didn't want to argue. We could hear the ice groaning again as the tide exerted pressure from beneath. There were more cracks. But worse, we couldn't see the shoreline ahead of us or the shore behind us. I was suddenly uncertain if my feet were still pointed toward our destination. I figured we were about three-quarters the way there.

"Are we going in the right direction?" Laura asked, panic rising in her voice.

"I think so, but I'm not sure now. The mist came in so quick. Let's trust the wind."

"It's out of the south, right?"

"South and east, I think. But as long as we keep it at our backs, we'll be heading away from open water."

"Are you sure?"

I wasn't certain. I'd seen the wind shift in the harbour. A south wind could easily bend east, an east wind could have funnelled by the land to turn north. My father would have known exactly how to use the wind at a time like this. I could only guess. "Yes, I'm sure," I lied. "We go away from the wind but angle our way toward shore."

But guessing was all it was. It would be a longer walk if we angled up the harbour, but it was my best shot. The mist grew thicker, colder, and more malevolent. Water began to form on top of the ice, making progress in our black rubber boots almost impossibly slippery. I began to fear the worst, that somehow we were walking out to sea. Visible cracks appeared with every step, spreading outward like crow's-feet on an old man's face. Sometimes it changed the ice into spiderweb patterns. After a few more steps, I stopped myself from looking down at all, but then paused to taste the water.

Salt.

"It's okay," I told Laura. "It's only the tide. We can't be far now."

"I can't keep going," Laura suddenly said. "We should have been there by now. What if we're going the wrong way?"

At that instant, with water up to my ankles, I was certain she was right. I was no master mariner, no expert at defying forces of nature, no gambler with any luck at all. "We're going just fine," I lied with the utmost conviction.

I held Laura's hand tightly, expecting one of us at any instant to plunge through the ice. What exactly could the other do? I had no plan. We would drown together or we wouldn't. It was entirely out of our hands. I don't think I had ever really understood the concept of fate until that instant, but I now knew precisely what a powerful blind force it was and it was our ruler at that moment.

Laura suddenly gasped and pulled on me. Our vision had been diminished by the mist to little more than ten feet in front of us. But within that range was the worst news imaginable. *Open water.* Every drop of blood must have drained out of my head at that moment. We didn't move. Before us the ice stopped and the water started. It was cold and it was salty. Had we been walking straight out to sea?

It was truly the first moment of pure terror in my life. I felt completely at the mercy of forces much larger than myself, uncaring powers that could destroy me. But it wasn't myself I feared for. Some part of my brain had already put me out of the picture. I didn't want to die, but I wasn't interested in my own watery death. It was Laura who must be saved at all cost. "Don't move," I told her.

Small waves lapped over the edge of the ice. The sun was blotted from the sky now altogether, and we were lost forever in this deadly world of mist and imminent destruction. I wracked my brain for a solution, and the best I could do was ask what my father would have done at a moment like this. The immediate answer was that he'd never get himself into such a situation, but I pushed beyond that message for something else, some glimmer of hope. *Study on it* was the way he would have put it. *Problems have solutions. Go slow and study all the information.* That had been his way out of any number of problems he'd encountered in designing or building or fixing boats. *Take your time and figure it out.*

Laura was shaking now with cold and fear. "It's okay," I said. "Trust me on this."

"I'm scared."

All I had to work with was my five senses. I smelled salt in the air. I smelled east in it, too. The wind, I was certain, was still southeast. We had been going up the harbour toward thicker ice and the eastern shore, just as planned.

I felt the ice getting softer under my feet, spongier. It wouldn't last long as the salt water worked away at it, and already the water was rising over the edge of the ice. The tide was advancing. I looked up. I now detected the silver smudge of the sun, but it was high above. No possible way to use it for direction. I studied the open water ahead and peered into the mist. I was desperate to see something, anything. Hard logic told me the eastern shore should be somewhere beyond that water. But how far? Ironically the ice seemed drier—and safer—to what it should have been to the south. Something wasn't making perfect sense.

The wind slackened for a fraction of a second, and I thought I saw something beyond the water before us. Something tall, dark, and sinister, but then everything around us seemed ominous. In a flash it was lost in the mist again. I knew then exactly what I had to do. I let go of Laura and stepped forward off the lip of ice and into the water.

Laura screamed as I felt my legs swallowed up by the frigid seawater. It filled my boots and then encircled my groin. It was unbelievably cold and painful, as if I had stepped into a million hot knives. I slapped down hard on the water with my arms outstretched and waited for the sea to swallow me, but it didn't. Up to my armpits in the harbour, I felt my rubber boots hit something hard. The harbour floor, the solid earth itself, had championed my cause and come up from beneath the depths to give me something solid. I fell forward and floundered in the weight of my heavy, wet coat, taking one clumsy step, then two, then three, feeling the water getting more shallow. I took two more steps and could see the dark, sinister shape I had first noticed—a lone, tall, gnarled spruce on the shore of the harbour.

The logic that had been delivered to me, the wisdom of my father, had suggested the water of an incoming tide would come up at the shoreline. It would eat away at the harbour ice, creating open water, even as the ice farther out might stay intact. I was a good gambler, after all. My legs were going numb, but I turned and forced myself back into the deeper water. "The shore's very close. Jump in, Laura."

"I can't."

"Yes, you can." The pain of the cold on my body was terrifying, but I couldn't leave her there. She held out her arm and I tugged her into the water. Together we made our painful, clumsy way to shore.

"I thought I'd lost you," she said. "When you jumped into the water, I thought you would disappear forever." She held me and sobbed.

"You'll never lose me. Now let's find someplace to get inside before we freeze to death."

There was a house nearby and an old solitary woman who took us in, stripped off our wet clothes, and sat us down on hard-backed wooden chairs by the cook stove. As the numbness seeped out of us like the water dripping onto the worn, unpolished floorboards, the woman said her name was Lyla and that she didn't get many visitors these days. "I was hoping someone might stop by today, but the weather's been some wicked." She fed us tea and soup and, when we were ready, she went to a store down the road to make a phone call that brought my father in his old Dodge station wagon. My father said not a word as he drove us home to Nickerson Harbour.

EIGHT

Somewhere in a poem I'd read the phrase "to make things whole again." If I stayed here long enough, that might happen, I hoped. California seemed to me farther away than China or Japan. Both remained possibilities for my secret escape—if all else failed here in Nickerson Harbour, I would go someplace where I was truly alien, where my looks, my skin, and my language betrayed the fact. California was just a bright, sunshine-filled bad dream. I wondered how I'd become accustomed to that life, that lifestyle, the money, the glitz, and those crazy, fun-loving people who would steal from me the one thing that meant anything at all in my life.

Spruce trees, tall and dark and sprouting new light green shoots from every tip, grew like weeds here and took over a farmer's field if you let them have a mere five years of neglect. They'd crowd each other out as they grew tall, spindly, and weak, literally starving one another of sunlight and nutrition from the soil. But if they had room to grow, each would explore the sky with majesty and grace, each would become Christmas in its own right, each would be green beauty incarnate. Red squirrels lived in their branches, bright yellow goldfinches returned to their favourite nests in the boughs each spring, robins chirped from the tops of the tallest, and blue jays cawed like street vendors from those undulating treetops on the edge of the fields. Spruce trees were of low repute locally, but I had always been in their fan club.

I walked away from the harbour, studying everything, alive or not, that still held the morning dew, a glistening fog-coating brushed on everything like nature's perfect morning varnish. An old rusted-out and forgotten Chevy truck was as beautiful in its splendour as was a rhododendron in pinkish bloom. The sheep sorrel bore magnanimous purple crowns of flowers and staged theatrics from Vance's backyard where it grew profusely, insinuating itself into his cluttered and uncared-for domain. And in the most barren of soils where someone had scraped off the topsoil to sell to a neighbour for enough money to buy stove oil, other ambitious and beautiful plants grew: dandelion and clover, coltsfoot and cinquefoil, and my favourite of all, a profusion of something we had simply called spring beauty—delicate little whitish-blue flowers that sprouted from a yard that was little more than raw red earth and stone. Spring beauties bloomed everywhere and advanced the theory that, in desperation, beauty will prevail.

My father would be at work in his boat shed by now and I would sit with him today and try to find a way to tell him about my mother's illness. But not yet.

A light breeze had arisen from the north. It would be a warmer day than usual without the chill of the sea. The sun would shine and drive away the fog and evaporate the dampness. The tops of the spruce trees tipped south with the first thrust of higher air, then bounced back and began a quavering dance that would continue until the sun went down and the wind abated. There was a sound that attended that first movement of treetops, a sound of release, a transfer of energy, a barely audible sighing that triggered the unlikely message from the old Jimi Hendrix song: "And the wind cries Mary." But, in my mind, I always replaced the name Mary with Laura. And so it did. The wind, from whatever quarter, in whatever part of the world, here or in China, would always carry her name.

And I was all too powerfully reminded of another sound, not unlike the first morning wind meeting the tops of the highest spruces, the sound of Laura as we made love, the sound of the air releasing from her mouth, spilling beautifully out of her lungs as I entered her during our lovemaking. She would exhale with delight, and the wind would be in my ear and we would both be united in something immaculate and precise, a place where pleasure and power melded. And I was always transported far away from California and from career, far from success and from music, into another dimension that was neither childhood nor adulthood, neither Nova Scotia nor America. It was the never-never land of our love and our togetherness that had its own simple geography of breathing and touching and folding ourselves into each other.

And it was about then that I had realized I had walked the length of the single gravel road that went from the harbour to the other end of the village of Nickerson Harbour, where the road took a sharp left at a big boulder and the pavement began for the connector road that went out to Highway 7, which led off to Halifax and the rest of civilization. A visitor would say this was where Nickerson Harbour began, but I knew it was where it ended.

Most of the time, as I walked, I had been looking up at the treetops. I hadn't even taken in much about the houses over the short distance from one end of town to the other, past the twenty or so houses that made up the village where I was born. I couldn't believe the place was so minuscule compared to my memories of childhood. Nickerson Harbour had been, in its own way, a large and bustling borough as I remembered it, and I had known everyone in the town. I'd known the personality of every dog, every cat, every nook and cranny of anyone's yard or the exact state of repair or disrepair of each automobile.

And again the wind cried "Laura" as I heard her sighing in the treetops, exhaling in my ear, and I was reminded that I hadn't made love to a woman, not even really touched a woman, since her death. Nearly five years of celibacy. Desire had fled to another sector of the galaxy. It was my own private, tragic joke that I was probably among some rare L.A. elite whose members were celibate of their own volition and weren't the slightest bit interested in changing that status.

The pavement met my feet, and it seemed intrusive and foreign. A mile or so down this stretch and I would come to Number Seven Highway, as it was so ingloriously labelled. Once there I could put my thumb out, erase my presence from Nickerson Harbour, avoid staring down the souls of this kitchen community who wouldn't forgive me for stealing Laura away, for sacrificing her for my own worldly aspirations, for returning home empty-handed with no justifiable excuses. I struggled with this temptation, then heard a car pull up behind me. I didn't have to turn around to know it was Paul Mascarene, prince of the Eastern Shore lead guitarists, with a poorly tuned V-8 engine and a leaky, stuttering exhaust system.

"Sure you don't want to hit the bootlegger and go cruisin'?" he asked. "Never know what we could stumble onto."

I smiled. At least there were two people in Nick Harbour who didn't hate me. Paul, in his own oblivion, would have been happy for my companionship. Together we could ward off the past or the future with homemade bootleg beer and drive around reminiscing about the old days, the dances, the girls, the music. But Paul's escape route wouldn't take me far enough to be of any good.

"Thanks, man. I can't."

"Well, you don't look like you're doing much. You look like you're lost or something."

"I am, Paul. I'm lost, but I'm working on a plan." What plan, I didn't know.

Paul looked as if he was feeling sorry for me. I guess I had sad sack written all over me. "Shit, pal, you just have to let it all go. People gonna think what they wanna think. Don't make no bloody difference. So just relax and enjoy being home. If it gets too weird, give me a call and I'll give you a ride back to California. If you can pay for the gas, I got the wheels."

"Thanks, Paul. I'll remember that."

Paul put the gas pedal to the floor, and he was still staring at me as the car hesitated, then spit a scree of gravel behind it. The tires squealed, the wheels came up onto the pavement, and a puff of grey-brown smoke, like downtown L.A. smog with a suntan, puffed out from behind the car.

Cross-country with Paul Mascarene in his old car. If worse came to worse, it might be one way out. We'd never make it to California; we probably wouldn't make it out of Canada. There would be some fun while it lasted, and it might be the most comfortable way to die if it came to that. Paul was an uncontrolled, exhilarating spirit who was as selfish as he was fun-loving, as villainous as he was vainglorious. It was a miracle he was still alive, a miracle he had only suffered as little as he had. In some small way he was still a hero to me, even though I knew he was one of the biggest screwups ever to breathe the salty air of the Eastern Shore of Nova Scotia.

And now he drove around with a shotgun in the back. If you were close enough to kill anything with a shotgun—no matter how bad a shot you were or how drunk—you just pulled the trigger and sprayed buckshot. Two barrels at once if it was your pleasure. Squirrels, rabbits, deer, ducks, and geese. Paul wouldn't have changed. He'd take pleasure in the dying and the blood even if he had no use for the meat.

I wanted to ignore the image I had in my head of Paul Mascarene arriving at the wharf tomorrow morning or the next and seeing Cobain waiting for his young friend. How long would it take Paul to get up from behind the driver's seat, hobble to the back of his car, and load the shotgun? Not all that long, I reckoned.

I had no trouble figuring out which house Wade lived in. It was the old Stephens place. There was a car in the driveway. Pennsylvania plates. A wind-worn fence with a gate rusted permanently open. I walked through and a dog started barking. It was the bark of the most ancient of dogs, and what waddled toward me was one of the most down-and-out, mange-damaged, low-slung, overweight miniature dogs I'd ever encountered. His bark was more like an echo or an afterthought of what a bark should be. His coat was grey and black and his back was balding with scales. As he neared, I saw the cataracts on the eyes. Here was truly one of the saddest creatures I had ever seen and I couldn't stop myself from sitting right down there on the grass. "Here, boy," I said. "Come here." I held out my hand for the dog to smell.

I'd never met a dog I didn't like except for those Hollywood Dobermans, and here was a dog I fell for at once. I loved old, beat-up mutts more than I loved an A minor chord.

"It's not a boy. It's a girl," Wade said, banging the screen door as he walked out of the house.

"What did you name this one? Morrison?"

"I didn't name her. Mom did. But she *was* named for a singer. Janis Ian. Folksinger, I think."

"Yeah, I remember. Long way back. She was good. What kind of dog is this?" What I saw before me could have been the remains of anything. My guess was a cross between a dachshund and a moustache.

"They're called Jack Russell terriers."

"Fancy. Never heard of them." The dog had sniffed me. I held her muzzle in my hand, cradled it, and looked into her cataract eyes with the large dark pupils. "You're a good dog, Janis," I said, although the name didn't sound quite right. Janis wagged her tail and I petted her back, scratching my hand across the scaly part of the skin.

When I looked up, Wade's mother was there. "What are you doing?"

"Petting your dog. Fine animal. Bet she's been in the family a long time."

"Long time, yes, but I've never been able to teach her not to talk to strangers. I guess my kid's the same way."

Wade called the dog and started to walk away; I hadn't yet had a chance to talk to him about the seal.

"What are you doing?" she asked again.

"I need to talk to Wade about something."

"Why would you *need* to talk to my son about anything?"

"Just trying to be friendly, I guess. This is my old hometown. Where I grew up. At one time I knew everything about everybody."

"Well, you haven't been around to keep up on the new neighbours. Why is that, anyway?" Her question had an edge, like the sharpened blade of a fish-gutting knife.

I stood. "Let me introduce myself."

"I know, I know. Trevor or Taylor or something with a *T*. Son of the guy with the boat sitting in his front yard."

"That's my dad. You know him, right?"

"People haven't been exactly friendly to me since I arrived."

"Could be the defensive weapons you carry." I was trying to be funny, but it wasn't working.

"I have good reason to be wary."

"I understand that, but I *am* trying to be helpful here. I'm not trying to sell anything, not asking for anything."

"That's what makes me even more suspicious." She was looking at me now, straight in the eyes. I didn't blink as she studied me to see if I was pure evil or just another local hick. She was younger than I was, but not by much. She had dark, intense eyes. There was fear there, but also fire, maybe even passion. I noticed now that her hair, tied up in the back, had a slight reddish tint, not altogether a natural hue. Her skin was olive-tan, almost Acadian in colour. I tried to envision her with her hair down full-length. I was thinking she was attractive, maybe even beautiful, but that she was keeping it hidden somehow.

She wore khaki pants and a shirt a woodsman might wear, as if she had adopted the uniform of the local peasants. Even though I had been born here, I knew there was some common ground between us. We were both outsiders. And I needed the friendship of someone who didn't know the whole story of my past.

Janis Ian whined, and I understood the language of a dog that craved more attention. I scratched her back again and patted her head, then sat on the grass and let the dog rest her chin on my leg. "You ever want to sell this dog just let me know the price."

She had no choice at that point. "You've made friends with my kid and my dog. I guess I can at least tell you my name."

"I'd be honoured."

She reached in the pocket of the flannel shirt and handed me a business card.

"Don't tell me you want to sell me insurance now?" I asked, then looked at the card. It was the oddest of formalities in a place like

Nickerson Harbour to receive a business card from a beautiful woman in her front yard. *Dr. Jillian Santino, English Department, Mount St. Vincent University, Halifax, Nova Scotia.* "You're a doctor?"

"Ph.D. in literature. I teach classes. I don't remove gall bladders."

"Jesus, Joseph, and Mary."

"Why does that surprise you?"

"What do I call you? Professor Santino?"

"Some people do. But not around here."

Wade was carrying a small portable video game. Quickly bored with us, he was sitting on the steps of the house, submerged in the throes of an intergalactic war. The vile little electronic toy gave off high-pitched sounds like amplified mosquitoes and black flies, punctuated with blasts of static that reminded me of a good car radio gone bad.

"It's a long drive to Halifax. You work there?"

"Two hours each way. But it's worth it. I wanted to live here. I only have to drive in two days a week."

"And you call that a job?"

"'Work is not man's punishment. It is his reward and his strength, his glory and his pleasure.' So said George Sand, who was a woman, not a man, by the way. And I don't think she really meant it to refer only to *men*."

"Funny name for a lady."

"Those were the times. Brilliant mind, but no one would have paid much attention if they thought the words were coming from a mere mortal woman."

"Professor, you got me out of my league here. I guess I don't know much about literature. But this is a pleasant surprise to find a beacon of culture in our dull little backward fishing village."

"Don't patronize me."

"Sorry. I just wasn't expecting you to be a university lecturer, that's all."

"What did you think I was? A single mother on welfare?"

"No. I guess I wasn't thinking."

"Typical."

"Typical what?"

"Typical male."

Back to square one. "I think you'll find that the son of Horace Colby is not typical anything."

"Maybe not." She folded her arms in front of her and looked at her dog whose head was still cradled on my leg.

Janis was fast asleep now and snoring. Her eyes were tearing, and drool ran out of her mouth onto my pants.

"What was it you wanted to talk to us about?" Jillian asked.

"I wanted to talk to Wade about his seal friend, Cobain."

Wade gave me a dirty look. I had promised not to tell.

"I didn't know he had a name," Jillian said.

Wade turned off his game. "I gave him a name. Big deal."

Jillian frowned at her son. "Why would you tell *him* and not me?"

Wade put his hands in the air. "I don't know. Who cares?"

I jumped in. "Anyway, here's the problem, Wade. If you keep feeding that seal at the wharf, he's going to hang around all the time."

"He's there every day now."

"Exactly.. You have to stop."

"You told me that once, remember?"

"Yeah, but I knew you weren't going to listen. And now I know you were right—about the guys down at the wharf."

"You have no right to tell my son to stop feeding a wild seal," Jillian burst out.

"Let me finish. I have an alternative."

Wade didn't want to listen. He switched on the Walkman game, but his mother flicked it off and gave him a dangerous look.

"The seal's going to get too comfortable there, and some asshole with a gun is going to blow his brains out."

"Why would anyone do that?" Jillian asked.

"Because the world is made up of any number of assholes who get genuine pleasure from killing living things. Besides, some of these out-of-work fishermen around here blame the seals for gobbling up all the fish."

"That's absurd. Human greed and deep-sea draggers killed off the fish, and you know it."

"I know it and you know it, but that doesn't mean everybody believes it. So I don't want to see Wade get attached to that nice little creature swimming around in the dark lagoon, then have to see it killed."

"Some asshole kills Cobain, I'll kill him!" Wade shouted, looking right at me, as if *I* were the asshole.

"You're a great influence on my son's vocabulary," Jillian said.

"Sorry. I apologize. I'm sure the boy has never heard the word before."

"Yeah, right," Wade cracked.

"Look, I have this old friend who drives around with a shotgun in his car just waiting for a target like that seal."

"Sounds like a great person to have for a friend," Jillian said.

"I can't help that. Some people are like that around here." I tried to describe Paul Mascarene to her, but I failed to convey the true image. "You've seen him drive by, I'm sure."

"So your solution is to stop feeding him and the seal will go back to sea and be safe?"

"That's the best option."

"And it sucks," Wade said.

"Big time," I added.

I looked at the professor again and saw new confusion in her face. Wade had the look of every twelve-year-old boy who had ever lost a friend or a big baseball game or seen the crash-and-burn demise of a dream. And I had to be the one to bring the bad news. Nobody spoke for a moment. The dog snored on, the wind exhaled again through the tops of the spruces, and Wade took his private revenge back into space, switching on his handheld cacophonic opera of deep-space destruction.

"Okay, there's another possibility," I said.

Wade looked up from his game. There was a final burst of static and then the voice of an electronic alien announced, "Game over. The empire has destroyed you. So long, sucker."

"What?" Wade asked.

"Tomorrow I borrow one of my father's boats and lure Cobain away from the wharf. We'll row down the harbour to a place that's safer. Mouth of a little brook with a big stone in the water. We call it Grandfather Rock. Feed Cobain there. Go back each day and feed him again. Seals are smart. He'll get the picture. That way maybe he won't go back to the wharf, Paul Mascarene or a vengeful fisherman won't see him, and Cobain will have a good chance at surviving without losing a friend."

"Excellent," Wade said.

Jillian looked at me hard. "You want me to send my son off in a rowboat into the wilderness with you?"

"It's not a rowboat. It's a dory handcrafted by Horace Colby. I'll bring life jackets. I'll make him wear one."

"I need to think about it."

"Aw, Mom," Wade whined, "don't be an asshole."

I cringed, patted Janis Ian on the head, and said soft, soothing nothing words to the old beast as Jillian walked back into the house. Wade gave me a thumbs-up, but then turned back to his fantasy world of megadeath as if I weren't even there.

NINE

The double barn doors to my father's boat workshop were open, allowing the morning light to spill into this wonderland of fresh lumber, sawdust, and wood shavings. In the middle stood my father, a fine figure of a man with a full head of dark brown hair. He was slightly bent in concentration, sliding his right hand along the smooth, curved gunwale of a fourteen-foot dory. He was unaware I had walked in. There was study and concentration here and, to my eye, it looked as if the boat was already complete. He was making some final estimation to determine if the craft was just right or not. Whatever he was doing, I could tell it was of profound importance to him.

What happened in this shed wasn't what anyone would ever refer to as "work." It was closer to religion. As I stood in the doorway of my father's sanctuary, I realized I had known the sanctity of this place since I was a boy. There would be rare equivalent moments in my life when I could approximate this feeling of union: walking a sandy beach here at Quoddy Point or Santa Cruz with Laura, feeling the music play through me onstage before a giant audience on some perfect starry night outside at the Hollywood Bowl, or surfing with

Larry anywhere outside L.A.—taking off on a wave and becoming one with it. Love, music, and waves had been my religions. But I had lost the catechisms for all three.

My father had been a supplicant to family and to craft. Although it seemed the world no longer had a need for his skill, he continued to worship, having long ago lost his family.

"It's beautiful," I said.

My father turned to look at me without surprise. "It's pretty much the same as the one I made when you were a boy. No fancy improvements. Just a matter of pulling the wood together into the right design."

I stooped to study the line of the boat from the bow. The front end of the dory came to a point; the middle section bellied out in a gentle, firm, round pregnancy. It was a shape of something from nature, a seed case or an eye. I breathed deep of the scent of pine and spruce and ran my hand over the unfinished wood. "Yeah, I remember. You gave me one of these for my birthday once."

"It was the same as this."

"How many hours did it take you to make it?"

"Same as this one. About a hundred and twenty."

"I was fifteen, I think."

"Sixteen, to be precise, and more interested in music and cars and…you know."

A wave of guilt swept over me. "And I sold it to a guy for seventy-five dollars."

"You could have got at least two hundred for it in Halifax."

"How come you weren't roaring mad at me?"

"I'd figured you'd seen me making boats all your life. Another little boat was no big deal."

"A hundred and twenty hours down the tubes."

"Not really. You ended up with seventy-five bucks."

"Which I spent on gas to drive to Halifax, a case of beer, and a fuzz box."

My father gave me a quizzical look. "What the hell is a fuzz box?"

I felt embarrassed to tell him. "It was that electronic distortion gizmo for my electric guitar. It distorts the sound."

"I remember now. That thing that made you sound like you were tuning up a chain saw."

"Yeah."

He scratched his head and ran a hand down along his face as if he were tracing the road map of creases. "Gas, beer, and a fuzz box, eh?"

"That's what was important to me back then, I guess. I'm sorry."

"Don't be," my father said, tapping the boat on the side with his knuckle. "You have a second chance. I want you to have this one for all the birthdays I missed."

"The prodigal son returns. He's forgiven and presented with a new boat. I don't know if I should accept."

"You have no choice. I want you to help me finish it off, though, coat it with Varethane. Then you have to row the damn thing around the harbour like you love the bejesus out of it."

"I'd like to do just that."

"Then I want you to take your mother and me for a ride in it when she gets here. It'll be like old times."

I didn't want to discuss anything about my mother.

My father closed his eyes and took a deep breath. "I can't believe I've spent so many years inside this place. I feel like I finished building it yesterday. We'd just been married. I'd bought the house and was scrounging the lumber for this. All I wanted to do was live with Helen, come out here every day and work with the wood. How could I have ever believed it was all that simple?"

"It should have been that simple, Dad."

"I was a fool, I suppose. Could have seen she wasn't happy. That was as obvious as the frown on her face. And then she was up and gone and a lifetime slips by and I'm still out here like a damn idiot who can't see nothing but the nose in front of his own face."

I had no words to offer that would do any good. I wanted to hug my father, but I wasn't sure I was up to it. We hadn't been much of a physical family. Nobody ever hit, but nobody ever really hugged, either. My mother was a screamer, but the Colby men were usually the silent, suffering types. Instead of touching him, I ran my hand along the smooth, planed wood on the side of the dory. And it was as if I were playing a delicate, elegant jazz riff, stroking high up on the neck of my Stratocaster. My father had fine-tuned this dory like a well-made musical instrument. Soon it would be floating in the sea and an audience of waves would splash their applause at this song made of wood.

My father noticed Jim Dan McGillivray, Laura's father, in the doorway before I did. Jim Dan was over six feet tall with a barrel chest. The boat rested between me and my father-in-law. My father had grabbed a three-foot length of two-by-four and widened the stance of his feet as Jim Dan picked up a wide-blade axe propping open one of the doors. "Horace, I came to deal with your goddamn son."

I stood frozen, gripping the side of the dory. My father, though, remained remarkably calm. Jim Dan couldn't look at me or talk to me. I think deep inside he was holding on to his rage, throttling it by looking at my father whom he had known for over forty years.

"You got reason to be angry, Jim Dan, but you'll have to get past me first if you want at him."

"Stay out of this!" I shouted at my father, angry at him for getting involved.

Jim Dan inched forward, perhaps expecting me to run. But I didn't. The axe wasn't raised, but it was gripped in front of him, ready to be put into action. Jim Dan was looking straight at me now, his fiery, widened eyes paralyzing me with their loathing, but he still couldn't speak to me.

"He didn't even show up at her funeral," he said to my father. "She's buried three thousand miles from home. We hear about it the day before. We fly all the way out to that godforsaken place and he's nowhere around. Laura's dead and he's run away."

I closed my eyes and felt his hot breath on me.

"Stay calm, Jim Dan," my father said. "I hear what you're saying, but this isn't the thing to do." He put his hands on my shoulders and tugged me away. We tripped over some boards on the floor and staggered backward, losing our footing and falling onto a pile of rough-cut lumber. I opened my eyes as Jim Dan raised the axe and let out a savage, inhuman scream. The broad-axe blade sliced the air with a whoosh.

I heard the crash, felt it even, and saw the axe drive through the side of the new dory. The wood splintered and exploded. Jim Dan moaned as he pulled the axe out and drove it again through the gunwale until the blade was wedged into the side of the boat. Letting go of the axe, Jim Dan stared at his hands and rubbed them up and down on his haggard face, sobbing. As we got back on our feet, my father hugged me to him and repeated the words he had whispered in my ear as I'd lain in my bed the night my mother left: "It's all right, Taylor, my son. Everything is going to be all right."

My father said nothing about the damage to the boat, nor did he ask Jim Dan to leave. "Let's go into the house, Jim. I'll put some coffee on. I hope you don't mind instant."

Jim Dan studied the axe embedded in the planks, then blinked as if he had just been awakened from sleep. "I don't know."

We didn't ask him what he didn't know. It was unimportant. My father let go of me and led the way to the back door. Inside the kitchen, the kettle was filled with tap water and plugged in. A box of stale molasses cookies was set on the table, and I knew the words that needed to fill up the spaces in the hollow kitchen air would have to come from me.

"The morning Laura was to be buried," I began, "I started out alone driving to the cemetery in Glendale. My friend Larry offered to go with me, but I said no. I had friends. Laura and I both had good friends who would be there at the funeral. I drove up Santa Monica Boulevard and the heat was stifling. It wasn't any worse I suppose than many other days in Southern California, but it was awful. I hated myself. I hated L.A. I hated everything in the world. When I saw a couple of teenagers walking down the sidewalk—a guy and girl kissing—I felt this awful thing swell in my gut. I couldn't bear to think again about losing Laura." I tried to look at Jim Dan, but he had his hands clasped together as if in prayer, his head bowed.

"I didn't even call you, Dad. I did nothing. Larry made all the arrangements. I knew I couldn't confront anyone from back here, and I somehow thought we were so far away, so far out of all your lives, that I'd never see any of you again."

Jim Dan didn't look up. "But she was my daughter, damn you."

"I know. She was my wife. I loved her."

"Then how could you let it happen?"

"I don't know," I said, letting my mind drift back. That day I had just kept driving until I had come across a street called Canada Boulevard. I decided it was some kind of message. The boulevard led to Angeles Crest Highway, which took me up into the mountains. The air was cooler. I was headed out of L.A. I was running and I didn't plan on looking back. I felt a little glimmer of hope. An hour later I was still driving and had the radio on, pretending everything was okay. I was going to start a new life. I thought I could put Laura and everything else out of my head.

All around me were giant pine trees. There was snow on the peaks. I hadn't seen snow for a long time. And I'd never driven up there before. The air felt clean and pure, the sky was blue. I knew I was deluding myself. And then a big sign said the highway was closed ahead, blocked by snow. There was no way through the mountain pass and on east, away from L.A. That seemed inconceivable, so I drove around the roadblock on the closed highway until I came to a place where the snow spilled across the road. It didn't look natural somehow, as if someone had come with a fleet of trucks and dumped it there, just to stop me from escaping.

Even though the air wasn't that cold, you could feel the chill emanating from that big mountain of ice and snow sitting on the road. I was alone. Truly and absolutely alone in a way I had never felt before in my life. I climbed on top of that avalanche until I found a flat, smooth place where the sun had melted everything into a white sheet of ice. I took off all my clothes, lay on my back, and stared up into the empty, unforgiving sky. And I stopped thinking about anything.

I felt the cold coming up into my body, penetrating every pore, seeping into my blood, into my bones. I became snow, I became ice, I became winter. I felt alive for the first time in a long while. It was the icy cold of a Nova Scotian winter, and it was like being home, being at rest. I was prepared to die like that.

But when a breeze came up off the mountaintop and began to stir the pine trees, there was something in the sound that made me wake up out of the trance I was in. Then, of all things, a seagull flew overhead and its shadow traced down across my body. My mind clamped onto the oddity of seeing a gull here in the mountains, but I knew I was no more than fifty miles from the coast. I began to shiver uncontrollably, just a little at first, then I was shaking like an epileptic. I tried to move, but the cold had numbed my arms and legs. I could barely move. But I got up and put my clothes back on, then drove to the house Laura and I had lived in. When I got there, I closed the door, ripped out the phone, and went to sleep.

There had been an awkward silence while my mind wandered, then a piercing shriek from the kettle. My father unplugged the kettle and tried to pour hot water into three cups with instant coffee, but it seemed like a monumental task to him.

"We tried to convince the people out there Laura should be buried back in Nova Scotia, but it was too late for that," Jim Dan muttered. "They said we'd have to get a lawyer. I couldn't see putting Laura's mother through more than she'd been through. We let it go."

"Why didn't you come and find me then?" I asked. "Why didn't you pound down my door?"

"We didn't want anything to do with you. I had trusted you, and you had promised to take care of our girl. Look at what you did."

"I know. If we had stayed here in Nickerson Harbour, she'd still be alive."

"You don't know what would have happened if you'd stayed," my father said. "You couldn't have prevented what happened."

"Yeah, I could have. I could have saved her life, but I didn't."

TEN

After the silence grew too thick for any of us to stand, we went back outside. Jim Dan hadn't killed me, but we weren't exactly on speaking terms. It was as if he wanted to be around me to make sure I was still a human being, not some vampire that had sucked the life out of his daughter. But he still had a hard time addressing me directly, even though there were things he wanted me to know.

Somebody drove by in a pickup truck and blew the horn. He was headed to the harbour. The wharf was probably still a focus of daily activity, even though nobody was fishing. It was a place to talk, complain, gossip. By now everybody in Nickerson Harbour knew I was here.

"Did I ever tell you why I quit that last job, Horace?" Jim Dan asked my father.

"You didn't have to tell any of us, Jim Dan. A month after you quit, that hole in the ground blew up and killed a dozen good men. I know why you quit."

Jim Dan picked up a twig and snapped it in half, then quartered the little pieces and fiddled with them like a giant stacking firewood with his fingers. "I didn't quit when they wouldn't let us spread crusher dust on top of coal dust. I didn't quit when they kept promising to fix the air system but never quite got around to it. I didn't even quit when I was sucking methane gas thick enough to choke a mule.

"I finally told my pit crew I was gonna complain loud enough so that somebody would do something. And they all came down on me hard, reminding me that everyone else who complained had been fired. I said I didn't care. Then one of the men, a young guy named Warner from Antigonish, said I *had* to keep my mouth shut. They might end up shutting down the mine and we'd all be out of work. I went to the boss, anyway, then went to the mine safety inspector, and both said they'd look into it, but it didn't mean nothing. When I went back the next night for my shift, I had five of the boys telling me I'd be sorry for what I did. They'd see to it. That's when I quit."

"Any of them end up in the explosion?" I asked.

"A few. And now I wish I hadn't quit. I wish I'd let those sorry sons of bitches try to pound my ass into the ground and then I would have got right back up and kept on complaining until somebody fixed the damn mine or closed it down. Instead, I quit the job, took my pay, and drove back here to Nickerson Harbour. I'm as guilty of their deaths as the bloody company that ran that hellhole."

At first I didn't know why Jim Dan was telling me this story, but slowly it started to sink in. You tried and you failed, and if things went bad, you were still guilty as sin. You never walked away from it.

"Laura wanted us to fly back and visit," I said, not knowing why I had to offer up this information now. "It wasn't long before she died. She was pretty messed up and I didn't want you or people back here to see her that way. I thought we were going to pull things together, but it didn't work out."

"You should have brought her back here, Taylor," Jim Dan said, staring straight up into the morning sky. "You should have let her come back to us."

"I know that now." I wanted to explain why it was that I hadn't dropped everything and devoted all my attention to helping Laura. If I'd spoken the words out loud, though, Jim Dan would have turned back into a raging monster and killed me on the spot. The reason I hadn't brought Laura back to Nova Scotia was simple, even stupid. *I was busy.* It was a great creative phase for me and I was doing music with a dozen of the most adventurous and successful musicians in Southern California. I was thriving on the energy, the crazy adventure of it all. There was money in it, good, challenging work, amazing people, and an outrageous good time. *And I didn't want to close down the mine.*

My father had begun to stack split logs that were lying around the chopping block. He didn't say a word, but I think he already knew what connected Laura's father and me. Sometimes the truth of a thing got out and seeped like osmosis through a small town, even if nobody came right out and said it. Lies worked the same way, but everybody expected rumour and half-baked accusations to reach every nook and corner of a small town. The truth of the matter, however, like the story about why Jim Dan had quit the mine, had already leaked out and everybody knew. They knew why he'd quit and why he felt guilty over the accident, even though it wasn't his fault.

"Helen says she's coming back," my father announced to Jim Dan. He had hope and even pride in his voice.

"I don't believe it."

"Taylor, tell him it's true."

I nodded. "Good old Mom. Coming home."

"For good? You mean she's returning just like that?"

"I guess," my father said.

"And you're gonna take her back?"

Horace Colby stopped stacking firewood and straightened. "I guess I am. No questions asked."

"Your father's either a fool or a saint," Jim Dan said to me.

"Maybe both," I said.

"All the Colby men are like that," my father said.

"Not all of them," I insisted.

Jim Dan shook his head and handed a couple of pieces of wood to my father. "Nobody offer you anything for that boat yet?" he asked, nodding toward the *Helen VI.*

"Not a soul. Who wants a new fishing boat if there's no fish?"

"Maybe the fish are just hiding," Jim Dan said.

"Could be. But I think I'll hang on to the boat for now. When Helen gets here, she might like to see it sitting there fresh-painted and all."

"What happened to the *Helen V*?" I asked.

"Sank on the rocks at Roaring Bull in the hurricane a couple of years back," my father said. "The two Stephens boys were chancing it big-time. An August blow come up out of the south, warm as anything, and they got cocky. Said the boat would have made it back to port if they hadn't misjudged and run her up on that reef. Still, it held together while it was being blasted by the waves. The boys hunkered down in the cabin and got on the radio. Coast Guard dropped a man in a harness and scooped them both up. Then, they say, a thirty-foot wave came down like the fist of God and blasted 'er apart in a matter of seconds."

"Maybe it was her name," I said, feeling cruel again. "Made for bad luck."

"Nothing bad comes from something that's built with love," my old man said, effectively silencing me.

Jim Dan laughed. "The words of a fool," he said, but there was a touch of gentleness in his chiding. "I'm out of here, boys, before you two start up a philosophy course."

My father had a good sweat up now as he continued the rhythm of stacking the firewood. Jim Dan put a foot up on the chopping block to tie the lace on his work boot, then he turned to look straight at me. It wasn't what I expected. I thought we had struck some kind of an accord. I didn't expect him to become my best friend, or treat me like family, but I thought we were past the worst of it. His look, however, said it wasn't over. I wasn't forgiven. Jim Dan wouldn't forgive himself for the men buried in the coal mine, he probably couldn't forgive himself for letting Laura go off with me, and he'd never let me off the hook, either. That was what he was telling me with his eyes.

Then again, maybe he had decided not to kill me just as a polite gesture to my father.

"I'm sorry about the boat, Horace. I'll pay for it."

"Ah, forget it, Jim Dan. Take me no time to fix it. Let it go."

"No, a fella's got an obligation to pay for a thing he damages," he said, then walked off.

When he was gone, I started picking up the split wood and stacking it alongside my father.

"Why do you really think she's coming back?" he asked suddenly in a deadpan voice.

I knew why, but I wasn't ready to tell him. "I don't know. Maybe it's like what Jim Dan said—an obligation to pay for a thing damaged."

"I don't hold your mother to blame for anything. It was all my fault."

"Jesus, Dad. It wasn't your fault. You know that. It was her goddamn fault. She ripped this family apart because she was a selfish bitch. Don't try to paint it otherwise."

"Don't talk about your mother like that," he said, breathing heavily. "And I insist you don't speak to her like that when she gets here."

That afternoon I sat down with my father and watched American TV talk shows. By the miracle of television, I was instantly transported back into the vanity-driven, egocentric, neurotic world of Los Angeles. Subjects for the day: women who loved men who didn't love them, teenagers with unusual tattoos on unlikely parts of their anatomy and, my personal favourite, young men willing to marry older women—of any age—as long as they were rich.

"Why do you, of all people, watch this crap?" I asked.

"Escape. I like hearing other people talk about how complicated their lives are. It makes me feel good about my own simple life."

"Nobody's life is simple, especially not yours. Our family is as messed up as anybody's. That's the nature of a family. Most kids are simply lucky if they survive growing up with minimal psychological damage. We start out pure and healthy and then parents inflict pain, suffering, and irrevocable problems that take the rest of our lives to sort out. Only most people never resolve their feelings about growing up."

"I didn't know you felt that way."

"Well, I wasn't really referring to you. You did pretty good under the circumstances."

"I was a failure."

"Give it up, Dad. Now you're starting to sound like someone on Oprah's show." I held an imaginary microphone up to him. "Tell me, Mr. Colby, how often did you beat your wife?"

"Get out."

I pretended to answer for him, mimicking the way he spoke. "Well, Oprah, I never did beat my wife, but it's possible I might have one day if she pushed me far enough. So I guess you could say I was guilty of the possibility of beating my wife and therefore I was responsible for the breakdown of our marriage and turning my son's life into a mess."

My father laughed and switched channels, then turned off the TV and headed for the kitchen. I followed him and changed the subject. "You got a rowboat out there or a dory without holes chopped in the side I can borrow for tomorrow?"

Boat talk always made my father more comfortable. "Got a twelve-footer you can use. Been sitting around gathering dust. I think it's watertight." Just like him to say he *thought* it was watertight when, in fact, it was probably nothing short of perfect.

"I want to put it in the water tomorrow if that's okay with you."

"Fine by me. We'll put it in the truck now and she'll be ready to go. Just don't forget to grease the oarlocks—and take along a life jacket."

"You taught me that a long time ago. I never forget the good stuff you taught me."

"Is that so? What about forgiveness? Didn't I teach you never to carry a grudge? You gotta forgive everybody of everything sooner or later. You gotta forgive your mother about leaving, and you have to learn to forgive yourself about your wife, too." He stopped there and then looked a little embarrassed. My father was scared to death even to say Laura's name. And I never once remembered him telling me anything before about forgiveness.

"That's bullshit and you know it," I said. "You've been watching too many TV shows. Besides, look who I'm talking to. You've never been able to look in the mirror and forgive yourself for her leaving, even when it wasn't your fault."

My father was at the kitchen sink, running hot water. "None of that matters now. Everything will come back together here in a few days."

As I walked out into the backyard, I kept thinking that L.A. had been a long vacation compared to returning to the insanity of my boyhood home. I was sure my father was the biggest bloody fool on the earth, and I was cursing myself for my inability to tell him I loved him more than any living soul on the planet. I pitied him, I admired him, I blessed him for his patience and his willingness to take me back as a son without any questions asked. But I also cursed him for having taught me yet another one of those great lessons of his: hide your deepest hurts and don't go overboard with expressing your affection, for fear you might push someone you love far, far away.

Eleven

I watched my father fall asleep after dinner in his chair in the living room. He woke up again at eight o'clock to announce he must be getting old.

"Sleep's a good cure for being tired," I said.

"Sleep's a righteous escape. I always dream when I fall asleep sitting up, but never in bed at night."

"You dream. You just don't remember. That's what they say."

"What do you dream about, Taylor?"

"I'll spare you an answer. Too weird. Too ugly. I don't really think any of it makes sense."

In my dreams I was haunted by days I didn't get to experience. Such as what it would have been like to continue a life with Laura if she hadn't died. We would have moved back north to British Columbia and lived somewhere on Vancouver Island, or beyond, in the Queen Charlottes. Or we would have returned to Nickerson Harbour and built a house together. Dreams about my mother were less vivid, but I also dreamed about other unlived moments with her. They were dreams about a continuation of a normal life, imaginary moments that never occurred because of her exodus from my life. My mother taking me shopping at the IGA. My mother congratulating me for a good high-school report card. She was always fuzzy, never in focus. But that was the mother I still loved, not the one who would return in a few days to throw us all into chaos again.

I slept well that night for some reason, refusing to endure the physical gossip of my old room and insisting to my subconscious it would do no good at all to envision a reunion with my mother. I was secretly pleased Jim Dan had come after me with an axe, but also genuinely satisfied I had survived the incident. I had been accused and convicted of Laura's death. That seemed more honest, more direct than anything anyone had tried to say to me about my role in her demise back in L.A.

I think I had somehow profited as well from spending time around two men who had suffered. Blessed are the meek, for they shall inherit the earth. And all the rest.

Wade was standing at the end of the wharf again with two tins of B.C. salmon when I arrived the next morning.

"Got a boat," I said. "Seen Cobain yet?"

"Not yet."

"What do you think about my plan to keep him away from here?"

I was hoping Wade might see me differently and lighten up. I couldn't let Paul Mascarene or anyone else kill the seal and mess him up any more than he was. "My mother doesn't like you," he said eventually.

"What about you?"

"Why do you care?" he almost snarled in a voice as hard as a ten-penny nail.

"I don't know. I guess I need all the friends I can muster."

"Now you sound like my father."

"Yeah?"

"Yeah. He always said he wanted to be my friend, but he was hardly ever around. He had some fat-ass job working for the city.

He hated my mother, I think, but he liked me okay. We got along cool when he was there."

"Miss him?"

"Yeah. I'm thinking of going back."

"What do you mean?"

"I mean, just going back. She can't stop me if I want to go. You saw what she's like. She hates men."

"All of them?"

"I think so."

"That's a lot of people to hate."

"Mom's got problems. But what's it to you?"

"Nothing. Just nosy, I guess. Help me with this boat, okay? We'll row out and find Cobain. You've got to wear this, though." I tossed him the orange life jacket.

"No way. I'd look like a freak in that."

"Who's watching?"

"Doesn't matter. I can swim."

"You wear this, or you don't go in the boat."

"Fuck you!"

I saw Cobain surface at that instant. The clear, dark water of the harbour opened, and the sleek figure of the seal emerged. He swam toward the dock and came up not seven feet away, his eyes dreamy dark pools of childlike wonder. I could never get over the pettable, doglike faces of seal pups, the curiosity in their expressions, the feeling that welled within me that I was somehow linked to them in a personal, almost familial, way. I checked my watch. Eight forty-five. By nine o'clock Paul or somebody else would be showing up here to talk and get bored in the company of other men with nothing better to do. Wade was opening one of the tins with a can opener and talking to Cobain.

I walked back to the truck and checked to see that the oarlocks weren't seized with rust. Throwing the oars and the lone life jacket into the bottom of the dory, I slid it off the back of the truck and made great gravel-crunching noises as I dragged it to the shoreline. Then I rowed the boat to the end of the wharf, scaring Cobain. He hadn't been fed yet.

"Look what you did. You scared him, asshole."

I decided Wade was ready to relate to me in a new way. "You want to keep doing what you're doing and watch him get blasted apart? You think those bastards onshore will give a shit if they kill your friend?"

The kid looked genuinely scared. I'd pushed him.

"Get in," I insisted.

"I'm not wearing that stupid thing."

"So don't wear it," I said, backing down. "Get in. Or are you afraid of being in a boat?"

"I'm not scared of nothing."

"Then get in."

Wade gingerly climbed down the wooden rungs along the wharf and nearly dumped us as he clumsily wobbled about in the dory, trying to get a seat. It was obvious he'd never been in a boat before. He held one hand on each gunwale and had a haunted look as we drifted away. It had been a damn long time since *I* had been in a boat. Today was the second clear morning in a row on the Eastern Shore, something just shy of a miracle. Being in a boat adrift in the harbour brought me back again to the beauty of my childhood, the magnificent splendour of growing up in a shore community, the freedom, the passion for the smells of salt and fish and spruce and wild roses. A dreamer's paradise. I let the oars kiss the top of the harbour water ever so gently as I closed my eyes and pulled two arms together, felt the tug of liquid resistance, experienced the small shiver of the dory beneath me as we glided out into deeper waters on a brilliant early-summer morning.

Wade was looking over the side, hypnotized by the flowing, fluttering seaweed beneath us, seaweed that danced in the eddies like exotic girls with feathery dresses and scarves. We could see schools of tiny herring and other flashing silver fish finding their course along highways of harbour currents that only they could understand. "I don't see Cobain," he finally said.

I dipped the oars and held them stiff, stalling the boat as best I could, then worked them slightly backward against the tide, suddenly feeling the mighty power of water in the grip of a lunar pull.

It was one thing to slide with the tide gracefully, adding your muscle to its own. But turn and try to go in the opposite direction—that was a whole other matter.

Wade was nervous, for sure. The life jacket lay on the bottom of the boat. I wanted to tell him to put it on, but I wouldn't try that a third time. "How's your backstroke?" I asked.

"Don't worry. I can swim fine. My father used to take me to a pool on Saturdays. We'd swim for hours."

"I could never stand the chlorine in swimming pools," I said. Los Angeles had been the land of backyard swimming pools. They always seemed sterile, artificial, and wrong. The clear, insipid, chemical-infested lifeless clarity of a California pool seemed so much the opposite of the rich, dark, amber presence of the water beneath us in an arm of the sea that was the very lifeblood of the planet.

"There he is!" Wade shouted, rocking the boat too much for my liking. Cobain surfaced back near the wharf, and Wade waved frantically.

"I'll angle in toward shore and we can row more easily back in his direction." My muscles tensed as I rowed hard out of the channel and into the less-insistent waters near shore. I pulled hard and felt the muscle burn with a pleasant sensation. Lifting off my seat, I worked against the natural flow of gravity and water and moon and tide and then, as if by a miracle, found a sluggish little back current near the shore that actually returned us to where we'd come from.

"How'd that happen?" Wade asked.

"Nature works in funny ways."

We were near the wharf again, and Wade tossed the first piece of fish into the sea. Cobain shot for it like a freshly launched torpedo and caught it with his mouth, then dived. I feathered the oars and we shifted out toward the channel. When I saw pickup trucks arriving, I knew it was time to make our exit. Maybe they had already seen Cobain on other days. Maybe I was wrong about them wanting to kill a young seal. But I couldn't take that chance.

Wade kept tossing small pieces of fish into the water. Cobain was wary of the boat, but he loved these tasty gifts provided by the boy from Pennsylvania. We were nearly a half mile away from the wharf when I saw the men get out of their trucks and walk toward the end of the wharf. Somebody waved in our direction and I saluted back. Cobain wouldn't be apparent—just a man and a kid in an old dory rowing around the harbour.

When we were far from the wharf, Cobain came up alongside, pacing us in the outgoing current. Wade kept luring him closer to the boat. I wanted to explain the logic to him again. *Don't get him too adjusted to people.* But I couldn't bring myself to say it.

Wade beamed. "Cobain thinks this is excellent," he said, opening the second can of fish.

"Cobain is wondering why he's eating West Coast salmon in a harbour in Nova Scotia."

"Fish is fish."

"It sure as hell is until it's all gone." Up ahead I saw Scarcity Brook running into the harbour mouth. I glimpsed a small patch of sandy shoreline and noted the one large boulder in the water. "Grandfather Rock. That's the place."

I tugged the boat to the western shore, with Cobain hot on our trail. Wade jumped out when we were close, getting soaked to his knees, but he didn't care. Nor should he. I beached my father's well-made dory and watched as Wade hopped onto the big rock and then tossed his final three pieces of fish to Cobain. The seal made half-circle sweeps around him. When all the fish was gone, the seal poked his head straight out of the water and, motionless, studied the boy who had fed him. I hung back onshore where I felt happy, almost silly. This small event was so fine and easy, so simple.

A city kid, I thought, could never really go back to the ugliness of an American city after this. It would seep into his blood and he would become one of us. He would become hooked on this vision of sea life and salty clean air. Even if he was ever to go back, to be with his father in Philadelphia, he would always want to return here. Only a fool would leave a place of this much magic.

And one of those fools was lying on his back now, feeling the warm sun on his face, allowing the water to dry on his hands, and sensing the most delicate crusting of salt left behind. I watched Wade as he talked to Cobain. The seal circled in wider arcs now. The fish was gone; a seal pup had other concerns. Soon he was in the middle of the harbour and drifting near the surface, on his back with his sea-dog face to the sky, drifting away and gone.

"Let's follow him," Wade said.

"Not a good idea. Let him go. He'll be back. We'll do the dory routine one more time tomorrow and then we'll walk out after that and see if he finds us when we don't show at the wharf. He's hooked. He's gone West Coast seafood gourmet now and he'll find you. We have to keep him away from that wharf."

"How do I know you're not just making all this up?"

"I guess you don't. Just trust me. Want to row?"

I held the oars out toward Wade. He looked curious, interested, a little frightened. "I don't think so. It doesn't look like that much fun."

"Suit yourself."

We rowed back along the shoreline again. I soon realized just how out of shape I was. I couldn't find the side-shore backcurrent at all this time. Each stroke was a full-on challenge. The kid could tell. "You don't look like you're gonna make it."

"I'll probably do okay."

"Want me to take over?" Wade's question was more than just adolescent male bravado.

"You and the University of Pennsylvania rowing team maybe. Otherwise, sit tight and watch a pro make headway against one of the most awesome forces of the planet."

Wade laughed, scanned the water for any sign of Cobain, and then pulled his Phillies cap low over his eyes as if nothing else could interest him.

When we pulled the boat ashore near the wharf, I was amazed to see Vance Beaudreau and a couple of Nickerson Harbour's finest and least-employed fishermen trying to get Beaudreau's old thirty-foot Cape Islander into the water. They had a cable attached to a winch on Vance's truck and had knocked the blocks out from under the *Vivian* and were letting it skid down the embankment on logs. It was a pretty comical scene: Vance was simultaneously burning out his clutch, brakes, and tires trying to keep the boat from slipping backward too fast; the other men where hooting and hollering and having a great time.

I recognized the boat my father had built for Vance the year the ice had crushed *The Casual Observer*. This old beauty had been handmade by my father almost a quarter century ago. It was worn and weathered and had lichen and moss alive and prospering on certain upper reaches of the planking. But when she kissed the water arse-first, did she ever want to float.

At some point in the launching Vance's brakes gave out and the rear of the truck entered the water until the harbour filled two-thirds of the truck bed. The *Vivian* was still tethered to the truck and floating free in the deeper water.

"They say salt water might make a truck rust!" somebody was shouting to Vance. Vance got out and tied the boat's cable to a bulkhead, drove his truck back up, and parked it by the sheds. When he and two men dragged a rowboat to the edge of the water and got in, I couldn't help but notice they had three rifle bags with them.

"Fishing gear," I lied to Wade.

"Yeah, right." The kid wasn't stupid.

"Cobain won't be around. He was only here because you were here."

We watched as the men got into the bigger boat, heard the engine cough and sputter and come to life. Vance gunned it, the water boiled around the propeller, and the boat moved off. Somebody aboard let out a yahoo.

As we walked away, I hoped like hell Cobain had stuffed himself enough to get far away, that his curiosity about humans was satisfied for today.

TWELVE

Jillian found Wade and me as we were walking away from the wharf. I didn't care for the look on her face and was hoping real hard she wasn't carrying any of her own firepower. I figured she'd seen me and the boy in the boat, him without his life jacket on, and now she was steamed again.

"Go home, Wade," she told her son.

"What now?"

"Just go home."

Wade threw his hands in the air and walked off. "See ya," he said to me.

"Later." I smiled and waved to the kid and decided I liked him, even though he was a master-class smart-ass. Or maybe I liked him because he was just that.

"I don't want you to talk to my son again."

"I know. You think I'm a child molester."

"No, I think I know who you really are."

"Great. You're one step ahead of me. Let me know the news."

"Don't try to be funny."

"Okay, I won't be funny anymore. It's not my strong suit, anyway.

What did I do to offend you now?"

"My neighbour told me you killed your wife."

"Jesus."

"Well, maybe you didn't kill her outright, but she died from drugs, right? The two of you were into it pretty heavy and you let her overdose. Do I have it right?"

"You have one version of the story, but I don't think you understand anything about it."

"I can't let my son go out in a boat with someone who uses drugs. I brought him here thinking we could get away from all that."

"Look, I got a history, you got a history. I can't change that. I'm clean as a whistle. No dope. No coke. No heroin. Hell, I don't even touch aspirin. You want to know the story about my wife, I'd be happy to tell it to you, but then you're going to think I'm the sorriest loser on the planet and you won't let your kid hang out with me because you'll be afraid it will rub off. So what do you want me to do?"

She put one hand in the air as if to halt traffic. "Look, I'm very sorry about your problems, but I've got to worry about my son. He's been around drugs in the city. Kids in Philadelphia don't just smoke marijuana. I can't take any chances."

I wanted to turn and walk away from her. I didn't need this crap from a lady I hardly knew. I suddenly didn't want anything to do with her, but I knew if I bowed out of Wade's life, the kid was going to be all alone against the witless seal-killing fishermen of Nickerson Harbour who would try to kill Cobain. "Tell me one goddamn thing in life that isn't about taking chances," I snapped back, my voice a little too loud for a two-person conversation on an empty village street in the late morning.

Suddenly I saw just the slightest hint of fear in her eyes. I'd frightened her. *Shit.* I lowered my eyes to the ground, lowered my voice, as well. "Why is it you're so afraid of me? I'm not the sort of guy people tend to be afraid of. Look at me. When I was a kid, bullies liked to pick on me. When I got older, people wanted to be my friend. Everybody loved to take advantage of me. Said I was such a nice guy, all I ever did was roll over. Now you don't even know me, but you're coming at me like I'm some hardened criminal, like I'm the enemy. I don't get it."

She had composed herself now. She still didn't trust me. I could see that. "Maybe you are the enemy, Taylor Colby. Maybe you can't see it from where you stand. Now I admit I don't know much about you. I do know now you were living in California. You were some big-time guitar player and you worked with a lot of famous people. I've probably even heard you on CDs I have at home."

"Yeah, you probably have. You might not have known my name, but you heard my music. I was in considerable demand for a while."

"But I'm not impressed, understand. Men become successful at the expense of people they love."

"Men do that, do they?"

"Yeah, they do."

"Men do lots of silly things. Lots of dirty rotten low-down scum-sucking things, but it doesn't mean we're all there with the dregs of humanity."

"Men brutalize and kill."

Cobain was on my mind now. I was thinking about every wounded seagull I'd ever tried to restore to flight. I was thinking about the hunters blasting away at flocks of Canada geese on the harbour. "Yeah, they do that. But I don't. Lady, you're looking at the walking wounded here. I don't know why I'm telling you this or why I even care, but I can tell you've been hurt, deep down in some way that makes you scared and protective of your son. You ran off here to Nova Scotia, hoping you could get away from whatever the hell scared you in Philadelphia. But I don't think it's that easy. I don't expect you're going to tell me exactly what made you this way, but I can guess it had something to do with a man, not just a bunch of kids sniffing glue on the sidewalks outside the 7-Eleven store."

I heard the locks snap into place on the door, saw the window shades being pulled down tight. "I don't think I want to continue this conversation with you." Her voice had changed. This was the tone of the professional. The professor speaking to a lesser mortal, saying the audience was over.

"What are you going to do when your son grows up to be one of those men you think are so bloody awful?" I asked, but she had already turned and was walking away.

After that I felt supremely sorry for myself. I'd still work on a plan to get Cobain as far away from Nickerson Harbour as I could. If I couldn't be there to help Wade teach the seal to keep his distance from the fishermen and the wharf, I'd make sure Wade didn't have to watch his friend get murdered by bored jackasses like Vance Beaudreau or Paul Mascarene, who would inevitably kill Cobain for the sake of a little entertainment.

I drove my father to the Halifax airport in near silence. The radio in my old rusty car had been bad since the time I'd driven home to Nickerson Harbour. You couldn't get any stations, but you couldn't turn it all the way off, either, so it emanated a low white noise that filled in for conversation on the hourlong drive. I half expected to run into the original owner of the old Subaru in the parking lot, returning home from a Toronto job search, but he was nowhere to be seen.

My father wore a suit and tie. I had refused to dress up. If anything, I dressed down. He had acquired a shy nervousness about him, and I didn't want to hazard a guess what was going through his head. When I tried to talk about a game plan as to how we were going to handle this most awkward of family reunions, all he said was, "We'll take it one step at a time."

The flight's arrival was delayed, and I bought my father a doughnut and a cup of coffee. The sugar spoon shook in his hand as he asked me if his hair looked all right. We finished our coffee and he left a tip on the table, two dollars, even though we had bought our food at a cafeteria queue.

We were near the back of a small crowd as the doors opened and arriving passengers streamed through. I pretended I was far away, sitting in the surf lineup at Malibu or Steamer Lane. Mental surfing had always been my escape route from dentist chairs and other unfriendly environments. Paddle, stroke, drop down the face of a smooth wall of Pacific glass, then push myself up onto my feet and arc a bottom turn.

The crowd thinned, the tide of travellers ebbed, and we watched as one final passenger, an old woman, walked toward us, accompanied by an overly cheerful flight attendant. I hadn't told my father yet what I knew about the "tests." I'd never found the courage. I studied her face as she scanned the crowd. My father touched my hand and moved forward. She saw him, then smiled at the Air Canada attendant and thanked her. My father had his arms out. I felt dizzy and lacked the ability to breathe.

A lifetime collapsed in upon itself as a compression of time, event, and emotion coalesced before me. Nothing about the past quarter century seemed real. I stared at the strong, broad back of my father, my mother's arms around him. I couldn't see her face, but it had already been etched in my mind from the brief glimpse of her as she had come through the doorway: old, tired, soft around the eyes, pale, pale skin. She was a woman who had diminished in some way I couldn't define. Even her hair had been cut short. As I watched her hugging my father, I imagined an incandescent glow, a transfer of energy, of life force, from him to her. Or it might have been the other way around. It wasn't real—it was just a contrivance of my mind—but I was startled by the intensity of their reunion.

I hung back and waited until they released each other. Now she advanced toward me. I didn't know what to do with my face as she tried to look straight into my eyes. She pulled me to her with what seemed to be two strong arms, and her hair brushed my cheek. My mother's body was soft and frail, smaller than I remembered. She buried her face in my chest, but then pulled back slightly. "I'm dying, Taylor," she said in a hushed voice. "I had to come home."

I squeezed back the tears that were a medley of anger and sadness and hurt. "I haven't told him anything yet."

"I know. I'll tell him." My mother pulled away but continued to look into my face. She emanated pure joy at reuniting with us, and it was infectious. But even now I couldn't forgive her. I preferred to keep my distance and my grudge. "I'll pull the car around front," I said, leaving her with my father.

When they emerged from the airport, a chill north wind made my father put his jacket around his wife and usher her into the back seat. He loaded her single suitcase into the trunk, then sat with her in the back. I felt like a taxi driver. "Where to?" I asked, trying to sound cheerful, but cynicism inflected my words.

"Home, please," my mother said.

"Nothing much has changed since you left," my father said. It was a thoroughly absurd statement under the circumstances but rang true in many ways.

"I like the car very much," my mother said.

"Thanks," I said. It was a hunk of junk, and she probably assumed it belonged to my father, not me, but it didn't matter. My mother was trying to be nice. "It's new. Or at least I bought it recently." The white noise of the radio took over. I drove south on the four-lane, then east on Highway 7 until we were beyond the suburbs of Forest Hills and headed toward Musquodoboit Harbour.

In the rearview mirror I could see that my father was holding her hand. Dressed in his suit, he looked as if he were prepared to attend an Anglican Sunday-morning service. My mother was wearing what I assumed to be a fairly expensive dress. It was one of those brightly coloured, flowing affairs that a matronly woman might wear to a Santa Barbara cocktail party. I wouldn't question her sartorial selections for the voyage home.

So my mother was in the back seat, dying, slowly, I presumed. My father was like a teenage kid in love for the first time and I was the idiot prodigal son who felt he was driving them to a high-school prom. "I wanted to come out to you in California when Laura died," she said to me out of the blue.

"Then why didn't you?"

"I wasn't sure if I was welcome."

"Sure. Another person in the audience to watch me go insane would have been most welcome."

"I might have been able to help."

"I know. You were always there when I needed you," I said with as much throttled cruelty as I could pack into the words.

"Taylor," my father said, "can we at least save all that until we get to know each other again?"

"Right, Pop. Outside the music world my timing has always been bad. I'll just drive."

"No," my mother countered, "I deserve whatever there is to be said of me."

"It's all right, really. Everything turned out okay, didn't it?"

My mother pretended not to hear my sarcasm. "It's so good to be back with you two."

I stopped to fill the car with gas and watched the silhouettes of my parents in the back seat. They were talking and I couldn't imagine what they were saying to each other. The gas overflowed the tank and spilled onto my shoes before I could shut it off. As I went into the station office to pay, for the thousandth time in my life I considered simply walking away. The keys were still in the car. I would walk through the service bay and out the back behind the garage and disappear into the forest. It wasn't a mere whim; it was a serious alternative.

I was fumbling with my wallet, trying to pull out money to pay, when I looked out at my parents. They were both smiling as if complete repairs had already been satisfactorily completed to the family. My father and mother were together again. As I handed over a twenty-dollar bill, the image of Jillian swam into my mind. It shocked me as if someone had taken a hammer and thunked me on the side of the head. Walking out of there, I wondered what had come over me, but admitted to myself that I found Jillian quite attractive.

I got in the car and started it up again. Looking in the rearview mirror, I saw my mother kissing my father full on the lips. The chauffeur dutifully returned his attention to the road ahead and tilted the rearview up and away. It was then that I started to suffer from the reawakened knowledge that I hadn't kissed a woman since Laura's death. Not only had I been celibate, without female companionship and living a monastic sort of life, but the real shocker was that I hadn't even had the desire to kiss or make love to a woman, *any* woman, since that time. Living in that distant lotus land eternally programmed for romance and sex, I had learned to become truly oblivious to passions of the heart and the libido. And I had adjusted well to my loneliness as if it were an exquisite and cherished form of torture.

THIRTEEN

When I was eight years old, I was standing by the harbour edge one afternoon when I saw an old, big, black-and-white, mean-as-Satan seagull dive toward the water to harass five baby eider ducks. There was no mother duck around, and the little ducklings dived under the harbour each time the big gull attacked them. Then I saw a thing that shocked me. The gull plucked one of the tiny ducks from the harbour and flew with it a hundred feet away to perch on a tree stump where it killed the poor creature and swallowed it whole.

My onetime respect for seagulls was shattered. When the bird pulled its bulky frame up out of the water and assaulted the ducks again, I threw a stone at it, missed, threw another. I watched again as the gull repeated the murder of another baby. The ducklings that still survived were disoriented, frightened, and scattered farther out into the water. I yelled at them as only a foolish eight-year-old would yell at them to come back to shore, that I would protect them, but I didn't stand a chance.

Three small birds were still alive, and I knew now the gull wouldn't be satisfied. He'd kill as many as he could. I ran back to the wharf and located one of my father's dories. I threw in a couple of half-shattered oars that were lying nearby and shoved hard against the heavy boat with my insignificant weight until it floated and I threw myself in. Then I rowed like a madman as quickly as I could, which wasn't fast enough. I screamed at the damn gull. I cursed it long and loud so that the men left standing on the wharf thought I had lost my mind. Not one would have considered interfering with the natural way of death. I was too young to presume the detached attitude of adults. I had no choice but to react. The surviving ducks were now my responsibility.

I carried no rocks to toss at the gull, and as I splashed my oars and yelled, it was obvious I was scaring the tiny survivors. Their adversary, the biggest and meanest of gulls living on the East Coast of North America, knew I was of no consequence. All too soon there was only one survivor. I was within ten feet of the tiny eider when he dived, unable to comprehend that I was the good guy, here to save him. I feathered the oars and waited for the duck to surface. "Come here," I pleaded. "Please come here." The gull was high in the sky, gorged but not giving up, flying around in easy circles. A dip of the wing and he could swoop fast, despite his heavy meal. His killer instinct made him the calmest and most self-assured of nature's murderers.

The eider surfaced, thirty feet away. These little guys were amazing underwater swimmers. I paddled near him, warding off the gull. The eider dived again. I waited for him to surface, slowly rowing in his direction. Still the gull spiralled above, occasionally casting a travelling shadow across the ripples of the harbour until the predator blocked the sun for an instant and I felt the cruel, dark weight of its presence.

I tagged after my friend, and finally the gull gave up and flew off, allowing me to declare a small victory. The eider surfaced within inches of my dory now but, shocked at his miscalculation, dived again. I waited, scanned all four quarters, and waited yet longer. And then I saw the tiny feathered creature surface, a limp, lifeless-looking body. Quickly I rowed to him and scooped the little bird up in my hand. He was still warm, near weightless, and I gently cradled him inside my jacket. I unbuttoned my shirt and held him against my chest as the dory drifted toward open sea.

As the bird awoke, fluffed about, and peeped with a high, sharp trill, I felt the strangest of sensations. "It's okay, little guy. You're going to be all right." I cupped the eider in my hands again and looked into his eyes. My heart melted, but I felt like a failure, having saved only one out of five. I wondered at the awful terror of a bird watching siblings snatched up into the sky and swallowed whole. I troubled my mind into a tourniquet of confusion as to why nature would tolerate such an easy conquest as this, how it could permit such an imbalance of power.

Now, however, the problem was how to get the eider ashore and home. He squirmed and chirped and peeped loudly for his long-lost brothers and sisters, and the human voice of a boy wasn't likely a comforting song to his ears. I couldn't hold him easily, for I had to row as we were drifting farther and farther from town. There was water in the bottom *V* of the boat and a slatted rack for feet above that. Cupping the bird with one hand, I lifted the slats and gingerly set my friend in the space beneath, then gently replaced the flooring in the rack above him. He had little headroom but settled in the several inches of water and looked up at me strangely as if from behind prison bars. "It's necessary," I told him. "That's all I can tell you now, little guy."

I rowed toward shore and found a slacker current against which I made some headway. I realized then I had never gone out alone during a fully escaping tide. My father wouldn't have allowed it. I struggled and fought but barely moved, even near the shoreline. The eider continued to chant messages to his missing family, or perhaps it was his plea for rescue to his absentee parents, but there was no sign of any other of his kind.

Finally I admitted defeat and beached the boat, not far from the mouth of Scarcity Brook. I left the duck in the boat, let out a long rope from the bow, and towed the dory back to the wharf with great difficulty, for I believed it would have been wrong to leave the vessel ashore so far from home where anything might happen to it.

The hangashores back at the wharf saw me towing my father's

boat and laughed with much public pointing and flashing of teeth in the sunlight. I didn't have the word for it, but I felt they were in league with the gull. The world was divided between the powerfully cruel and the rest of us—the weak. I didn't believe at that point in my life, however, that the weak need all be victims. I ignored the men as they watched me drag the dory onto the stony beach and tie it with a good, dependable knot. Next they saw me lift the flooring and scoop out the tiny eider.

"Gonna make soup out of it?" somebody asked, but I wouldn't answer. Nor would I look up at any of them. I held the fiercely squirming eider inside my jacket and headed home. As I opened the back door, my mother saw a look on my face that revealed both despair and hope. If this commingling of emotions actually existed, then they could only live in the features of a child. The eider popped his head through an opening between the buttons of my jacket, and my mother's eyes lit up. "What do we have here?"

I cherish that day as no other, I suppose, because the woman who greeted me and my eider orphan seemed so much like the best of all mothers in the world. There was no question in her mind that we would try to help the bird after I told the tale of the evil black-and-white gull. She emptied a laundry tub, set it in front of the oil stove, and filled it with water from our well. When I settled the duck into the water, it swam immediately around and around. It didn't try to get out. He swam silently but with intent, ducked his head under and drank long and hard from the water in which he propelled himself.

My mother cut up tiny pieces of raw fish and, miraculously, the bird ate the morsels right from her fingers. I put my head down low and stared into the dark eyes of the eider. The faces of ducks the world over are extremely beautiful, even sensual. My mother was as fascinated by our new tenant as I was. She gave me no lecture about the foolhardiness of trying to raise a wild creature by human hands. She even generously failed to remind me that thousands of these birds grew up and were shot by hunters each fall. Instead, she shared in the wonder of the houseguest swimming in the clear, cool waters of the laundry tub.

My mother warmed up a bowl of soup—a heady, heavenly mixture of cod tongues and herring fillets, beach peas and dried kale, with slivers of sliced kelp, Irish moss, and dulse. It was a recipe that was an oddity even for a fishing community where most families had little respect for the taste or texture of seaweed and yet supped and sated themselves with monstrous intakings of salt fish, salt pork, and fried fat. My mother had inherited a special compendium of near-organic recipes from her own mother, and I was a singular fan of her sea-based soups and exotic chowders. As I ate, however, and maintained eye contact with my eider pet, I heard the words of the man from the wharf and vowed that, whatever I would eat in my life, I wouldn't devour duck again, ever.

The baby eider grew quickly accustomed to us that day and seemed perfectly content. We became family. It was a golden time. I knew nothing of my mother's needs for finer clothes, a better house, a more active worldly life. Nor did she express those needs. The next morning I woke up at six-thirty and ran to the kitchen. My mother was already there looking into the tub. Her footsteps in the hall had probably awakened me. We both studied the lifeless baby eider afloat in the water. She reached down first to pick it up and then I touched the stiff, cold form she was holding.

"I don't get it," I said. "He was doing fine." The tears came as my mother hugged me tightly. I closed my eyes, and we were locked in that embrace when my father came into the room. He put his arms around both of us, and I felt hot tears fall onto my head but had no idea whose eyes they fell from. I felt mad and I felt cheated and I didn't have anyone to blame. But, at that moment, I felt closer to my mother than I had ever experienced before or after.

At noon my father returned from the wharf where he had been talking to the fishermen. Vance Beaudreau had told him that salt-water ducks could only drink the water they lived in. If they drank fresh, they died. My father tried to explain this to me in a clinical, matter-of-fact manner.

"That's ridiculous," my mother said. "He's lying. How could such a thing be true?"

"I don't know if it is or isn't," he said. "Maybe he just died of loneliness. Ducks grow up spending all their time with their families. Maybe they can't survive alone."

"I never heard of such a thing," my mother countered.

"It doesn't matter," I said. "It's just not fair."

And there was a deep and abiding scar from that small tragedy, made more awful by the fact that I discovered later that Vance Beaudreau was right. Survival was an extremely fine-tuned instrument. One string out of whack and disaster followed. My mother and I had killed the little eider orphan with our own best intentions.

A surreal atmosphere hung over us in this house of a family reunited after so many years. My mother had put on a cheery face; her voice spoke only of positive things. We slipped into a time warp and relived days and moments before my twelfth year. We reshaped and refitted our private history, making alterations and fabrications that created a pageant of our lives primitive and pure. I asked my mother if she remembered anything of the small duck I had brought home, and all she said was: "You were always bringing home some stray thing or other, some poor wild animal with a broken this or that."

My father had a hard time making conversation and spoke with an odd formality but with the greatest sense of respect toward his wife. They had never divorced. The matter, as far as I could tell, had never been discussed between them over the years. My mother had remarried, illegally I gathered. In the eyes of the law she was a bigamist, but such a word seemed ill-fitting. Once, in a dark moment of despair and revenge, I had toyed with the idea of getting on the phone in California and calling up an Ontario lawyer to file charges against my own mother. But I couldn't bring myself to do it. I knew it would involve my father and hurt him deeply.

So my mother had been remarried to her new husband, a shoe salesman. A man named Frank. I had never met him, but I envisioned a slick, worldly, handsome Casanova who had swept my beautiful mother off her feet. Once I had learned the creep had a name, I discovered that I fully hated the name Frank and anyone who shared the moniker.

My mother asked if it was okay to make supper, and my father said it was fine. I watched as she opened cupboards and reached for ingredients that were still located in the exact places where she had once kept them. She found cod in the freezer and potatoes in a bin where they had always been stored. The potatoes had long sprouts on them. She trimmed off the white "legs," carved out the eyes, and boiled the potatoes with the cod until they were soft and pale. There was no seaweed in the house. All manner of dried seaweed except for dulse had long since gone out of fashion in our more modern community where even fish was a luxury these days, often bought in the IGA and having origins in Iceland or British Columbia, rather than the "real thing" caught two miles beyond the mouth of the harbour.

With my father safely gone for an hour or so to finish varnishing the repaired dory in the shed, my mother and I could talk freely.

"I can't bring myself to tell him," she said, removing a scarf from her head that revealed her hair to be fashionably short. But the short hair on my mother was still a bit of a shock. "It's because of the chemo," she told me, noticing my surprise, then laughed. "You think this is bad. You should have seen the hideous mess I was a while ago."

I pretended not to be appalled by the sight of my old mother with short, straggly hair on her scalp, where once flowed long, dark locks. She could tell I was uncomfortable and generously returned the scarf to her head. "Your father didn't even pretend to notice I had changed."

"You know he's like that."

"I know what he's like. And I know exactly what I did to him and to you. That's why I'm back here."

"What about Frank?"

"Frank is Frank."

"You can just leave him?"

"No, I can't. Frank is a good man. All I knew was that I had to be back here. I don't know what I'm going to do about that man in Ontario. He told me I should come here, though, if it was what I needed to do. He said he could handle it."

"Maybe he's happy to be rid of you," I said, but as soon as the words were out, I felt guilty for saying them.

She smiled and peeled some more leggy potatoes, then reached deep into the cupboard and, without even looking, found the pepper in the same spot it had been in for thirty years. "I wish it was that easy. I really do."

"How do you expect anything to be easy after the mess you created?"

"I don't expect anything to be easy. Except dying. I think dying will be easy."

"You don't look that unhealthy."

"If I can keep a good attitude, I can look fit as a fiddle."

"So does that mean you could stay like this for quite a while?"

"No. It doesn't. I've been living with cancer for nearly eight years. It started in the pancreas. Then it spread. I've done radiation, chemotherapy, shark cartilage, acupuncture, herbs, macrobiotics, psychic healing, every possible thing—scientific or quack-stupid. I did it all. Frank made me. I had no choice."

"You see that boat in the front yard with your name on it?"

"I did. It's a beauty."

"But no buyers. He built it, named it, anyway, and set it there in the front yard for everybody to see. And he didn't care that every soul in Nickerson Harbour would probably laugh at him for being so hung up on you after all these years."

She was cutting onions now and sniffling. I had watched her give up paring potatoes and reach for an onion, stab into it, and hang her head slightly as if to use it as an excuse for her tears.

"I want *you* to tell him," she said finally. "I can't do it."

"I have to warn you. I don't deal well with death. I run and hide."

"Doesn't everybody?"

"I don't know. I know I'm worse than the average schmuck off the street."

"I'm really not afraid of dying," she said, pouring onions and potatoes into the pot on the stove, then looking at me with glassy eyes as steam rose before her.

"How can that be?"

"I went through a lot of pain in all these treatments. I know what pain is and it scares the living daylights out of me."

"You should know there's several kinds of pain. Not all of it is associated with cancer and hospitals."

"I know that. And I know what you're saying. I caused you a lot of pain, Taylor. I hurt you and your father. I need you both to forgive me."

"Great," I said. "You think it's that simple?"

"No. It isn't. And I can't justify what I did to you both. It was something I felt I had to do, and you'll hate me for saying this, but for me it was the right thing."

"Go to hell," I said.

My father was on the back steps just then, his hand on the door. My mother glanced at me with frantic appeal in her face, then turned and went back to the cutting board and sliced clean and deep through another onion.

I looked away as my old man walked in through the door and bent to take his work boots off. He hadn't taken his boots off upon entering the house since she had left. In his fallible, faulted, but ever-optimistic mind, the Colby family was still picking up where it had left off. His twelve-year-old son had somehow been transformed into a middle-aged man, and his wife had cut her hair and taken on crow's-feet. Aside from that, though, he wasn't remotely concerned about the lapse of years. He had walked out that door less than twenty minutes ago and upon returning had discovered the world had gone fast-forward. Nevertheless, he was smiling. He was a father, a husband, and a craftsman and he had family. What else was there that could possibly be worth worrying about?

FOURTEEN

For the rest of that day and the day that followed we lived peaceably together with little talk about any past wrongs or what life might have been like had we all stayed together. My father and mother shared a room and I think my mother pretended her life in Ontario hadn't existed. When she and I were alone, I tried to convince her to tell my father the truth about her illness. I still refused to have any part in delivering the bad news.

"Let's go out in the backyard," she said.

I followed her down the steps and she began to walk slowly toward the workshop. She looked at the wood grain of the door, then turned and walked to the edge of the forest. It was as if she were getting reacquainted with everything. Very little had changed here—physically at least—since she had left, since I had left.

We strolled to the side of the house, and she stood silently staring at the boat with her name on it in the front yard.

"I had to come back here," she said. "You know that."

"I think I understand."

"It seems so cruel when I look back on what I did."

I said nothing.

"I kept trying to think of some way to fix it, to make it up to you and your father. But there was nothing. That's when I decided I'd just come back. It doesn't seem like much, does it?" Gulls were circling the boat now. You could smell the salt in the air. "I don't know. It's just good to have us all together right now."

My mother described how she found out about the cancer that had begun in her pancreas and then spread. She described in detail the treatment and the pain. She also asked me several times, when we were alone like that, to tell her about Laura, but I wouldn't. Although I had agreed to a workable truce with my mother, for my father's sake, I wouldn't allow her to be my confidante or my confessor when it came to the greatest tragedy and regret of my life.

I did not, however, want to allow her to remain mute about this other mysterious life in Ontario, the life I envisioned with the handsome, sophisticated stranger who had been able to supply her with whatever worldly possessions, excitement, and cosmopolitan thrills she had craved as a younger woman. "What did you tell Frank when you left to come here?"

"I told him I was coming here," she said, standing at the stove again, stirring a pot of beef stew. The smell was extraordinary, like nothing I had experienced in the house since she had left. It was more than just the basics. There were spices in there that didn't register, spices she must have brought with her from Ontario.

"And he accepted that?"

"Frank is Frank."

"You keep saying that. What the hell is it supposed to mean?"

"He's a very understanding man."

"All of your men have been that way," I said with an edge to my voice as sharp as a beach-rock barnacle.

She let out a long sigh and looked at me apologetically. I just left the room.

The following morning the three of us were sitting down at breakfast. My mother had a look of pain on her face but refused to admit anything was wrong. Instead, she took a pill, then a second pill. "It's nothing," she kept saying. "Nothing much at all."

That was when someone pounded frantically on the back door,

then wrenched it open before I had a chance to get up. It was Jillian. I immediately registered the panic in her face. "Have you seen Wade?" she asked.

"No," I said. I had decided Jillian was trouble, big trouble. If she didn't want me around her kid, I was going to stay clear.

"I told him not to go back to the wharf. Yesterday he didn't. But now he's not in his room. I don't know where he went. I think something's wrong."

"I'll help you look," I said. "I've got a couple of hunches where he might be."

My father was on his feet. "Let me help, too."

I looked at the worry in my mother's face. There was something about this scene that tugged at her memory.

"No. Stay here. I'll call if I need help. I think I know where he's at." I suspected Wade had succeeded in weaning Cobain from the wharf and was meeting him at Grandfather Rock.

I followed Jillian to her car and she raced us to the wharf. I expected to see the place empty, but I saw Paul Mascarene's car parked with the trunk open. At first I didn't see Paul. Instead, I saw Vance Beaudreau and Max Snell studying something that was blocked from our view by a shed wall. Then I heard the gunshot, and someone let out a loud war whoop. "What the hell?" Jillian cried. I jumped from the car to have a look. Jillian was close on my heels.

Neither one of us was fully prepared for the grotesque scene. Hanging from a large wooden frame, one used to haul out car and boat engines, were the dead bodies of two large harbour seals. They were hanging from the frame with cables threaded through their necks. Someone had taken a knife and slit their bodies full-length, spilling their stomachs and intestines onto the ground. And the two fishermen laughed as Paul Mascarene fired at one carcass and then another with his shotgun. He was unsteady as he pulled the trigger— from booze or from his car injuries, I wasn't certain.

The carnage of the seals was enough to make us both sick. I knew why they had killed the seals. I had a vague understanding of their perverse misbelief that the seals had stolen their livelihood, but I couldn't even begin to fathom why they would string up the creatures and blast away at them. Paul loaded two more shells, waved his gun at the sky, then let go with two barrels peppering into the poor dead seals who once so gracefully swam this harbour.

Jillian put two hands over her face. I walked over to Paul as he dropped two more shells into the gun and closed it. Grabbing the weapon, I yanked it out of his hands. It went off, and buckshot whizzed past Paul's head up into the branches of the spruces. The blast of the gun scared us both, and I realized I had made a very rash move. I knew nothing about guns. I could have killed him or me or somebody standing nearby. I looked at the shocked, cock-eyed expression on the face of the guy who was once my musical idol. Then I glanced at the sad disgrace of the corpses that had been used for target practice.

"What the hell are you doing, Colby?" Paul demanded. "You nearly blew my brains out!"

I was holding the gun, examining it as if it were some kind of inscrutable living thing. I also knew there was one shell still in the barrel. Not a good thing to have hanging around when two shore boys got into a quarrel. I swallowed hard. I didn't know what to do. Give it back to him, point made? Or walk away with it? I saw a glimmer of an insane little smile spread on Paul's face. He wiped a grimy hand across his mouth and looked unsteady again. Paul was sizing me up, and I knew I was out of my depth.

Vance and Snell were watching us. They'd stopped laughing. "Just a little fun there, Taylor. Don't get so riled. Me and Snell caught these bastards this morning, put a bullet in 'em, and brought 'em ashore. Two less of 'em to steal our fish. Paul isn't hurting anyone."

My eyes were on Paul, and we were both caught off guard when Jillian came up beside me. "Give me the gun," she said.

Now I had a big problem: Jillian, the man-hater, in the midst of this scene of masculine cruelty. Was it a good idea for a woman with a grudge to have a shotgun in her hands around any of us?

"Please, give me the gun," she repeated.

"Give her the damn gun," Paul said. He saw the confusion in my face. Paul didn't have the foggiest idea what was going on.

Gingerly I handed Jillian the weapon. She took it out of my

hands like an old-time schoolteacher, indignant at the behaviour of her students, taking away a water pistol from the belligerent boy in the back row. Then she deftly unloaded the gun. We watched as she calmly strolled to the side of the harbour and threw Paul's shotgun ten feet out into the water.

After that she walked back in our direction, brushing off her hands. With a clear, calm voice she asked, "Sorry to interrupt the fun, but have any of you seen my son, Wade? Twelve years old, wears a Phillies baseball cap."

Paul snickered. "He's yours, is he?"

"Do you know where he is?" I asked.

"He was here," Paul said. "He come onto me with language like I never heard around here. Kid has no sense of respect for the handicapped at all. What've you been teachin' him?"

I saw fear in Jillian's eyes. I could just imagine Wade arriving to see the dead seals strung up and these jerks standing around laughing or shooting. The kid would have gone wild.

"You didn't hurt him?" Jillian asked.

Vance walked over as Paul started to laugh hard. "No, miss. That little boy of yours started cursing at us and giving us a lecture. We let him go on but didn't pay him much mind."

"I have a feeling the kid had good reason to be upset to see a couple of God's beautiful creatures like that strung up and dripping their guts all over the ground," I said. "Vance, where did he go?"

"Look, we didn't ask him to come down here and watch."

"Where is my son?" Jillian demanded.

"He took that dory of Horace's that Taylor brought down the other day. He untied her and he rowed off."

"Least he tried to row off," Snell said. "He was pretty upset. Don't know where he thought he was going in a boat. Tide going out and all. Just wanted to get away from us, I guess. But he didn't look too lively with those oars. I know I saw you teaching him how to row, Taylor. But, if it was me, I wouldn't let him out there on his own quite yet."

Jillian flashed me a look that said I was going to burn in hell if she had any say in the matter.

Paul had gotten over being angry already and didn't seem to care that his shotgun was sitting in about twelve feet of salt water. "Anyone want a beer?" he asked as he hobbled toward the open trunk of his car. "You, miss?" he asked Jillian.

I walked to my father's fish shack and looked inside. The oars were missing, but the life jacket was still there. I picked it up and gave it to Jillian. On the shoreline I saw only one small boat, Vance's little beat-up plywood skiff. "Come on," I said to her.

She got in, looking unsure and unsteady. I shoved the little rowboat hard off the pebbly shoreline and jumped in. "Vance, I'm borrowing your boat."

"Bring it back in one piece," he said, following Paul to his car.

As soon as we were afloat, I realized how poorly the rowboat had been constructed. Vance had made it himself. It wasn't the work of my father, but a hasty, haphazard makeshift thing. A make-do-until-you-can-buy-something-better sort of boat. It leaked water from all corners, and one of the oarlocks was broken. "Put on the life jacket," I told Jillian.

She looked at it on the floor of the boat but didn't pick it up. "Don't worry about me. Just take me to where Wade is."

I shook my head. "You're as stubborn as he is. But then I guess he got it from you."

"What do you mean?"

"I mean, I tried to get him to wear that thing, but he refused. Said he was a good swimmer. Swam every Saturday in a public swimming pool back in Philadelphia with his father."

Jillian had a hand on each side of the boat, keeping herself steady, looking unsure, however, about being out in the harbour in a leaky boat with me. "His father always promised to take him swimming but almost never did. His father was a very *busy* man. Didn't have much time for his son."

"So Wade's not much of a swimmer?"

"No, why?"

"Nothing. Keep your eyes peeled for a dory."

Now she wanted to turn on me again, her only ally. "What was he doing in a boat with you?"

"I know, I know. I overstepped my bounds. It had to do with that seal friend of his. You saw those idiots back there. If they came across Cobain playing around the wharf, waiting for Wade, they'd shoot the seal and ask questions later."

The first traces of the morning sea breeze fanned out across the water in front of us. Jillian couldn't suppress a shiver that ran up through her body. Cold sea air and fear for her son commingled. She leaned over and put on the life jacket. I pulled hard on the oars, trying to compensate for the broken oarlock.

Then something appeared in the water. Jillian was startled and wobbled the little boat so bad I had to make a quick, flat slap with the oar on the opposite side to keep us from tipping. We both watched as the seal surfaced and drifted alongside, pacing us in the current, blinking salt water out of his piercing dark eyes.

"He was here this morning," I said. "Wade found him and tried to row him away from the wharf as far as he could."

"And you taught him how to use a boat?"

I hadn't taught the kid a thing. We hadn't had time and it wasn't really on the agenda. "Yeah, he picked it up pretty quick."

"Why didn't he tell me?"

"Kids don't tell their parents lots of things. Yo, Cobain," I called to the little seal. "Take me to Wade."

Cobain, unfortunately, hadn't grown up watching TV shows about domesticated dolphins or movies about tame killer whales. Cobain was simply a hungry seal who would keep company with any kid carrying a tin of fish from the IGA. I tried to keep his attention, but he had already decided we had no food for him. He dived deep and swam off, up-harbour. Wherever Wade was, it was unlikely he would have ended up in any direction opposite to the current. I zigged and zagged across the harbour to try to cover as much ground as possible. But I couldn't ignore the gnawing feeling in my gut.

FIFTEEN

"We should have called the Coast Guard or someone," Jillian said.

"It would take too long for them to get here," I countered. "Besides, we're here. Wade's probably ashore somewhere. It'll be okay."

She looked at me then and I absorbed the entirety of her fears for her son. I couldn't let the depth of the terror in her eyes overwhelm me. If I did, I'd be of no use. She held my gaze for seconds, and I knew then the barriers had come down at least in that brief instance. I was her ally now, her only hope in finding her son. She needed me desperately and she would no longer push me away as the enemy. "Please help me find him, Taylor."

"I will. Wade's a smart kid. Resourceful."

"I know."

But I knew it was a big harbour with tricky currents. There were islands and there was too much territory to cover. I hoped he remembered about the plan to attract Cobain to Scarcity Brook and the big rock. I angled off toward that precise location but, as it came closer into view, I saw no sign of Wade. We went in tight to shore, but there was still no sign of him. I decided that if he was on land he was okay, but if he was still on the water, he would have drifted farther out. I was to take no chances and row on. We'd figure a way back somehow. The sea breeze was stiffer and that, in one respect, was a good sign; it would help counter the outgoing tide, slow down the approach to sea.

I checked my watch. Twenty minutes had passed. Jillian hugged herself to ward off the chill. We were a long way from the wharf. Once past Settler's Island, we would be out of the protected part of the harbour. Silently we slipped past the east side of the island without a sign of a boat or a boy. When the first wave of the open sea slapped into the boat, the frail plywood craft shuddered and seawater splashed into it.

Jillian looked scared, and for good reason.

"It's okay," I said. "I did some surfing in California. Big waves. These are nothing. I don't think Wade would have come this far, but if he did, he's in a dory my father built, much stronger than this. All he has to do is stay in it. You can't sink the ones my old man makes. It's been proven. The Canadian navy used to use them as targets at sea, but it was too discouraging for the artillery men. They'd pound one of my father's dories with enough ammunition to sink the fleet, but it would still be there bobbing in the waves as if nothing happened."

Jillian tried to smile, but it was a failure.

Then I saw the dory in the breakers on the rocky shoal known as Roaring Bull. "Look," I said, and began to row hard against the waves.

"He's not in it," Jillian said.

"He's probably lying down. The boat is fine. He should be okay."

I was truly hoping the kid had gone ashore somewhere way back and that the dory had just slipped to sea. I wouldn't tell Jillian I had my doubts about even getting ourselves back out of here in the flimsy plywood boat. I watched the wood screws loosening in the frame behind where she was sitting, but it wouldn't do much good to complain about the quality of the workmanship now. Best to get to my father's dory and get us all in it. I hoped like hell the kid was safe ashore, though.

Jillian began yelling for her son, but it was hard to hear anything above the sound of the waves slapping over the side of the boat. "I think you'd better start bailing," I told her. We had salt water up to our ankles, and the rowing was getting very hard.

She cupped her hands and started scooping out water. I wasn't lying about my surfing skills. I used everything I knew about waves to skim up the face of the incoming waves and over, then pull hard into the trough of the next one to make some headway. The dory was at the whim of the waves, but it still seemed to miraculously go straight into them as if by instinct. Anything connecting sideways to a wave out here was certain to swamp.

"Wade!" Jillian yelled. There was still no sign of him.

In the next instant we slammed into another wave and it broke on top of us, the cold water drenching me first as it swept over my back. "No problem," I said. "We're almost there." Whatever would happen next, my plan was to ditch the little rowboat that was coming apart at the seams and climb into the safety of my father's dory. We were almost upon it when a second wave smacked hard into our skiff and left us half-filled with water. I knew we had almost no control.

The dory had shifted around, and we could now see Wade in the water, clinging to the side of it. I yelled out to him and tried my best to keep control of our own craft as I spotted another larger wave about to engulf us. "Hang on!" I yelled to Wade, but I saw the swell lifting the dory into the air. The wave feathered at the top and started to break. The boat was safely above the top and about to slide down the back, but the force of the breaking wave tugged at Wade and he lost his grip. Before I could do anything Jillian was over the side and swimming toward her son. "No!" I screamed at her, but it was too late. The wave crashed down hard on top of her, then swept over me. I toughed out the blast of salt water that wanted me out of the boat, too, but I quickly realized it had been a moot victory. Frothing seawater filled to the gunwales. The water was predictably icy cold, and I watched as Jillian struggled to keep her own head above water and make her way toward her son. My boat was being swept away from them, and I realized my plan to hang on to the oars and get into the other boat wasn't going to do much good. I leaned over into the water and began to swim with ferocious determination, trying to catch up to Jillian.

As I reached her, we both watched in horror as her son struggled to stay above the water line, only to drop beneath the surface as he flailed his arms. I knew we were in the relative shallows of Roaring Bull, but there was no footing to be had. It was a bad piece of work, this shelf of savage stone that had taken its toll on incautious fishing boats for centuries. Even though I had grown up here and gone to sea a hundred times, I had never once been right here at this spot. We'd always steered clear for good reason.

Jillian struggled to swim. I didn't even want to get close to her, fearing the horror I would encounter in her eyes. She would be pummelled by the waves, but I couldn't help her now. The boy surfaced, and I kicked my feet hard, ploughed the seas with my city-softened muscles until I was an arm's length away. Jillian screamed something unintelligible at me as I reached out and grabbed, only to find my hands clutching air. Wade had slipped below again. I dived deep but couldn't see a thing, had little control as the turbulence over the reef pushed me this way and that. My hands finally scratched on the rocks of the bottom just as my lungs were about to explode and the cold was about to rip open my brain. I realized I had even lost my sense of down from up.

As I pushed off the bottom of this raging sea for the surface, I ran smack into Wade, clutched at the back of his shirt, and dragged him to the surface. A wave caught me full in the face as I was about to breathe, and I coughed and sputtered salt water. Wade was coughing, gagging, and wrenching himself around. I could barely hang on to him just as his mother arrived. She hugged him to her even as he vomited seawater and flailed about in panic. I clasped Jillian's life jacket as two more waves smashed over us.

She held tightly to the boy. I knew she wouldn't let go, and although I could see they were certainly not safe, the jacket was keeping them both afloat. Wade was crying now, wailing something incomprehensible.

The worst of our plight was this: we were being held in position just over the reef, locked there by the outgoing tide and the incoming waves. It seemed impossible to go farther out or farther in to deeper water and relative safety. I tugged at Jillian and Wade, trying to drag us east, away from the fury of the pounding sea, but it was like towing lead. "Just hang on!" I screamed again, only to find myself assaulted with another mouthful of frothing white water. I coughed, spit it out, then began a torturous swim across and through the powerful waves to where the dory bobbed. I tried once to heave myself up over the side but discovered my arms had gone limp. I tried a second time and failed.

I couldn't believe how the sea had sapped my strength in so short a time. I watched in horror as another wave swept over mother and son, and I vowed to God and all the dirty evil natural forces of the planet that I wouldn't let them die. I allowed the next wave to hoist me as it lifted the boat, then I went up over the side, fell into the bottom in a shallow pool of seawater, and tried quickly to steady the dory and get my bearings.

There was two feet of seawater, but the boat was intact. One oar was floating inside it. I got to my knees and drove it like a weapon into the sea. A set of waves had just passed us by, and there was plenty of chop but a lapse of swells. I dug hard with that oar like a demented canoeist. It would be twenty seconds at most before the hammering of the next set of murderous North Atlantic waves. Mother and son were silent and looking the other way, unable perhaps to turn around. I tried to shout but found I had no voice, then decided I would save all my lung capacity for the task at hand.

As I drove that oar into the sea, desperately wishing I had two to make this dory sing the way my father had intended it to, I watched two heads, mother and son, bobbing in front of me. This woman, Jillian, wouldn't let go of her son. Facing away from me, she must have believed they were alone now. Wade no longer struggled, and I knew that was a bad sign.

"Get in!" I screeched as I approached, my voice like that of a frightened boy. But Jillian didn't move. I leaned over and grabbed her.

"I can't move my arms," she said.

"I know. I'm going to turn you so I can grab Wade."

I tugged on her life jacket and slowly pulled her around. Wade's face was white, his lips blue, his eyes closed. I braced myself to keep the boat balanced, then pulled hard on the boy until he was up over the side. It was as if the sea were trying to suck him back below, though. I was amazed at how heavy he was. Just as I felt the ocean give up its grip, he tumbled into the bottom of the dory, his head resting on the seat. Then the next batch of waves arrived. I reached over to grab Jillian, but she slipped away. I was forced to grasp my oar and use it as a rudder to keep from getting swamped by the first wave and then the second. Wade was stirring now, shivering, in the bottom of the boat. He shook his head and vomited again as another wave broke over us. I could do little more than keep us afloat until seven waves passed by. The harbour current kept pushing us back into the face of breaking waves even as the waves themselves tried to wash us landward.

During the next lull, I dug hard again with the oar to make my way to Jillian, vowing I'd never again have anything to do with the sea. My love for waves had turned to vile hatred. Wade was shaking violently, and I heard him call out for his mother. I hadn't lost sight of her. When I came up close a second time, I saw that her eyes were open, but it was as if a fire were slowly going out. "Jillian, get in," I said.

"I can't."

"You can." I dragged on the life jacket until it ripped and I feared she'd slip again into the sea. Try as I might, I couldn't pull her into the boat. Seconds mattered. More waves would be on the way. I hated what I had to do next, but it was my only solution. I took the rope from the bow of the dory and tied it around her, looping it through the damaged life jacket. "I'm not losing you," I said, noting again that faraway look in her eyes.

As the first new wave lifted us, I jammed hard on the oar, stroke after stroke, then held it stiff at the rear of the boat, using it as a rudder. I could feel Jillian being dragged behind us, and I knew she would be assaulted by more icy water as each new wave slammed down, but I couldn't think about that now. I used as much of the force of the wave as I could to get us inside the shallows, then I paddled hard, hard, harder to get us those precious hundred feet east of the Roaring Bull.

Once in deeper water, we were still slowly drifting toward the open ocean, but at least we were free of the grip of the crashing waves. I tugged at the rope and pulled Jillian toward us, then lowered myself into the sea and gradually, painfully, lifted her over the side and into the boat. She looked drugged, but she immediately clung to her son as they lay huddled in the water at the bottom of the dory, both crying and shivering.

I prayed silently for the miracle of a second oar that would get us ashore, but none appeared. I saw that Vance's plywood rowboat had been smashed apart in the waves and all that was left was unsalvageable lumber. There was no sign of those oars, either.

The harbour was broad here, the sea wind working to our advantage now. The sun was out, and I felt the most generous warmth spread throughout me. I used the oar again as a paddle and we moved ever so slowly eastward.

When I landed the dory at Stoney Beach, a good mile beyond Scarcity Brook, I picked up Wade and carried him to a place sheltered by the wind but exposed to the bright morning sunlight. Then I went back, led Jillian out of the boat, and untied the rope. "I'm sorry about this. I wasn't strong enough to lift you into the boat out there in the waves. It must have seemed like the cruellest possible thing to do."

She put her arms around me and pulled me toward her. "You saved my son first. That was the right thing to do. Even if you had to sacrifice me to do it, it would have been the right thing."

"I wasn't sacrificing you," I said, and suddenly I found I couldn't say another word.

"I know," she said. I felt how cold her body was.

"Sit down over here."

We sat by Wade, who was warmer now but exhausted. He was sleeping. His breathing seemed normal, and when I roused him once, he awoke and said, "I'm tired."

Jillian was still shivering, but we were both beginning to feel the effect of the warm sunlight feeding life back into us. "Hold me," she said. "Please just hold me."

SIXTEEN

Jillian had her arms around her son, and I had my arms around this strange, frightened woman who had come into my life. I blessed the sun that granted us the warmth and I thanked the compassion of the great boulder behind us that sheltered us from the sea wind.

And then I felt a door open inside me. I was holding a woman in my arms again for the first time since Laura had died. I was grateful and I was very, very afraid, but I saw myself walking through a doorway that led me back into the household of humanity. I was becoming human again. Inside the first room was a remembrance of things too painful for anyone to desire to remember, but I would have to walk through there before I could enter the other rooms of that house.

We had all nearly drowned. I had played yet again a masterful role in assisting fate to create a vicious, mortal trap, this time for a twelve-year-old boy and his mother and me, as well. Life, I reminded myself, was such a treacherous and dangerous game that at times I wasn't sure if it was worth playing at all. You were up against a force that changed the rules from under you whenever it liked.

My own selfishness and apathy had killed my wife. Back here in

Nickerson Harbour, however, it would have been my involvement, my concern in the matters of Jillian and Wade, that would have led inadvertently to their demise. Any decision, I now knew, any action, could lead to pain, suffering, death.

The sea itself had been my friend. Atlantic or Pacific, it had been relatively benevolent in my life, brought me visions of beauty, provided a backdrop for love, granted joy, freedom, and even escape through surfing. Now it had tried to swallow the three of us. Nothing was to be trusted.

The cynic's voice was loud and clear in my head, but I was still opening doors, moving from one room to the next, in this hovel of human existence. I was holding Jillian in my arms. She *wanted* me to hold her in my arms. Her words. As the last shiver of Atlantic cold left my body, I closed my eyes and entered into a room in the sacred central core of the house that was my mind and soul. It was a room safely insulated from the pain, but it wasn't a place of apathy. It was a room of love, a sanctuary within my heart that I hadn't visited for a long time. I closed my eyes tightly and pressed Jillian to me.

The wind continued to rise, and small waves slapped at the pebbles along the beach. Eventually I heard the engine of a Cape Islander. I looked up to see Vance Beaudreau's cabined boat headed our way. We would all be removed from our holy asylum here in the warmth of the sunlight at the edge of a cruel but beautiful sea, our isolated world of survival and, dare I say, love. I expected that whatever bond had been forged was temporary and would be broken once we returned to civilization. I grieved for that loss as I let go of Jillian, stood, and waved for Vance to come our way. He may have been a soulless fisherman when it came to killing seals, but he would do all he could to help us. Even the most heartless of hunters on this shore would risk his own life to save anyone in trouble. I'd seen that before as I was growing up.

As Vance's boat neared, I saw him and my father more clearly. Jillian leaned forward and whispered something to Wade. We were much colder as we stood in the wind. Wade shook loose from her as he stood up, then pushed her away, while I summoned my strength and tipped the dory on its side to empty it of water.

Vance's Cape Islander was now as close as it could get to shore. I ushered Jillian and her son into the dory again and pushed off with my oar, poling the boat until we were free of the gritty bottom. Within seconds we were beside the bigger vessel. My father lifted Wade and Jillian aboard. I tossed him the rope, and he tied the dory on, then took my hand and pulled me into the Cape Islander.

My father led the three of us into the little cabin where we were immediately saturated with the warmth of the tiny cook stove. Wade pulled away from his mother, folded his arms around himself, and gave my father a dirty look, then slouched off into a corner.

"Everybody all right?" were my father's first words.

"I think so," I said.

There was a blackened metal pot on the stove, and my father poured tea from it into a ceramic mug with the words GO FISH! printed on the side. He gave the tea to Jillian, who curled her hands around the cup and held it to her face as if it were a sacred religious object. Then my father handed me a cup of tea. I blew my breath across the wisps of steam rushing from the surface.

"Vance wanted me to tell you he's sorry about the seals," my father said.

Wade said nothing.

"I won't be the one to defend him," my father continued. "But I don't think he did the killing. Still, Vance should've had more sense than to let Paul get involved with anything."

"I hate them. I hate everyone who lives here. I want to go back to Philadelphia," Wade said, looking defiantly at his mother.

"Let's not talk about that now," Jillian said, then looked away from Wade and directly at me. The old contempt was gone. Something else had replaced it, but I couldn't read it clearly. It was something composed of equal parts pleading and apology and not what I was hoping for.

Paul wasn't at the wharf when we came ashore, and I was thankful for that small bit of good fortune as my father drove us away in his pickup truck. When Jillian got out at her doorstep, she touched me lightly on the face with her hand. "Thank you," she said in a voice unlike anything I'd heard her use before. "We'll have to talk."

"I'd like that. I really would."

And then she and Wade were inside their home and I was alone in the truck cab with my father. As the door closed to her house, my father leaned over and let his forehead rest on top of the steering wheel. "I thought I'd lost you, Taylor," he said, his voice betraying all the emotion he had been holding in. Leaning back, he put his hands over his face and tried to look directly at me but couldn't. Quickly he turned away.

"I'm tough," I said. "Take more than a little seawater to snuff me out."

He pulled himself together, straightened, and rubbed his hands on his neck. "You're like me. Don't matter what happens, you survive. My father was tough, I'm tough. You inherited the Colby stamina. We're a bunch of ragged-ass survivors, if nothing else."

I never really thought of my father as tough, not in the physical sense. "Might be a curse more than a blessing," I said. Survivors had to endure all the pain of life. How often I wished I hadn't "survived" Laura's death. Why the hell was it I had blundered forward, rudderless, with my own life after that, anyway? Why was it I could survive my mother's desertion? I never really cracked, never truly let go. Neither had my father after my mother left—or at least he never showed it. We bloody well survived and plodded on with our stupid lives. In survival was suffering. The tougher you were, the more you hurt.

"Let's go home," I told him. "I need some dry clothes."

"Your mother's probably worried sick."

I couldn't stop myself from laughing at all the irony inherent in that remark.

"Did I miss something?" he asked.

🮫

My mother hugged me to her when we came in the door, and this time I reciprocated. For the time being I was truly glad she was with us. "Get yourself out of these wet things and into something dry," she said. "Then we'll eat."

I guess she had always been that way. Fix whatever was wrong with you with food. Pickled beets to pot roast right on to rhubarb pie. And, Lord, over a feast of good food—fresh-made rolls, German potato salad, sauerkraut, fiddleheads steamed and buttered, haddock steaks thick as rough-cut two-by-fours—did we eat. My mother devoured her meal like someone who had just walked away from a famine, and I failed to comprehend how she could possibly be dying of pancreatic cancer if she had such an appetite. My father matched her ferocity as he fed his face, looking up from every other bite to smile at her. Myself, I ate like a man who had never seen a plate of homemade food before and couldn't bring himself to quit until his stomach exploded. Then we drank dark, rich coffee that made the room smell like an Arabian palace, and polished off the repast with a heavenly pie made of apples and cinnamon.

My mother appeared vibrant and alive, satisfied by my story of how I had averted disaster. She was pleased as well that it was my father who had gone looking for us in Vance's boat and knew exactly where to search.

"She seems like a nice enough girl," my father said after the coffee and dessert. I knew who he meant. I had little trouble picking up my father's intent in the midst of his thought stream.

"A bit feisty at times," I said.

"Feisty is good," my mother chimed in.

"True," I agreed.

"But I think that boy has problems," my father said.

"Think so, too," I said. "Kids get messed up for all kinds of reasons," I added, wishing I hadn't said it that way. My mother stopped the cup halfway to her mouth and looked at me quickly, then away. Guilt was the name of the pattern on the wallpaper she was staring at. "He's afraid his seal's going to get killed by Paul Mascarene or one of the other idiots around here."

"He's probably right," my father said.

"I don't know if there's a damn thing we can do about it. I'll talk to Paul, but I'm not exactly on his good side right now."

"Paul doesn't have a good side. He's got the mistaken notion there isn't much to live for except causing grief and having a good time."

"He always was like that."

"Yeah, but it's different once you grow up. Ever since his accident Paul has had a habit of messing with things, breaking things, and generally screwing up anything he touches. If he sees that little seal friend of yours, he'll kill it just to make you feel bad."

"I don't understand how a guy with so much talent could have messed up his life so badly," I said. Once again there was an eerie double meaning to my statement.

"Just the way some people are," my mother said. "More coffee?"

"I got an idea," my father said.

But I didn't have a chance to hear his plan. Someone was knocking on the door. My father started to get up, but I waved him down. I was secretly praying it was Jillian coming to offer further generous thanks for my help in saving her son, but when I opened the door, I found myself staring at a short, somewhat flabby-faced bald man wearing an old pinstriped suit that looked as if it had been slept in.

"Hi," I said.

"Hello," he replied awkwardly. "Can I come in?"

"Who are you?"

"Frank. I hope I'm not disturbing anything."

There were no particular syllables anxious to find their way out of my mouth, so I opened the door wider and allowed the stranger into our kitchen. As he entered, I looked away, out the door, watching the warm air of our kitchen mix sweetly with the mist that was settling outside. Everything out there was green and vibrant. The spruce trees had inches of new growth on every tip. I took a deep breath and gently closed the door. My father was wiping his mouth with a napkin as my mother got to her feet. She showed no signs of surprise whatsoever.

"Taylor. Horace. This is Frank."

"Pleased to meet you," Frank said, giving a little half bow. "I'm sorry to interrupt your meal. I hope I'm no trouble."

My father looked at my mother's other husband. He was still dabbing at the corner of his mouth. Blinking several times, he tried to form some sort of greeting with his hands out of the empty air in front of him. Frank had shocked us both, not just by his mere presence but by the fact that he was clearly not the suave, debonair, sophisticated lady's man we had both expected. He was at least a half foot shorter than my father. He might have been more of a looker when he was young, but not by much. Frank appeared to be a shy, meek, sweet "little" guy with no hair and a really bad suit.

"I had to come see how she was doing," Frank said.

"Frank's like that," my mother offered.

"I didn't know how to get here," Frank said. "I thought there'd be a bus or something, but no. So I had to take a taxi. Two hundred dollars they charged me." Then he added, "But it was worth it. I had to see how she's doing."

"I'm doing okay, Frank," my mother said, smiling at him.

The word *awkward* couldn't begin to describe the situation.

"Sit down, please," my father said. "What can we get you to eat?"

Frank looked at the coffeepot. "Just coffee. I ate on the plane. It was a bad meal, but after that I don't feel like eating anything. I don't fly that often. Too many things can go wrong, too much to worry about."

"Frank worries about a lot of things," my mother said.

My father smiled just then at Frank, who shyly smiled back. I stared at this man who I had envisioned so differently, this guy with a name I had learned to loathe. Sitting at the table before me were two men who were both still legally married to my mother. She was pouring them both coffee and, despite Frank's admonishing, she was pushing a piece of apple pie in front of husband number two. My mother looked as if she had been expecting him. My father clasped his fingers together, then studied the lines in the palms of his hands. The silence could have been sliced up in large, thick chunks to make for the final course of the meal.

Eventually my father cleared his throat. "What's the weather like in Ontario?"

Frank's mouth was full of pie, and he spit some crust as he answered. "Hot. It's awful hot there. You people have much nicer weather here."

SEVENTEEN

"I can stay in a motel or something," Frank announced.

"No motel around here," I said.

"Bed-and-breakfast maybe."

"None of them, either."

"Doesn't matter to me. Put me out with your chickens or cows or whatever. I'll be happy."

"Stay in my room," I said. "I'll sleep on the chesterfield."

"I couldn't make you do that." An uneasy silence ensued. The sleeping arrangements would be an uncomfortable topic of discussion. Which husband would my mother sleep with?

"Helen," my father said, "you take Taylor's room. Frank can have my bed, Taylor can sleep on the chesterfield, and I can make a bunk in the boat shed."

"I can't let you do that," Frank said. "I'll call a cab."

"Forget it," my father said. "Cost you another two hundred dollars. We're a long way from Halifax."

"Taxi drivers must be wealthy men around here."

"Not really. People just don't take cabs much in these parts, is all."

"I've got it," I offered. "I'll spread out a couple of blankets on the kitchen floor. Frank can have the chesterfield in the living room. Mom stays in my room and you stay put. I like sleeping at floor level. That's what we did in California all the time. Learned it from the Japanese."

"The Japanese are always so clever," Frank said, trying to make small talk.

"I'm awfully tired," my mother said. "So much excitement for one day. Is it always like this around here?"

"Not all the time," my father said. "Some days are slower than others."

My father was sound asleep and my mother was, too, by the time I finished washing the dishes and dialled Information. Jillian Santino had an unlisted phone number. I wanted desperately to talk to her. I'd ask if Wade was feeling okay. I'd ask how she was and then I'd ask if I could come over and get to know her better. But she wasn't listed and I knew I shouldn't show up at her door late at night, uninvited. I sat in the living room as Frank brushed his teeth with great commotion in our washroom. Plucking at the strings of my old cowboy guitar, I roughed out "Malaguena," which I hadn't played for a long time. I rediscovered the chords to a couple of traditional tunes I'd grown up with and stumbled onto the melody of something that had been buried deeply in my memory, a Scottish song called "Neil Gow's Lament for the Death of his Second Wife," usually played on a fiddle. As far as I could remember, there had never been a tune entitled "Neil Gow's Lament for the Death of his First Wife." The tune was so perfectly sad that I had to quit lest I dredge up my own fathomless pool of grief, from which I still drank long and hard by the hour, day by day.

Frank came out of the washroom in a set of comedic pajamas. "Boy, you have a lot of iron in your water," he said. It wasn't a criticism, just a statement of fact.

"No chlorine like city water, though. Some people think it's healthier this way."

"Healthy? Heck, yeah, how couldn't it be healthy? That stuff probably lets you live forever. In the city, water all tastes like medicine."

"My father dug the well himself. It's out back."

"You mean he dug it with his own two hands? This man dug a well?"

"That's my father, but he did use a shovel and pick."

Frank sat on the chesterfield and looked at me. I wanted desperately to hate him, this creature who had stolen my mother. I had lived for so long with the myth that there was pure evil lurking in the world and that sometimes it existed incarnate in individuals. Frank should have been one of them. He should have been a handsome, greedy, lust-driven maniac who would snatch a little boy's mother away. But he was none of that.

"This is bound to be uncomfortable for you," he said.

"Why? Having my mother here under one roof with two husbands? Me having a conversation with a man I never knew and grew up hating? Why should that be uncomfortable?"

I'm not even sure Frank registered my hard edge of sarcasm. "I can see what you're saying," he said slowly. Frank was a patient man, not smart, not clever, but like my father he seemed patient and prepared to solve the world's crises one step at a time. "I wasn't even sure you'd let me in the door. I thought somebody might hit me over the head with a hammer or whatever."

"We were never a very violent family. The Colby men tend to suffer in silence and pretend nothing's wrong, even when the family falls apart."

"You know I love your mother."

"I believe you. She was very beautiful when she was young."

"She's still beautiful."

"But very sick. So she says."

"Oh, she's sick all right. I've been there with her, every minute of it, through thick and thin. Your mother has had a lot of pain."

"So she says."

"Your father must know the truth by now."

"No, he doesn't. She refuses to tell him."

Frank's jaw dropped in shock. "She was supposed to tell him first thing."

"She couldn't."

"But the plan was that I wouldn't come here until she told you both."

"She told me but not him."

"Why didn't *you* tell him?"

"I don't know. I guess I couldn't bring myself to hurt him. Again."

"I thought the only reason you let me in was because you knew she was dying."

"What can I say? We don't ask questions of strange men claiming to be my mother's other husband from Ontario. We're very polite that way."

"I think the two of you are…wonderful. I can see why she had to come back."

"Oh, yeah, right. Took her long enough to find her way back, eh?"

"Your mother idolizes your father. She talked about him all the time. She says he's the best boat builder in Nova Scotia. He has skills other people can only dream of. Now you tell me he digs wells. He must have been an incredible father."

"Yeah. He *is* an incredible father. I can't believe she told you stories about him."

"And about you. Both of you. She told me everything."

"This is nuts. She never called us once after she left. She never wrote letters. If we were so great, why the hell did she desert us?"

Frank looked down at the floor, then rubbed his hands together. "You know what I did for a living before I retired?"

I said nothing. What was there to say?

"I sold shoes."

"So?"

"That's what I did. I sold women's shoes, kids' shoes, shoes for men—teachers and accountants and secretaries and airplane pilots. They bought shoes from me."

"What does this have to do with anything?"

"It has to do with the fact I'm not a man like your father who can take wood and turn it into a boat that'll go out to sea. That has to be some kind of miracle."

"It's what he does."

"And what I did was sell shoes. I could never match anything about your father."

"Then why did my mother leave us to go live with you?"

"It's not that simple. It's complicated. Let me tell you about your mother. She hasn't told you?"

"Told me what?"

Frank leaned forward and looked a little uncomfortable again. Then he straightened and rubbed his back. "I'm not in as good shape as I used to be. All those years of bending over looking at people's feet. What size shoe are you? Nine?"

"Nine and a half."

"That's a good honest foot size."

"What hasn't my mother told me?"

"Why she left. She hasn't told you the truth about why she left."

"That part of the story I know. She said it out loud over and over. She wasn't happy. She was bored. She wanted a better house, she wanted more excitement, she wanted more…things. Right before she left, that's all she could talk about. I couldn't believe it was my mother. She'd always been unhappy about something, but I couldn't understand why she was throwing her life away because she didn't have a new dress or because we drove an old car."

Frank raised his hand and asked me to lower my voice. "You're missing one important piece of information, Taylor. When I met your mother, she had just been released from hospital in Toronto."

"What do you mean? She didn't have cancer back then."

"It was the mental wing of Toronto General. Your mother had checked herself in. She left here because she knew there was some-thing wrong with her. Mood swings. She couldn't control them. So she had to get away from you and from Horace. She had some kind of breakdown. She was afraid that if she stayed in Nickerson Harbour, she'd drag all of you down with her. She was very, very bad off. She'd even received electric shocks. Mental hospitals were much more crude in those days. I didn't meet her until after she was released. She worked in a store next to mine selling flowers."

"How do I know you're not lying?"

"Why would I lie? Go to Toronto, check out the records at the psychiatric wing of Toronto General. You're her son. Maybe they'll let you look at them."

I took a deep breath. "Go on."

"She changed after she got out of the hospital. She got better, but she couldn't bring herself to come back here. She knew she had hurt you both so deeply and she thought it would be worse if she returned into your lives."

"You knew she was married?"

"Yes. She told me."

"And you married her, anyway?"

"Yes. I loved her. I wanted what was best for her and I wanted to be with her. Can you understand that?"

I rubbed my eyes and tried to rewrite the history of my family, but I couldn't fit the new information into the package of half-truths and faulty conclusions I'd been carrying around in my head. How could I have been so wrong?

"She always expected your father would come after her and bring her back. She thought he would do that."

"We thought she hated us."

"She loved both of you."

"Why didn't she tell us what was happening?"

"She had a mental illness. She was sick."

"Then why didn't you call us?"

"By the time I knew there was a son and a husband back here, I was already in love with her. I wanted to help her, but I was also very lonely. I needed her. I guess I'm also a little surprised your father never went looking for her. After a year passed from the time she left, I assumed her life here was over. I asked her to marry me."

I got up, paced the room, and stared at an old painting on the wall of the *W. D. Lawrence*, one of the largest wooden sailing ships ever built. Launched in Maitland, Nova Scotia, in October 1874, it was a legendary vessel many naysayers of the day had said would never sail. It was too big for a wooden ship, they insisted. But it worked fine and made a small fortune for its owner. My father had told me stories about the *Lawrence* and its construction. He had memorized specifications and carried them around in his head as an English teacher might memorize lines from Tennyson or Wordsworth. I looked away from the painting and toward my father's bedroom door. Why *hadn't* he gone after her? Why hadn't he at least tried?

The Colby men, I was beginning to realize, weren't as tough as I thought they were. My mother had left us to spare us her madness and he hadn't even cared enough to bring her back. My mother hadn't deserted us; my father had let her go. And it was all a horrible mistake.

"Don't blame your father. He's a good man. But someone has to tell him she's dying."

"Is she going back to Ontario with you?"

"I don't know. It's up to her."

"What are you going to do if she wants to stay here?"

"I don't know. It's not important. I'll do whatever she wants. I'd like to stay around, though, if I can, until the end. She's been in remission before, but it's not likely to happen again. Doctors say this will be the last one. The cancer has spread into the bones. Once she starts to go downhill, it'll probably be the end."

"I want her to stay here in Nova Scotia. She can go to the hospital in Musquodoboit Harbour when the time comes or get home care and stay here."

"If she wants, I'm behind it a hundred percent. This is her home. She grew up here. Ontario never really felt like home to her."

"I want you to stay here, too," I said.

"You want me around?"

"Yes."

"What about your father?"

"We'll work something out."

"I'd like to get to know him."

"You will," I said. "You're going to tell him she's dying. Then you'll get to know him."

EIGHTEEN

My mother didn't look so good at breakfast. I started to say something to her in front of Frank and my father, but she read my mind and began talking before I had a chance. "I think I love this kitchen more than any place on earth."

"She said the same thing about the Eaton Centre," Frank said, trying to make a joke. My father mustered a polite smile, and Frank added, "I think she was only joking then. It was Christmas and all, you know."

Frank appeared much more comfortable this morning. My father seemed slightly baffled but not unhappy. My mother had put on too much makeup and was working hard at trying to pretend she felt okay, but I could tell she wasn't feeling well.

Frank told a story about a woman in Scarborough who had come into his store and bought a new pair of shoes, the exact size, exact style, exact everything, every single month. "The only thing that ever changed was the price, but she never complained and I never asked her why."

"She probably just liked the attention," my mother said. "Frank was a very sensitive salesperson."

"Salesman, please."

"Okay, salesman," my mother conceded. "Anyway, people do funny things and you never know exactly why."

I guess my father figured he would flesh out the conversation with his own thoughts on the matter of how "funny" people could be. He told the story of "some fool" farther down the shore who built an entire Cape Islander using only brass nails and not one screw. "When the first wave hit that poor boat, she started to come apart at every single seam. Pretty soon the guy was in big trouble. He got her back to shore with the help of a tow from the MacIsaac brothers but, by then, about all he had was a swamped Chevy engine and a pile of wet lumber."

Frank went out to join my father in the boat shed that morning as he proceeded to paint the repaired dory. My mother returned to my room and fell asleep. At nine o'clock I walked down to the wharf. At the end of the dock sat mother and son; the seal was beneath them in the water, and Jillian had her hand outstretched, but Cobain couldn't quite get far enough out of the water to take the canned mackerel, so she dropped it into his open mouth.

"That guy's got teeth like a shark," I said as I approached. "Better be careful."

Jillian turned and, for a brief instant, I thought she was angry again, that she was going to tell me to leave them alone. But it was just surprise. "Don't sneak up on people sitting on the edge of a wharf."

"You're right. If Cobain saw something falling toward those sharp teeth, he might take a bite. It'd be like *Jaws*."

"Yeah, right," Wade said. "Cobain wouldn't hurt anyone."

"How are you guys doing, anyway?" I asked.

Jillian put her arm around Wade, even though he tried to shake it off. She smiled at me. It was a warm, genuine, beautiful smile. It was the first time I'd seen her teeth. And I liked them. I decided I liked everything about her. "*Us* guys are doing okay," she said. "Thanks again."

"Hey, no big deal. I'm from here, remember? We did stuff like that every day when I was growing up. Usually before school. You get enough exercise and then you can settle down for a long boring day of education."

Jillian frowned. "You saying you don't think education is exciting?"

"Oops. I forgot. Lady professor and all that. I didn't exactly mean it the way it sounded. Hell, I was in love with half my high-school English teachers. The ones that were women at least. They all seemed so damn smart. And the grammar. Loved it. And all that other stuff—everything from diphthongs to diatribes." Jillian was smiling now. I sat beside them. "That's good. I knew you had a sense of humour. English teachers always have an excellent sense of humour from reading all those Shakespeare comedies or whatever it is."

"I haven't read Shakespeare for over ten years."

"Guess he's out of fashion, huh?"

"No. My area of specialization is feminist literature."

"Oh, got it. That would be my *area of specialization*, too, if I was getting my Ph.D. now. I think men have screwed up literature something awful. Especially all those damn long boring poems."

"Boring is right," Wade added.

"See, the boy knows his books as well as his marine life."

"Wade likes to read. Unfortunately it's mostly comics."

"Not comics, Mom. Heavy-metal magazines."

"Didn't know there was such a thing," I said.

"Violence and large-breasted women scantily clad," Jillian said.

"Didn't have those two things when I was growing up."

"I'll bet."

The harbour was a field of blue-white diamonds shuffling themselves over and over. Cobain appeared beneath us again, and Wade tossed him the last of the fish. "You should select better reading matter, Wade," I said with a fake serious tone. "Get up to speed on some of your mother's old favourites like, um…help me out here."

"Mary Wollstonecraft Shelley. Gertrude Stein…"

"Those were two of my favourites. Out in L.A. everybody talked nonstop about Gertrude Stein. Wasn't her husband manager of the Yankees for a while before he ran his car into a tree?"

Jillian smiled. The sunlight danced on her face. I tried to guess her age but couldn't. She was younger than I was, but when she smiled she looked like a teenager. I couldn't believe the transformation.

"We'd like you to come over for dinner tonight," she suddenly said, not looking at me but away at the shoreline on the other side. I followed her gaze and found myself staring at a rocky tip of land on the far shore where I could barely make out the crooked-neck silhouette of a cormorant. As I watched the bird lift his wings and flap them in the air, not trying to take off, just exercising his muscles and feathers, panic welled inside me. I didn't dare let it show in any form.

"You're just trying to be polite because I pulled your son out of the ocean," I said.

"Something like that."

Cobain rose from the water, did one of those funny seal standup acts of lifting himself straight out of the water as far as his sculling flippers would allow, then splashed back down, rolled onto his side and onto his back, spiralling himself into the cold, clear, kelpy forest of the harbour waters below.

"Did you see that?" Wade asked.

"He's a showoff," I said. "He knows you're watching."

"Cobain ate a piece of fish right out of my hand today," Wade boasted. "He never did that before."

"You have a friend for life," I said, but the words had an ominous ring for me. Nothing, I knew, was for life. Not family, not love, not happiness. Here today, gone tomorrow. Anything could happen. Like yesterday. Wade's good intentions and rash decision could have left another lifetime scar on his mother. Yet maybe *some* things were permanent-press. Pain and suffering, for example—friends for life. "By the way, Vance said he'd talk to the men around here and see if they'd lay off the seal hunt. He felt bad about his part in what happened yesterday."

"If anybody hurts Cobain, I'll kill him," Wade said. I saw the fire and anger in the eyes of this boy and understood it well. It wasn't unlike the look I'd seen in the face of Jim Dan not too many days ago when he came at me.

"The male solution to just about everything," Jillian said to me as an aside, but she didn't criticize her son.

"I honestly think they'll lay off, maybe find some other form of entertainment," I said.

Cobain was gone now. Wade looked once at me, but it wasn't exactly a gaze of friendship or gratitude. He pulled the bill of his Phillies cap around to the front of his head and tugged it low, then plucked the video game out of his pocket. The tinny artificial electronic beeps and explosions sounded impossibly alien against the raw beauty of the land and sea around us.

"You didn't answer yes or no," Jillian said. "About my invitation, I mean."

I glanced at her, tried hard to look straight into her eyes but couldn't. I lowered my voice, so Wade couldn't hear. "I didn't kill Laura, you know, but I was responsible for her death," I said, as if using my grievous past as a shield to push Jillian away.

Her response surprised me. "You can tell me about it tonight."

I said nothing. There were no words in my head offering up assistance. I didn't want to recount the story. I had run and rerun the sorry tale of Laura so many times it almost seemed to come down to one statement: there was nothing to tell. Laura was a nice girl. Grew up in a nice family in a great little town. She found herself a boyfriend who took her away and got her involved with a bunch of screwy people. They didn't know when to stop having "fun" and it killed her. The boyfriend, now husband, was too busy with his own life to stop it from happening. End of story.

I hadn't said yes or no. One word was commitment, one was total denial. I didn't want either and couldn't find the language of middle ground. Getting up, I walked back to the land end of the wharf where I heard Paul's car approach. He pulled to a stop and the door to his old car creaked open. Paul stuck out a cowboy boot with the help of his two hands and glared at me from the seat as he focused his eyes on another morning in Nickerson Harbour. I didn't want enemies. Hell, I wasn't sure I could even handle friends, but enemies I knew I didn't need.

"Morning, Paul."

"Son of a bitch," he said, spitting something onto the ground.

"Remember that dance at Moose River?" I asked

"Yeah, the one at the Legion Hall. I had just bought my first Marshall amp. The Savages were at their best."

"And the RCMP tried to shut the dance down, saying you were too loud. Neighbours were all complaining."

"Right on. So we cranked the music louder and started doing a medley of Stones tunes."

"Until the constable pulled the plug on your amp."

"No one messes with my equipment."

"You wasted a good guitar on him."

"It was my third Stratocaster. It needed new strings."

"Mountie didn't know that. He just thought someone had levelled him with a lethal weapon."

"Guitar in the right hands *is* a lethal weapon."

"Everyone freaked and they tore that place apart."

"It was one of those nights." Paul was smiling now. I was like a skilled fishermen. I teased and toyed and then reeled him in. Put him in a good mood, anyway.

"Whatever happened to that Marshall amp, anyway?" I asked. "I saw that big old mother sitting there onstage and I had to have one after that. Nearly lost my hearing as a result."

"I kicked it in one night when I got pissed off at the guys in the band."

"Why'd you do that?"

"I didn't like the musical direction the Savages were moving in. We were losing our edge."

"Never want to lose your edge."

"Better believe it," Paul said, standing now, reaching out for a hand as he heaved himself out of the driver's seat. I figured Paul lived most of his life at the steering wheel of that car. He fumbled with a pack of Player's and inserted one into his mouth, then offered a second to me, but I declined. He lit his smoke, squinted, and stared at Jillian. I didn't like that. "What's her problem?"

"She doesn't like men," I offered.

"She a lesbian?"

"I don't think so. Just thinks men are a little crude. She's American. She can't help it."

"She likes you, right?"

"We're getting on."

Paul leered. "You only been back in town a few days. And this?"

"We're just friends."

"Thought you said she didn't like men."

"Paul, that lady has at least one thing in common with you and me."

"What's that?"

"We're all walking wounded. So give her a break."

"What the hell is she and her troublemaker smart-ass kid doing out here this morning, anyway?"

"They like the view, I guess."

"What view?" Paul asked, waving his cigarette toward the harbour. It was a crystal-clear, early-summer morning. Not a trace of wind or fog. The sun was rising and the water looked dark and magnificent. Reflections of spruce trees fringed the harbour and, farther out, a lone sailboat tried to tack in almost no wind at all. "Ain't nothing out there," Paul continued. "Not a damn thing."

"She's from the States, remember?"

"Right. Thinks she's at friggin' Peggy's Cove probably."

"Something like that."

"She's not that bad-looking, ya know? Maybe if she could lose the attitude."

"I think she just wants to be left alone." I didn't know how to gracefully convince Paul not to mess with Jillian or Wade or the seal. The less I said the better.

"Bitch owes me money for my gun." I recognized the timbre of his voice now. I knew all about the Paul Mascarene who was suave and smooth and friendly as could be, but I also knew that deep down he was still one of the true savages of the world.

"I owe you money for the gun," I said. "How much?"

Paul laughed, butted his first cigarette of the day on his boot, and lit a second, his Bic butane lighter sending out a long blue demonic flame. "Fifty bucks." He paused, sucked nicotine, sized up his opportunity. "No, seventy-five."

I opened my wallet and pulled out five American twenties. "All I got is Yankee doodle."

The hand that had once played magnificent riffs on a Stratocaster, the hand that had played Chuck Berry to Bob Dylan, Pink Floyd to Aerosmith, took the money and stashed it in his pants pocket, then looked up at the sky.

"Everything's cool, right?" I asked.

"Sure. Everything's cool."

NINETEEN

I knocked on the door. The Jack Russell dog, Janis Ian, barked and the door opened, revealing Jillian in a long, flowing dress. She had let her hair fall onto her shoulders. And she was smiling.

"Excuse me, I must have the wrong house," I said.

"You're early."

I looked at my watch. She was right. "It's one of my worst faults. I've suffered this affliction all my life. Lost friends over it. Some people in L.A. couldn't tolerate me. I'm either always on time or early."

"Don't worry about it. What's ten minutes? Come in."

I leaned over and petted the old sad-sack dog with the miniaturized body and oversize head, mangy fur, and four-star personality. Janis licked my hand, and I scratched her behind the ears.

Wade came into the room, said a cursory hello, and fled for the safety of a television sitcom. In another room.

"Now I'm a little embarrassed. You're all dressed up looking like you stepped out of a movie and I just have on my old duds."

"I like those clothes."

"I didn't pack much when I left California to come here. These belong to my father. He doesn't dress up much. Spends most of his time talking to lumber and marine paint."

"You look fine. You want something to drink?"

"Have any Yoohoo?"

"What?"

"It's a chocolate drink. Wade would love it."

"Sorry, no Yoohoo. Settle for a glass of white wine?"

"Only if it's Canadian. If it's French, Californian, German, or Australian, I refuse, 'cause then we'd have to discuss it. Where I came from people would pour a glass of something and then talk about it for several hours until the paint began to peel off the walls. To me, wine is wine. I can tell the difference between red and white, but that's about it." This was all nervous talk on my part, but it helped cover for the panic settling into my brain like a frost during the first real cold snap of late fall. The room smelled of garlic and tomato sauce with basil.

Jillian had walked into the kitchen and back. "I checked the label. It was the cheapest bottle I could find. Comes from Ontario, I think. Cheers."

"Cheers." I closed my eyes and let the wine slip down my throat, gulping it until my glass was empty. When I opened my eyes, Jillian was looking at me and laughing. "What?"

"Where did you go?"

"What do you mean?"

"You closed your eyes."

"I did."

I was embarrassed. It wasn't as if I savoured drinking wine. "I don't know. I just did, I guess. Look, I know I'm acting weird, but I think you're making me nervous."

"Somebody told me you've played guitar and sung at the Hollywood Bowl, Carnegie Hall, Madison Square Garden, and the Philadelphia Spectrum. How could I make you nervous?"

"Those were all strangers out there and the lights were in my eyes. I couldn't see them. Besides, I was only playing backup. The up-front guys took all the pressure."

"No, it's something else. What is it?"

I held out my glass for a refill. "I'll take seconds if you're feeling generous. We can always go to the bootlegger's if we run out. Most people think he only stocks Black Diamond rum and Moosehead beer, but I think he's got a special wine cellar full of Chardonnay for when special customers come knocking."

Jillian was laughing now as she retreated for my second glass. The TV—*Fresh Prince of Bel Air*, I think—was coming through strong from the next room. *California, oh, California, I'm still haunted by all your trash-trivia commercial success, fun-and-frills death-making madness.*

"I haven't had much to do with any women," I said, "since Laura died." I presented the information in a flat, matter-of-fact manner, which was the only way I could get it out. I knew I had to put this news to her now, not later.

Jillian picked up Wade's running shoes, which were lying in the middle of the living-room floor, and deposited them in a closet. "I haven't had much to do with men since I left Thomas. Actually I haven't had that much to do with men for longer than that. Thomas was almost never around. I'm not complaining on that count. Things went better when he wasn't."

"Men are like that sometimes."

"Thomas was a true professional. His job came first, then family. No, I think family was farther down the list. He was a lawyer. Worked for the city for a while. Then climbed the ladder of success defending criminals. Now he's got his own firm. I don't know precisely when it was that we started falling apart, but I think Wade and I were pretty low on his list of priorities."

I cleared my throat. "You grew up in Philadelphia?"

"No, I grew up in a little place called Cinnaminson, across the Tacony-Palmyra Bridge—just on the other side of the Delaware River from the City of Brotherly Love. My father was a farmer. So was my grandfather."

"Get out! Farmers in New Jersey?"

"They grew tomatoes and corn before the ground was paved over to allow for parking at the malls."

"The nice thing about Nickerson Harbour is the lack of asphalt. Ever notice the paving stops just before you actually get to this little village?"

"Why's that?"

"Civilization refused to cross into the land of cod scraps and rusty cars."

Jillian held her glass in the air. "Guess that's why I'm here. Wanted to be someplace without skyscrapers, malls, or paved roads." Suddenly she turned serious. "I came here to escape. I admit it."

"Escape what? You had a job, didn't you? A life?"

"I taught part-time at Temple University. I was writing academic articles about Elizabeth Barrett Browning while my son was getting beat up by drug pushers and my husband was making us rich by defending thugs and murderers he knew were guilty."

"Come again."

"After he quit being a prosecutor for the city, he got that job with the big law firm. He was very good at what he did and he believed with all his testosterone that every American had the right to a so-called fair trial and a good lawyer no matter how painfully obvious it was that the accused was guilty. Thomas was very proud of the fact that a pimp who murdered a prostitute wasn't sentenced thanks to his representation. He got the creep off due to a technicality involving the arresting officer. Thomas was that kind of guy."

"Maybe we could throw him in Nickerson Harbour in a seal costume some morning when the locals are feeling real bored. What do you think?"

"I think he would be getting off too easy."

"Maybe one of the big bull seals would mistake him for a female of his own kind and try to mate with him first."

"Now you're getting closer to justice. I've got to finish dinner. I'll see if Wade will come in to keep you company."

"No, don't do that. Never separate a boy and his TV. I'll go sit with him for a few minutes."

Wade looked up when I joined him. The laugh track filled the room. I sat on a wooden chair and waited for a commercial. "Pretty scary stuff yesterday, huh?"

"Wasn't so bad until I threw up."

"Near drowning will do that to you. But you were pretty tough."

"I'll never go swimming in the ocean again. And I'll never, ever, go out in a boat. Any boat."

"I'm not sure that's the right approach. You had a close call. A little respect for the sea can go a long way."

"You sound like my father."

"Ouch."

"My father was always telling me I should have more respect for him and for what he does."

"I hear he was...sorry, *is*...a lawyer."

"And a damn good one."

"I'm convinced of that. You and him got along pretty good, right?"

Wade crossed his arms in front of his chest defensively. "We got along good. He just wasn't around a lot."

"Well, he had a job and was good at it, right?"

"I'm gonna go back and live with him. I can't stand it here. It's boring. Nothing to do."

"Seems like you've had quite a bit of excitement."

"I'm only here because of my mom. If I didn't come here with her, she'd have been all alone."

I wasn't going to ask the kid for more information about Jillian or her breakup with Thomas. I sure as hell didn't want him to feel I was using him. *Fresh Prince* came back on. "How many times have you seen this episode?" I asked.

"Three, I think."

"You know what they're going to say next?"

"You don't want to get me started," he said, smiling.

Jillian popped her head in. "Dinner's served."

We walked into the kitchen where the walls and windows were glazed with condensed steam. Wade piled his plate high with spaghetti and returned to television land. Jillian and I sat across from each other. "This will be good practice for the both of us," she said almost formally. "Associating with the opposite sex, I mean." It came out sounding absurdly proper and professorial. I was afraid it might be bad form to laugh.

"I was just thinking the same thing. So far so good." I munched on my green salad and took a bite of spaghetti. "This is delicious.

Not one thing here with scales or bones or eyeballs staring back at you. You must be Italian."

"Yes, I am. My mother was second-generation Italian. Her father was from Abruzzi."

"Anybody with roots in Abruzzi can probably make pasta while they're sleeping. This is damn good."

"Hope you don't mind garlic."

Garlic to the highest power was the name of the game. "I usually eat five or six big cloves at breakfast just to ward off vampires."

"It thins your blood and makes you live longer, too."

"People in Abruzzi must have the thinnest blood of anybody anywhere. They probably never have artery problems or heart attacks. What do they do—just die from getting bored with living too long?"

"Something like that. You're sure you like the food?"

"Love it. But I didn't think feminists cooked food for men."

"A true feminist feels free enough to choose to do whatever it is she wants to do without fear of anyone, including herself, thinking of the act as being antifeminist."

"That's true. That's exactly what I've always said."

Jillian stopped eating. "Think we can be friends?"

I preferred to keep the conversation on the light side. I was real good at one-liners, at comebacks in intellectual word games, penmanship even, whatever the social occasion called for. The friendship thing had an ominous ring for some reason. It pointed out to my befuddled brain that I had somewhat more serious intentions. My soul was crying out for something, for someone, and it had been for years now. Jillian had opened a door, and there was a flood of something close to being unleashed, an outpouring from within. Friendship seemed like a door opened with one of those safety chain locks still dangling across the airspace. Yet I realized, as I stared into my garlicky spaghetti, that it would have to do for now. And if someone wanted to take off the chain from inside, they would when they were ready. "Yeah, I think I can manage that. I don't have a lot of friends in Nickerson Harbour."

"That makes two of us. Now tell me about Laura."

I shook my head. "No, not yet." I was afraid that if she heard the whole story too soon, the door would close again in my face. The two of us were carrying enough emotional luggage to sink the *Titanic* a second time. "I'll throw it back on your side of the net, though. Tell me more about Thomas. Your son seems to think he's a pretty good father, a regular swell guy."

Jillian sipped some more Canadian white wine. "Sons like to believe only the best about their fathers."

"That's true." I was reminded of something I had learned from Frank about my mother's mental problems. *Why hadn't my own father gone after her?* If he had, history would have been rewritten. I might have grown up with a mother. I might not have left with Laura for California. She might be alive today.

"Hello?" a voice was saying.

"Sorry. I drifted."

"You okay?"

"Yes and no. But go on. You were going to tell me about Tom."

"Not Tom. I was never allowed to call him that. Only Thomas. Thomas was very formal sometimes, very proud of his career. Very successful. He saw himself as being a good father. When he was with Wade, which was rare, he was just that."

"A boy needs a father full-time."

"Not according to Thomas. Anyway, we met in college. I worked while he went to law school. When that was done and I went on to graduate school at Penn, he footed the bill, but he resented it big-time. We drifted apart a bit, I got too serious about Virginia Woolf and Christina Rossetti. Thomas had a couple of big cases with lots of media attention, and his career skyrocketed. Up, up, and away.

"I hated how he lost all his ideals. I can't believe he wanted to become a lawyer to help the poor and then changed into a monster. Oh, he can talk about all sorts of convoluted crap about how noble his profession is, and I even know he's done some good things along the way. But now he defends men he knows are guilty of violent crimes. He's so damn good, he wins time after time, and then he's bloody proud of it. I couldn't bear it if Wade grew up to be the same."

"Wade will grow up to be different," I said.

"I hope so. I really do. It's all part of why I had to get him out of Philadelphia, away from the U.S., but particularly away from his father. He's mad at me for that."

"It's only natural. Problem is, now he might idealize his old man, whether the bastard's down there emptying the jails of murderers or not."

Wade headed back toward us, but when he figured out we were having a conversation about his father, he left his plate on the table, gave Jillian a dirty look, and returned to the TV room, closing the door and turning up the volume.

"Thomas was a very good man when we met in college. He did volunteer work in legal clinics. He marched with welfare recipients to city hall. We both did. He cared. He had compassion. I don't know what happened to him. After his big success in getting the pimp off, he got a big raise and was asked to become a full partner. In the midst of his glory he came home and I tore into him. I told him full-out for the first time in a long while how I really felt. He went into a rage."

"Men don't take criticism well, especially when it comes to their job. What did he do, hit you?" I was sure Jillian's arctic reaction to me was the result of some violence done to her by a man. Wife abuse, I had come to believe, was a close second to baseball as the great American pastime.

"No, he didn't. I almost wish he had done something physical and then begged for forgiveness. Instead, he started to close me out of his life. He stayed at his office longer, took on more cases, spent less time with Wade, as well. That was all part of his punishment."

"All lawyers should die a slow, painful death."

Jillian's eyes were watering. "Too much garlic, I guess," she said. "I should stop there. I'm sorry. I'm ruining the meal."

But we were both finished. The food had been good, but something else had already happened. I felt as if we'd gone two steps beyond friendship. I reached out and touched her hand, and she held on to it. Her hand was sweaty.

I led her to the sofa in a sitting room farther from the noise of the TV and we sat, both of us staring at the floral pattern on the wall. "There's more, isn't there?"

"Yes. I got my first job—part-time teaching night courses at City College. Wade was only four years old. I had to hire sitters because Thomas was never there in the evenings. I loved teaching. The first year is always the most exciting. I was all fired up about everything to do with literature. It was extraordinary. I would meet with some of my students. We'd talk about John Keats, Jane Austen, Walt Whitman, Doris Lessing. I'd never experienced anything quite like it. I let one of my students, a young man, get close to me. We had coffee together. Talked the talk. He made a pass at me, and I cut him off. End. Over. Not what I had in mind. But then he followed me to my office at the college one night, and when I refused to have sex with him, he raped me. I hated him for it. I hated myself. I couldn't bring myself to go to the police. I went to my husband first."

"Thomas should have been there to help you."

"He listened to me tell him what happened. I was pretty incoherent. But he listened as if I were a client of his or a witness on the stand. He wouldn't even put his arm around me. When I was done, he looked at me, his eyes cold. He said it was my fault. I shouldn't have led the guy on. If I went to the police, he said, I'd probably lose my part-time job at the college. Young Ph.D.s who needed the work teaching freshman English were a dime a dozen. He was right. He also said that in court it might be pretty hard to make the case stick. I had met with my student on several occasions privately. 'How could you be so stupid?' he asked.

"So we acted as if nothing had happened. I had been raped, I had been brutalized, and I went along with what the great attorney, my husband, thought I should do. Thomas had even less to do with me after that. He rarely touched me. We started sleeping in separate beds. We never talked. I know this all hurt Wade, but I felt fragile, victimized, and totally defenceless in the world."

"Didn't you have anyone you could talk to?"

"I got involved in a women's group, but I felt guilty about the time away from Wade."

"You needed something, some kind of support."

"I needed a husband, I needed love, but I couldn't get it at home. I nearly had an affair with another woman. I was desperate, but I realized it just wasn't me. I wished I could have, I really do, but I just couldn't."

"What happened to the guy?"

Jillian's face went hard. "He kept coming to class. It was as if he was testing me. I saw no look of remorse on his face. I did a lousy job teaching my classes after that. Every student could see something had happened. Some asked. I said nothing. I plodded on. I finished the year. I passed the bastard even. I couldn't handle any confrontation. I hated myself, and if it hadn't been for Wade, I don't know what I might have done. Nothing in my life, not even the rape itself, was as bad as the isolation and fear I was living through.

"I tried to talk it through with Thomas again, but he pretended as if the whole incident were ancient history and of little consequence. I couldn't comprehend what had happened to him. His job had made him completely immune to other people's pain, even his wife's. And then my student, this bright young man who looked like the most normal of normal men in his early twenties, went out and raped again, this time another student. She fought back more than I did. He strangled her. She died. I went to the police when I heard he was charged.

"Thomas pleaded with me not to get involved. I was insane. It was my fault she had died because I hadn't come forward sooner. It turned out that someone else had accused him of rape before and a lawyer, no, not Thomas—but there's plenty more of his breed out there in the courtrooms of America—got him off on a technicality. If it wasn't for my testimony, he wouldn't have been convicted this time. Afterward, I received all kinds of threats from the guy's family. Thomas cursed me for putting Wade at risk. Thomas never hit me, not once, but he knew how to be cruel to me in ways that were far beyond physical pain. When it became impossible to live with him, impossible even to live in the same city where he lived, I quit my job, I left everything, and I came here. I left behind everything except Wade."

"Why Nova Scotia?"

"I've always loved the sea. I wanted Wade to grow up near the ocean. I wanted to be outside the United States in case Thomas tried to pull some legal tricks. And this was the first place I came to where the pavement ended just short of town."

Jillian touched my face and ran her hand down to my mouth, tracing my lips with her fingertip. It was a powerful sensation that sent a chill down my spine. She closed her eyes and leaned forward, but I stopped her by taking hold of her wrists. I didn't mean to be rough, but I guess my movement had been quick, abrupt. *I* was the one, after all, still most fearful of physical contact. I wasn't sure I was ready for this. She opened her eyes, and they were filled with confusion.

"Sorry. Not yet. I have to tell you about Laura first. You might feel differently then."

TWENTY

Laura. Over and over. *There was a girl once…*
No.

There was a girl once, and there was a boy. There was only the two of them and they lived in a very private world of sea and sky and deep forest, and there was sunlight and there came snow and ice and a long, cold winter.

And then one perfect cold clear morning the two of them stood at the harbour edge just as the ice broke up to signal winter would soon be over. There was for them the smell of the ice, the sea, the salty, salty air and, along the shoreline, crystalline exaggerations of beauty. They stood like that, alone, watching islands of ice set sail for the sea, watching an armada of blue-white jagged ice pans drifting, drifting. And the sun was warm on their faces as they gazed into the clear dark waters that now had been unlocked from the winter prison.

It was only the third day of March, but Laura said, "It's the beginning of summer."

I remembered clearly *who* I was then and dutifully held on to that prototype of me, even as I changed through all the inevitable manifestations to follow. That person standing there with Laura was the core of me, and I could never lose that. I loved being alive. I loved that dangerous, beautiful harbour. I loved being with her. I loved Laura. And I even loved myself. It was all quite extraordinary and simple, and I locked those moments into my heart forever.

Laura went from being taller than I was and skinny to something else. Her freckles all but disappeared. She grew her hair longer and longer. Flowing down her back, it was a rich, lustrous brown waterfall of hair. She lost the tomboy look altogether as her body changed. Older boys and men noticed her beauty as the tomboy girl lost the battle with womanhood and physical maturity triumphed over youth. Soon I was taller than she was, but I still looked very much like a boy while she had blossomed into a goddess. At least that was how I remembered it.

My father tried to prepare me for disaster. "You two have been together ever since you were little kids. It gets really tough once you get into high school. Something might change that's beyond the power of either of you. It won't be anybody's fault. Just don't blame her and don't blame yourself."

"I don't think that'll happen," I said with the greatest conviction. "I think we'll be together for a long time. We'll live together after we get out of school. I don't know if we'll get married." Laura and I both mistrusted the institution of marriage. I had good reason to do so from my own experience, but she had "philosophical reasons."

"Two people who love each other don't need a piece of paper," she said.

When we were sixteen, I walked Laura home one night and entered her kitchen where Jim Dan sat alone in a pool of light, listening to Cape Breton fiddle music on the radio. The mill had closed on him and he had been forced to go back to the mines. He had just arrived home after working a week in the shafts near Stellarton. Now he was drinking. While Laura was out of the room, Jim Dan sat me down. He had an exhausted, almost angry look, and I thought he was going to tear into me for keeping her out too late or seeing too much of her, but it wasn't that. "Taylor, the world's a dangerous place. A girl like Laura needs someone there for her all the time."

"Sure."

"I've known you for a long time, Taylor. Known your father. You and him have one important thing in common. You're both steady, both have character. You don't flit from one thing to another. You don't change your minds like the wind changing directions. You figure out one thing and you stick to it."

I wasn't sure this was all complimentary, but there was truth to it.

"Promise me you'll never go down into a mine."

That one caught me off guard but, hey, that was no big deal. "I promise I'll never go down into a mine."

"Number two. Promise me you'll always be there for Laura. If she needs you or not. Even if she says she doesn't need you at all. Promise me you'll be there."

Number two was almost as easy to go along with as promise number one. "I promise."

The fiddle sang sweetly in the kitchen air. I breathed in the perfume of his rum-laden breath and felt bonded to this good man who was Laura's father, this man who earned his family's keep by rummaging for black rocks deep in the bowels of the hard, cold earth.

Laura's mother came into the room then and shook her head indulgently. She had on an old flower-print housecoat and her hair was in curlers. She had a soft, round face and wore rimless glasses that always made her look much older than she really was. "Jim Dan, you needs your sleep. Give poor little Taylor here a break. The boy don't need so much of your nonsense."

"Come here, woman, and give me a kiss," Jim Dan said. He cracked into a grin and his eyes went a little funny. He pulled his wife to his lap and kissed her hard on the mouth.

Laura walked back into the kitchen and laughed. "Would you two cut it out? That's gross. You don't have to do that in front of Taylor."

But there was nothing gross about it. And Laura wasn't serious. We both enjoyed seeing her parents make happy married fools of themselves. I felt the ache of my own loss of a mother yet again, but before it had a chance to settle into my heart like a cold block of ice, Laura said, "Taylor and I are going for a walk."

"Again?" her mother asked.

"It's early," she said.

We walked out into the dark night beneath the canopy of the Milky Way, toward Orion, all the way to my father's boat shed where we went in and smelled the pure pine shavings from a day's hard work on a new boat. Without turning the light on, we climbed to the little overhead loft, bumping perilously into razor-sharp saws and woodcutting tools that hung along the wall. When we lay down on the single khaki blanket above, I lit a small kerosene lantern I had strategically placed there two days earlier.

We lay side by side, kissed, moved our hands up and down the length of each other's body. Everything looked softly radiant in the light of the kerosene flame. I could see our reflection in the little window and beyond that only darkness. We were alone, the two of us. Safe in our embrace, in love, yes, but not yet obsessed with sex. That would come later. It was a private, shared ecstasy that diminished time to absolute insignificance. The clock stopped here.

"Remember the time that…" I was sure I said it or she said it and then we repeated tales told to each other ten times apiece or more until the stories were moulded and reshaped by the telling. "Remember the time out on the ice…" I said at one point.

"It didn't happen that way at all," she said after my telling. "It was your idea to cross the harbour." The magic was suddenly breached, but I refused to let our tryst be broken.

"Right," I said.

The kerosene ran low and the flame diminished but didn't go out. It remained a low blue moan of a flame for nearly ten minutes. We lay there for a long time. No more words. Just touch. I traced my hand across her face—her lips, her eyes, her nose, her throat. In the near total darkness we tried to look into each other's eyes and felt a powerful, subtle energy link us. We were one in ways even sex couldn't approximate.

We survived the intrusions of the community in which we lived. Laura ignored the entreaties of the older guys—the football playing jocks, sons of fishermen and loggers. I didn't need to push the limits of my own macho glory to "defend" her from any of them. She was "a lovely girl," her mother would say, but she was tough, witty, quick with an insult or a joke that could defuse the most hormone-crazed barbarians in our crowd.

Music came into our lives and we'd sit for hours learning songs from the radio. I faked my way on the guitar through song after song, and Laura would sing. She had inherited a sweet voice from her mother, and I dubbed her "Joni or Judy or Joan." I had learned to finger-pick, and to ourselves we sounded good, better than anything recorded. Sometimes we'd try harmony on "Four Strong Winds" or "The Circle Game," and we didn't care *whose* generation any music came from as long I could play the chords and she could find a scattering of the words to a verse and most of the chorus.

My first car, a Ford Falcon station wagon, changed all that. We drove to dances in Sheet Harbour and concerts in Halifax. We drenched ourselves in loud, live music, not the least of which came from Paul Mascarene's Savages. I'm sure no one outside Nova Scotia knew anything about Paul's brash, intense brand of rock and roll but, watching him race his fingers across the neck of one of his many short-lived Fender Stratocaster guitars, I knew he was way ahead of me on some path to glory in this thing I had to do.

Laura and I didn't always have money for gas, so sometimes we'd hitchhike to Halifax. On one occasion I saw an electric guitar and a two-hundred-watt amp on sale at a Gottingen Street pawnshop. I had to have it. The man behind the counter was trusting enough to take my cheque, and Laura and I hitchhiked back to Nickerson Harbour with an Epiphone guitar and that big black amplifier. We were picked up by a a Baxter's milk driver in a blue-and-white van. The driver was one of the smilingest, friendliest souls I'd ever come across. "I wish I could be like you kids," he said. "Free to do anything you please. Walking down the highway with your electric guitar and not a care in the world."

I went into the back of the van, took out the guitar, and

strummed him a few chords—barely audible without electricity for the amp, and Laura sang Joni or Judy or Joan, but it would be one of the greatest of jam sessions for the two of us. The smell was all sour milk, but the music was heaven.

I formed my own band after that—the Messengers—and, for whatever reason, Laura didn't become our singer. The music we knew was male, and Laura never questioned that but dutifully followed us to our dance-hall performances from Sherbrooke to Lunenburg. She helped carry equipment and deal with the money, but there was always too much gear to be bought and not really enough cash to flow through our band to call ourselves professional.

And then high school was over and done with like a fleeting, fragile dream. The Messengers snagged a couple of better-paying gigs in faraway Truro, Moncton, and Sackville. We played cover tunes to suit the crowds, but as often as possible sneaked in a tune or two of our own creation. Our lead singer, Dave, wasn't much of a singer, but he had that Paul Mascarene style of showmanship that pleased everybody. He *looked* as if he knew what he was doing, so he always got away with it. It was obvious to me that I had more musical talent than the rest of the band put together, but I never said such a thing out loud, not even to Laura.

We smoked cigarettes, we drank a few beers, and we toked a little dope before and after and during the breaks. Laura and I both swore off cigarettes after a while. "Stupid is stupid," she said, but we were sure marijuana was somehow "good" for us.

In all too short a time we lost track of simple things like lying side by side in my father's boat shed, like watching the deep, dark tides of the harbour. When we returned from a road trip, it always felt as if we went back in time. Nothing ever changed in Nick Harbour.

Laura grew restless more quickly than I did. Like a fool, I didn't see it coming. One night she got royally stoned, and we made love for hours in a motel in Amherst not far from where Leon Trotsky had been held prisoner during World War I. The next day we returned to Nickerson Harbour. Just as the pavement ended and we were back on gravel, Laura said, "I don't think I can live here anymore."

"It is a little dull," I admitted.

But I didn't know she was going to leave, just take off the next day, an eighteen-year-old girl on her own, hitchhiking to Toronto. When her parents told me, I was stunned. "Go after her," Laura's mother said. "Jim Dan and I have all the faith in the world in you. I don't think she's ready for this." She handed me an address of a cousin in Toronto. Everyone in Nova Scotia had some relative in Toronto.

I drove day and night and arrived at the address on Brunswick Street. No one there had heard from Laura. It was a hot, sweltering summer night in the city as I sat on the front steps of that apartment building, praying and waiting for the miracle of Laura's arrival. It was a neighbourhood so different from my hometown that I might as well have been on the moon. The sound of cars racing up and down nearby Bloor Street was overwhelming. Neighbours argued publicly on their front porches and music poured out of windows. The streetlights gave off a cold, steely glow and hummed. There were no mosquitoes or black flies.

Sitting on the stone steps of a Toronto apartment building gave me time to reflect, and I soon realized why Laura had run off. Everything about our life had become predictable. Music had taken over and I was living my dream, which I thought was enough for both of us, but it wasn't. Into the night I worried more than anything about Laura's safety, but I also had time to wonder where we would go from here. If I could ever find her again. I knew I had been holding her back. She had been crying out to me that she needed to be more daring, take more chances. She craved adventure and there wasn't enough of it. Toking up and playing loud, frantic rock music in a Truro dance hall until 1:00 a.m. was my personal idea of living on the edge. But, to Laura, it had become a dull edge, a dreary cup of tea on a Sunday afternoon with the Anglican priest. And all the while I had been blind, blind, blind.

Then the fear settled in. *I had already lost her.* She was somewhere on the road, hitchhiking, getting picked up by God knew who. Maybe she'd met someone who could satisfy her quest for adventure. Some free-spirited vagabond with a van headed for

Mexico. A rich old guy who wanted to set her up as a mistress. Or maybe something worse had already happened. I wanted to get up and trace every mile again from Toronto back to Nickerson Harbour. But the miles were many, so I sat alone on that hot, obscene night and saw my life dissipate around me into something less than dust. I deserved punishment; after all, I had let my love for Laura become dull. I could see that I had even allowed sex to become more important to us than love, and perhaps that was a crime against all that was good in the world.

Somewhere in the distance drunks were stumbling out of Yonge Street taverns. Husbands were arguing with wives along this boulevard, as well. Cats were beneath porches stalking and killing mice and rats. Dogs barked at everything and nothing. Not since my mother had left us alone in Nickerson Harbour had I been willing to reopen negotiations with God. I didn't come from a religious family. Religion was something oddly absent from Nickerson Harbour. All the churches were six miles away in the next harbour town. God had somehow passed over Nickerson Harbour. That had been both a blessing and a curse.

Right now I wasn't sure how to address a deity. I thought of my father making a deal with an honest but poor fisherman desperate to buy one of his boats but not having enough money to pay for it. If God was up there and ready to make a deal, He knew I didn't have much to offer Him. So I begged for mercy and hoped God would somehow have the compassionate, negotiating soul of my father.

I confessed I had been living a selfish life and that I hadn't been taking proper care of Laura. I promised that if He was willing to return her to me safe and sound, I'd never let her out of my sight again, that I'd put love back on a shelf higher than sex and I'd love Laura for the rest of my life and well on into whatever afterlife might await us. If necessary, I'd sacrifice my life for hers, if such a balance would satisfy some celestial equation.

I put this forward to God and waited.

Two hours passed and nothing happened. I dozed, I fidgeted, I got up and paced the sidewalk. Then I sat back down, put my head in my hands, and wept. Then God appeared, overweight and wearing black. He had long grey hair and was riding a heavyweight Kawasaki motorcycle with a noisy exhaust system. He stopped in front of the steps where I sat, and I noticed he had a passenger on the back. Laura unsaddled herself from the big bike and gave her driver a peck on the cheek before he drove off.

TWENTY-ONE

We stayed on in Toronto for a couple of weeks. I borrowed an acoustic guitar, and Laura and I performed together at open mikes at coffee houses in Yorkville, calling ourselves Joni and Jeff, although I couldn't remember why. Yorkville had already become fashionable, and the best of the counterculture had long since been absorbed into commercial culture, but it was still a grand time for a fledgling pair from Nickerson Harbour.

Laura loved the big black squirrels of Queen's Park, the noisy streets, and the crowds on the subways we travelled for hours at a time just for entertainment. But when we grew restless, we'd always have to hike down past the CN Tower and under the highways to get to the lake. But a lake, even one as large as Ontario, was never enough to satisfy the water cravings of a coastal breed. "It's big and dull, flat as piss on a plate," she said. "You can tell it once had a soul but that it's been taken away."

The sun was setting, and I studied Laura's face, remembering my bargain with God. "What do we do next?" I asked her.

"I don't know," she said, turning to me, looking more beautiful than ever in the red glow of an Ontario sunset. "I don't know what

I want to do next. Now that I'm here, it's not as exciting as I expected. But I'm not sure I'm good for you anymore, Taylor. I have this feeling I'm gonna screw things up for you somehow. I've already hurt you once."

I relived the night sitting on those Brunswick Street steps and lied. "Not at all. I was just concerned. I love you, remember?"

"I don't know what love is. At least I thought I knew, but now I'm confused."

"What do you mean?"

"I don't know. I haven't really changed the way I feel about you. It's just that I don't have anything to compare it to."

We were back out on the ice again. She was daring me to move on, not to stay on the relative safety of ice near the familiar shore. "I *know* I love you," I said. "You do whatever you have to do, but it won't change my feelings. I'll still love you."

She pulled me to her and kissed me full on the lips, and I dissolved in her embrace. "Let's go home," she said.

People talked when we came back to Nickerson Harbour. But it wasn't as if we were still thirteen. We were both eighteen by then. Laura got a job working the checkout at the IGA, and I landed a job loading lumber in the warehouse of the building-supply store. We were saving money for something, but we weren't sure what. We saw the Savages perform one night not long after we returned, and they were legendary. Paul had bought a wah-wah pedal and a fuzz box, and the Savages' music was better than ever. The Messengers had, by now, passed up nearly a dozen gigs due to my day job, and I was green with envy watching Paul flail his guitar. Laura, I could tell, was very impressed, too. We danced to the music, but I wanted to perform badly.

Two days later Paul got busted for growing marijuana plants in his bedroom, and the Savages asked me to sit in on guitar until things settled down. We performed at a couple of dances and then at Dalhousie University and an outdoor concert on Spring Garden Road before Paul cleared up his legal problems and paid his fine. Naturally the bust gave Paul even more notoriety, and I was left in the dust as the band soared to even greater heights of Nova Scotian rock glory.

After a while the Messengers drifted apart, to jobs in the city, or fishing for cod or going to university. I didn't have much going except the idiotic warehouse job I'd hung on to. Laura hated the IGA. It was when I started to talk to her about forming a new, even hotter band than the Savages or the Messengers that she told me she was quitting her job and going to Vancouver.

I realized immediately that I hadn't kept my bargain with the Kawasaki God. "I was thinking it was time to move out west myself," I said. "Vancouver, maybe Vancouver Island. Time to make friends with the Pacific Ocean."

She smiled, but it wasn't sincere. "I need to grow" was all she said.

I knew what she was talking about. In some respects we had both held the other back by holding on to each other. But I didn't have the strength to give her up, addicted to her as I was. Vancouver, Tasmania, Mars, the Horsehead Nebula—the destination didn't matter. She would have a rough time shaking me and, even though I knew she wanted her freedom, if I wasn't about to give it, she'd refuse to break my heart. "I know you need to grow. I want you to. Once we get to the West Coast, you'll have a lot of opportunities you don't have here. It'll be a blast."

My father said he didn't understand why we had to go so far away. "Pacific, Atlantic, an ocean's an ocean. Why don't you just move in together in Halifax or someplace?"

Jim Dan understood better. He knew there was no holding her back. "Go with her," he told me. "Don't let her get away from you. She needs you, Taylor, to take care of her. We'll sleep soundly as long as we know she's with you. We trust you."

Both my father and Laura's parents knew we had been sleeping together at different times on our travels with the band or nights we spent in Halifax. No one seemed to understand why we didn't just get married. Twenty years old at that point and not quite ready to settle down. What the hell was wrong with our compass needles?

I would have married Laura at the drop of a hat, but I knew she still believed such a move to be "artificial."

We traced the Trans-Canada from Truro, Nova Scotia, to Burnaby, British Columbia, and when the old Ford Falcon gave out near Simon Fraser University, we took a bus to Granville Island and rented a converted apartment in what had once been an old paint factory. Laura took a course in creative writing, and I started hanging out with musicians I'd run into on the street. We both landed part-time jobs as waiter and waitress in restaurants, hers Greek, mine Japanese. Our life and lifestyle were about as far from Nickerson Harbour as you could get. I felt homesick often but tried not to admit it. I missed my father; I missed the feeling of being on the Shore.

We stayed up late and smoked a lot of potent marijuana. When the price of weed went up, it turned out you could buy opium on the street quite cheaply. We both tried it and found that it sent us reeling into a heavenly nowhere place, a psychic realm where time ceased to have meaning. One of my musical buddies, Chuck Coombs, who would later become famous as singer/songwriter for a punk band called the Nymphs, urged me to steer clear of all the opiates. "Read history, man. China. They had wars over opium. Stay clear of it."

I knew Laura was more into the whole drug thing than I was; it was just like her to take more chances, go one step farther. The day cocaine came into our lives it arrived free of charge as a gift from the owner of a downtown music club. I was doing fill-in gigs as rhythm guitar in a band called the Ego. The missing member of the group had gone into rehab for alcohol problems. The club owner was short on cash, or so he said, and he gave me a little vial of white stuff and showed me how to snort it. It was such a mild, happy, uncomplicated high that I decided to share it with Laura. But then I shared everything with her. When I discovered how expensive coke was, I decided to leave it alone. In fact, I was already tired of being around whacked-out Vancouverites, especially my musical friends, each of whom seemed to have his own particular passion for self-destruction.

Laura and I started spending quiet, sober, down-to-earth evenings wrapped up in our very private, ever-so-isolated cocoons of imagination and creativity. I bought a little transistor-radio-size amp for my new twelve-string Rickenbacker. I hung that little amp on my belt, plugged in my axe, and listened through the earphones, exploring new possibilities for my guitar playing as never before. Laura curled up on our bed and wrote poetry in a notebook. She refused to show me what she was writing. "It doesn't come easy, you know," she snapped once.

"Just keep practising," I said. "You'll write some great stuff." But Laura was convinced she had lived an all-too-happy, unsophisticated life. She now believed she'd grown up in a rustic enclave of fishermen where life had been dull, tedious, and dreadful. She wouldn't write about her past, only what she perceived to be her present. I should have taken note of her influences and tried to steer her otherwise. I'd met her writing instructor—a chain-smoking, overwrought, sullen intellectual who let me know with a flick of his cigarette ash and a sideways look that I was of little value. I think he had more than a literary interest in Laura, but when I suggested it to her she freaked and started giving me lectures about needing more "space," more freedom. Laura surrounded herself with books, and I wish I could have been a greater influence on her reading list. Sylvia Plath, Denise Levertov, Stevie Smith, Elizabeth Bishop—she wanted to write like them. She wanted to write from pain and despair and she hadn't had enough of either of them in her life. Her writing was going slowly and was a torture, not a pleasure. She blamed me and herself for having lived such a sheltered existence. Laura, for the first time in her life, was truly unhappy.

I bought a used Ford Econoline that had once been a delivery van for a florist. It smelled of flowers when we bought it—orchids, roses, gladioli. I wanted that smell to linger with us on our first trip out of the city. So I stopped at a nursery on our way to the ferry at Tsawwassen and bought live daffodils, pansies, baby's breath, and other flowering plants. Laura changed back into her old self. "It's like driving around in a flower garden," she said. "I've got to write a poem about this." And I knew we were on the right track. Once on Vancouver Island, we drove as far as the road would take us—a little town named Bamfield—then went hiking with camping gear on our backs along the rugged Pacific coastline. We slept overnight at a place called Cape Beale and listened to the roar of the wild ocean smashing against the ancient rocks.

Laura fell in love with me again that night, and in the morning she ripped up her notebook and tossed the poems one by one into our campfire. "It's all about being happy, isn't it?"

"What is?"

"This. You, me, everything. Why was it so easy to be happy before?"

"Because we were young and stupid."

"Now we're twenty-one. Old and stupid."

I did feel rather old. When you were just closing the door on being a teenager, age and the rapid passage of time were scary things.

"How come you and I are different?" she asked.

"One of us is female, the other male?"

"Idiot. You know what I mean."

"I'm not sure I follow."

"How come you're happy and I'm not?"

What she had said frightened me. I guess I didn't really believe she was truly unhappy, just unsettled. Now she'd said it and the words didn't want to rest easily in my brain.

"Hey, I'm the one with the messed-up childhood," I said. "Me, happy? You'd have to be a fool to believe that." But I was lying. I *was* happy. As long as I had Laura, I had everything. But apparently having *me* wasn't enough for her. It would be up to me to make the suggestion first. I would have to be one step ahead of Laura if I wanted to keep her. I poked the dying fire with a stick, shuffling the black-carbon remains of paper that once contained Laura's poems. Then I looked up at her and out toward the seagulls catching the updraft of wind along the cliff edge. I heard a musical phrasing in the back of my head, something high and wild, lilting and ascending, a guitar sound of a rising glissando that carried despair and longing and hope and possibility all in the same harmonic package. "I don't think Vancouver's right for us," I said.

"I'm not going back to Nova Scotia."

"I know. Neither am I. We have legs. We have a van back there full of wilting flowers. You pick a direction and we'll go."

Laura was smiling now. It was the little-girl smile, the daredevil, live-for-today one. The dark poetry was consumed by flame, the fire was dead, and the ashes were scattering in the wind, caught in the updraft and ascending toward the birds of the Pacific heavens. We were camped on a grassy little plateau near the cliff edge. Laura stood and closed her eyes. "Spin me."

I started to twirl her slowly. Giggling like a child, she wobbled, and twice I had to pull her back from the edge. I wanted her to stop so that she was facing north. I could already see us heading for the mountainous, isolated coastline of northern British Columbia, the Queen Charlotte Islands, or farther on to Alaska—Ketchikan or Sitka. Some place with monster trees and freedom written all over it. A place to build a log cabin and split firewood for heat.

Laura was cheating. She peeked. Or maybe she could tell the wind was coming at her from the west. She knew which direction she wanted to stop in. Her feet were precariously close to the edge of the continent when she stopped, lost her balance briefly, got her bearings, stuck out her arm, and pointed. Due south.

We watered the flowers in the van and watched as they came back to life miraculously. Laura would scout the side of the road and occasionally shout, "There!" I would stop, take out my hand axe, and cut a chunk of grass from the side of the road where we would plant flowers. Port Alberni, Parksville, Nanaimo, Ladysmith, Chemainus. When our private nursery ran out, we stopped and bought some more. In the middle of the night we planted flowers in the front lawns of suburban homes, outside the gates of a pulp mill, and at the doorstep of an RCMP detachment. And it felt good.

When we arrived back at our ugly little paint-factory apartment, it was clear Vancouver didn't want us and we didn't want her. We told the landlord to keep the deposit, loaded up my guitar gear and all our belongings, threw Sylvia Plath and the other depressing poets into a dumpster, and headed south. Oregon, I was thinking. Maybe some little town on the coast. I'd always had a good feeling about Oregon.

TWENTY-TWO

What I should have been looking for was the Great American Bypass, the one that took you right around the country so you ended up in Mexico. We crossed the border, intending to find happiness on the Oregon coast somewhere. But the music kept sucking me south. One band led to the next. All I could find on the coast—in Astoria, Newport, Coos Bay—was country-music gigs. I felt as if I were cheating on the music, cheating as much as in "Your Cheating Heart," or as much as cheating on your wife with a hooker at a truck stop. That bothered me; I'd always been faithful to my music. I still wrote my own tunes, however, staying up late with my Walkman-size amp to carve out new guitar territory alone while Laura slept.

Retreating inland to Portland, I lined up with a band about to record in a local studio—folkie tunes with brazen electric noises. Musically the Ledge was young and unfocused, but the demo found favour with a new label and the label got bought by a bigger label and it all happened overnight. Soon we were on the road. South, of course. Sacramento, Oakland, and finally San Francisco, where the band broke up and I was sure I was ready for something bigger.

Laura, who had forsaken writing, had begun to paint by then, and I was making enough money so she didn't have to work. She had begun by creating a series of paintings in which everything was made of flowers—a van first, then cars, then buildings, then whole cities and even factories. Next she created bold, sometimes lurid paintings and intense, intricate etchings. One day I discovered that her style of painting was not at all unlike my own trademark guitar style. Take a beautiful sound, work it over with a near overload of pumped-up energy, and stretch the sound as far as possible while softening the edges of the distortion to prevent burning out the audience.

A gallery near Berkeley put a few of Laura's works on sale, and they were snapped up for a couple hundred bucks each. Not bad for a brand-new artist. Laura would have been happy to stay in San Francisco. She didn't have many women friends, but the art scene had brought her close to a half-dozen gay men who became her allies. Having come from Nickerson Harbour, I had a hard time at first keeping my mind open about these men, but the rational part of my brain, underdeveloped as it was, told me they were, at the very least, safe. I needn't be jealous. What was there to worry about? Laura traded recipes, went shopping, and learned more about art from the gay men. And when I had to go away for a few days at a stretch to record or perform, she had friends.

And then, like a fool, I moved her away from there. The Ledge broke up, and I got a phone call from a producer in Los Angeles. Studio work. Lots of it. Some performers with big acts coming into L.A. needed an extra axe picker. More money. More glitz. More everything. They all wanted to make me jump and all I could say was "How high?"

We weren't prepared for Southern California. It swallowed both of us. Nickerson Harbour, our families, our old life diminished, dissolved, and ultimately ceased to exist. We rented a quirky little exotic house on El Sobrante Drive in the Hollywood Hills. All of our neighbours were lunatics, but happy-go-lucky people. The hills rattled once in a while from minor earthquakes, and we thought it was a great California tease.

Without the friendly Berkeley gallery owner and her old gay artist friends, Laura lost interest in painting, and I encouraged her to get back into singing. Joni, Judy, and Joan. I even brought her into a couple of practice sessions to do some vocal backups for a rising star, but she hated the tension in the air, hated the attitude of the militant producer and the repetitive process that, for her, sucked every bit of life out of a song until it was "too sanitary, too commercial and devoid of life."

I became very busy. And Laura gave up any thoughts of a career. She became a social animal instead. There were always plenty of interesting people around. We had more invitations than we knew what to do with. Californians were happy, crazy, hip to everything new, and I was just glad Laura was having a good time. Drugs flowed freely in my line of work, and I'd toke up to be polite or snort a line of potent white stuff to be sociable.

All too soon I learned that success could be debilitating. You lost track of what was important. I did. I had cut the ties completely with the young kid who had made a lifelong commitment to a young girl from Nova Scotia. I became the successful guitarist that people wanted me to be. I was a chameleon, and my brain became as reptilian as my skin. Where once I had the power to arrest time by simply *being* with Laura, now time had complete dominion over me. Time and managers and success. Money happened. It fell from the sky. I was no musical genius. I had a few good tricks, a style, and a sense of musical adventure. I adapted easily to anyone's musical attitude and, chameleonlike, enhanced the work of whomever I was playing for. And I was dependable. My father must have taught me that—craftsmanship and dependability.

We partied at night and I worked most days. Laura, however, partied in the night and partied through the days, as well. She shopped, she socialized, she socialized some more. She was always accompanied by "friends," so I believed she was doing okay. I deluded myself that she had it under control. I believed what I wanted to believe.

When Laura gave up drinking after the accident on Mulholland Drive that nearly took the life of a teenage girl, I was proud of her. And when she shunned psychedelics, tried and then rejected amphetamines and Quaaludes, I was even prouder. But I failed to take full notice when the subculture of cocaine around us began to change.

Coke was less expensive and more accessible in L.A. The high was a real nice buzz that didn't blitz you out. I was a classic casual user. Purely recreational. Coke was a musician's RV camper ready to roll. "Snow," they called it then. Perfect for a couple of Canadians, someone once said.

Laura had a "kit" that included a mirror, a razor blade, and a hundred-dollar bill. Or sometimes two hundred-dollar bills. One to buy the stuff with, one to use as a tube to sniff coke up her nose. Day in and day out. And I only knew about the tip of the iceberg. I had no idea how hard she was going at it.

I tried to talk to her about the drugs at one point when someone else had clued me into the potential pitfalls of too much of a good thing. But Laura assured me she had no problem. She wanted to prove to me everything was fine, so she took up painting again. She bought enormous canvases and tackled ambitious, impossible abstract images. The more she painted, however, the more the images made sense to me. She began to find form and substance, not just shadow and colour. Amazingly I discovered that the images, hard to decipher at first, were of Nova Scotia: rugged, rocky shore-lines, seabirds, spruce horizons. When I mentioned this to her, she said I was way off track. It was the colour and shading that mattered. They were purely non-representational images.

Over the years phone calls home to Nickerson Harbour had decreased. We had become Californians. Many Californians, especially those living around L.A., were citizens of the here and now. *Carpe diem* was our anthem and holy script. We had no past. We had Canadian friends in L.A., but for some reason Laura was always uncomfortable when around them and didn't like it when someone pointed out her accent or mentioned her home province.

I did a poor job of keeping track of the household money, so I didn't see it siphoning off into Laura's cocaine hobby. I guess I thought it was all going into rent, phone bills, and art supplies. Eventually I hired an accountant to help me figure out a tax mess I had fallen into. He had a bizarre suggestion for my woes: get married.

"What?"

"Get married, fool. Lower your taxes."

So I asked Laura if she'd marry me, and I did it *for tax purposes*. I was ashamed to admit that. We already had the lifelong commitment. It wasn't that I was afraid of marriage. So I asked her and she said, "Sure, why not?"

We had become so American, so Californian, that everything had gone casual in our lives. Even marriage. A marriage of economic convenience. We drove that cliché all the way to Las Vegas and stood in front of a justice of the peace in a tiny stucco chapel. Before and after the event we both sniffed a little snow, and I should have yet again read the road signs. But we were high and happy as we drove to see Hoover Dam and then on to the Grand Canyon on a whirlwind honeymoon.

The desert seemed like an old friend to us, and an air-conditioned, gas guzzling eight-cylinder car seemed like a perfectly normal means of travel. I was happy. I really was. I didn't care why we were married, but I liked the idea immensely. I always had. I guess it just took an accountant's logic to persuade the love of my life that we should be legally hitched. From a motel in Flagstaff, Arizona, I phoned my father to tell him. He was overjoyed. "When are you coming home?"

I muffled the receiver with my hand. "When are we going home?" I asked Laura. She suddenly looked completely disoriented, turned away from me, and stared at the closed venetian blinds. "I'll talk to Laura and let you know," I told my father, and heard an audible sigh of disappointment. As I hung up, it seemed impossible the crime that we had committed. We had moved away and not returned home to Nova Scotia for over ten years. There were letters, phone calls. We pretended to be in close touch. But we had severed ourselves from our home and our families. We had done it of our own free will and we refused to see the barbaric act of cruelty we had committed. I vowed silently that we would fly home soon. Very soon.

I tried to conjure up a picture of us returning. Husband and wife at long last. Me, a big shot. Laura decked out in the latest fashions.

It would be a blast. A hoot. We would be the envy of everyone in the old hometown.

No, that would be a stupid idea. It would be all wrong. We couldn't reconcile anything about who we were back then with who we were now. Or so Laura convinced me. "I'm not going," she said simply. "You can go if you want to."

It was a long, uneventful, air-conditioned ride back to the Hollywood Hills. The coke had run out. Laura was cranky and so was I. By the time we walked in through our front door, the only person still happy about our marriage was probably our accountant. For once a client had taken his advice. "Congratulations, you love-birds." His voice sounded so cheery but hollow on the answering machine.

What followed was more good news both from my accountant and from the recording studio, which offered me an opportunity to play on tracks for several important sessions. It seemed that, almost by accident, I had become very good at making music, making money, and making everybody happy. Everybody except Laura.

I wasn't home the evening she died. I didn't even know she was free-basing coke. I'd seen a couple of studio musicians doing something once that looked insane and weird to me, something involving a little butane torch that looked as if it belonged in a kid's chemistry set. But I never expected Laura to move ahead of me into the nether reaches of the get-high-and-get-messed-up drug games of my contemporaries.

Whatever she was doing right or wrong about the coke thing, she did too much of it too quick. The vapours of the altered cocaine were sucked into her lungs as she hunched over the blue flame. I can see it all so awful in my head as if I were there. It was a heavy hit, they said, not unlike injecting with a needle. The drug slammed into her lungs and volted through her system. She had a heart seizure and died. There in our living room, which we called instead our "music room." On each wall of that room was one of four enormous paintings by Laura. It was a room without furniture, only a deep pile carpet. It was a place where the two of us had once spent many hours alone, just holding each other. Sometimes high, sometimes not.

I came home at nine o'clock that night. It was a beautiful evening, but a little too warm. A wind was blowing off the land, a hot, dry wind that sometimes led to bush fires in the hills. I unlocked the door to the house, heard only silence, then walked into our living room and saw her on the floor. There was a burn mark on the grey carpet near where she lay. I knew instantly she hadn't just passed out.

She wasn't breathing. Her heart had stopped. She was cold. Later they would say she'd been dead for nearly an hour before I arrived. It had been relatively painless. She had been insanely high when she left this world. The medical examiner reckoned she wasn't truly familiar with free-basing and had overdosed. Nothing I could have done when I arrived could have helped.

I lay on the carpet and held her to me. I smelled her hair, touched her cheek, closed my eyes, and pretended we were only going to sleep. I wanted to sleep and awaken and find it all hadn't been real. To my horror, I realized I hadn't loved Laura enough. She had slipped away, and I had inadvertently pushed her from me. Slowly, almost methodically, I had invented and perpetrated her death.

No one would be able to convince me her death wasn't my fault. No court of law need convict me of murder, but it would amount to the same thing. Love required obligation. It required that you never took a relationship casually. I stayed on the floor, not moving for the rest of the night. I didn't cry. I was too angry at myself to do that. In the dim morning light that broke over the arid hills outside, I stared at the paintings that surrounded us and saw the Atlantic, the sometimes pale, sometimes dark, luxurious waters of Nickerson Harbour, rimmed with spruce trees, sunlight radiant through the branches and dancing on the water. I saw that the four paintings were one of each season in Nova Scotia: the crystalline world of winter ice; the foggy, opulent wetness of spring; the exquisite blue beauty of full sunlight on the open sea in summer; and finally, the one that riveted my attention, the one I didn't understand—fall. It wasn't like the others. The harbour's surface was pale and obscure, as if the colours had been layered on purpose by the artist to throw you off at first, to make you miss something buried in the watery image.

There were wisps of mist perhaps on the water's surface, familiar but ambiguous. No person was in the picture, but it was as if you were seeing this vision of beauty through the eyes of someone visually impaired. I turned away from the picture and, instead, focused on the painting of summer.

Through her art I returned with Laura to a morning long ago. I went back to being Taylor Colby, son of Horace Colby. Laura McGillivray was my close friend. As I closed my eyes, Laura and I listened to the sound of small, precise waves lapping the shoreline of tiny pebbles and sand. The air was still cool, but the sunlight was growing warmer on our faces and it was good, oh, so good, to be young and alive in Nova Scotia.

TWENTY-THREE

I was a wreck by the time I had finished my long, sorry tale. Jillian hadn't interrupted me. The TV was off in the living room now, and Wade had gone to bed. We were alone. Jillian touched my hand and looked softly at me, but her words didn't fit the message in her eyes.

"Maybe it wasn't all your fault. The way you tell the story, Laura was responsible for her own actions."

"But I should have been paying attention."

"Women want more than just to be protected and taken care of. Laura might have followed you to California, but she made her own decisions. Staying with you was a good decision. Going off the deep end was a bad one."

"But I should have seen it coming."

"Yes, you should have. But it's history."

"Not really. I live it every day."

"You need to get some help."

I looked around the room, my eyes resting on a piece of driftwood sitting on a shelf. "Maybe that's where you fit in." But as soon as the words were out of my mouth, I saw something in Jillian's face change.

"I'm not sure you should have told me this," she said.

"I'm sorry. Kind of a lot to drop on you. It's just that it had to come out some time."

"I know. It's just that my own life is already so complicated. Half the time I don't know if I did the right thing by bringing Wade here, or if I was just running away. I made a rule for myself when I left Philadelphia. Be selfish. Do whatever is best for Wade and me. Don't take any chances."

"And anything involving me would be a pretty big gamble, right?"

"Something like that." She couldn't look me in the eye anymore. I understood full well what she was saying, but I felt hurt and betrayed.

"It's okay. I understand, I think." I got up to go.

"Taylor, I really appreciate what you did for us. I'll never forget that. And if things weren't the way they are, I think I'd really want to get to know you better. I think I could even—" she stopped, paused, looked in the air for missing words "—get involved. But that's the last thing I need in my life right now."

I was crushed but part of me agreed with her logic. She would have been foolish to "get involved" with what was left of me after Laura, after California drained the life from me. "It's okay, Jillian. It really is. S'long."

"Bye."

The night was damp and chill. The gravel of the road crunched under my feet. I thought about walking off into the night. Anywhere. Nowhere. Somewhere other than here. I didn't want to run into Jillian again, and you couldn't live in a place like Nickerson Harbour without bumping into everybody—often. I reckoned that if I had kept my mouth shut or told a modified version of my story, I might not have scared her off. But she had the good sense to avoid someone as messed up as I was. It wouldn't take a brilliant, two-hundred-dollar-an-hour Beverly Hills psychiatrist to figure out how screwed up I was.

I didn't have the will to seek out Paul's bootlegger and get drunk. I was tired and beat. So I let my feet find their way home.

The kitchen light was on, but everybody was asleep. Frank was lying half on, half off the sofa and snoring. It was a classic, vaudevillian snore, like something from slapstick. I studied the appearance of the second man my mother had married. Bald head, round face, cherubic almost. I could take a guess at what his friends would say about him back in Ontario: "A little odd, but one of the sweetest guys you'd ever want to meet." I decided that this wouldn't be such a bad thing to be remembered for. Maybe someone would say it about me when I got old.

The door to my father's room was open a crack, and a night light was on inside. Before I turned out the kitchen light and prepared to crawl into the sleeping bag on the floor—the "buddy bunk" next to Frank—I looked in on my mother. She was sick, after all; maybe she needed something. I opened the door to my old bedroom ever so slowly and poked my head in. As the light sifted into the darkness, I could see the bed was empty. That seemed impossible. How could she be gone? For a second I feared she had died while I was out, but I knew that couldn't be. Frank was still in the living room. She couldn't possibly be dead. As I stood in the warm darkness of my old room, I wondered if she had disappeared on us again, run away perhaps from Nickerson Harbour for a second time. But that didn't make any sense, either.

I went into my father's room to wake him and find out what was going on. The door was already open, and in the dim glow of the night light I saw an amazing and startling image. My father and mother were in bed together. He had his arm around her. I heard the rhythm of their breathing. They were both sound asleep. I stood still in wonder and bewilderment. Two old people sleeping together as if it were the most natural thing in the world. A husband and his wife. All the intervening lonely, empty years erased. My father had been given back the only woman he had ever loved.

My father had always said she would come home one day. And here she was. Asleep with her man, her first husband, while the second snored loudly in the next room. What would the people of Nickerson Harbour make of this arrangement? They didn't know much, mind you, but they knew enough already to talk, talk, talk. But my father didn't care. He had his wife back.

Maybe I wanted to laugh. Or cry. Or just stand there for the rest of the night watching them sleep like that. My mother had her head on my father's shoulder. Her pillow had fallen to the floor. They were as together as any two sleeping people could be. Peaceful. Not a care in the world.

I tiptoed out of the room, but as I was about to turn out the kitchen light, Frank turned over, let out a loud, well-practised yawn, and rubbed his eyes with a fist the way a little boy would have. "Oh, it's you. Boy, did you ever stay out late. What time is it?"

"Near midnight." Before I said another word I switched off the light. Maybe he didn't know my mother and father were in bed together.

"You're young. Young people can stay up late. I always have to be in bed by ten. Sleep—the great escape."

I slipped into my sleeping bag and tried to pull it over my head.

"I told him," Frank said in the darkness. "I told your father she's dying."

I swallowed hard and wished he hadn't reminded me. "Well, now at least it's out in the open. How did he take it?"

"I think he knew something was going on. Your father's not a naive man. He wants to take her to some doctors in Halifax. He's sure there's something that can be done."

"Maybe there is. There's something in the news every week."

"Yeah. It's okay. I'm glad he's not giving up. I haven't, either. But we've been at this thing for a few years now. I think your mother knows the score. I'm in favour of anything as long as it doesn't cause her pain."

"How can you be so sure something can't be done?"

"It's spread. It's throughout her body. I've seen the results. I don't think you can reverse such things. They say it's happened slowly but that one day soon it'll be too much. Her body just can't fight it anymore."

I lay on my back and looked at the ceiling. The only light in the house was coming from my father's bedroom. You could hear the two of them shifting on the bed, turning over, an audible sigh. It was obvious two people were sleeping in that room. Neither one of us spoke a word about it, though.

"How can you handle this so well?" I asked Frank. "This must all seem like madness to you."

"I'm just thankful for the time we've had together. I don't ask why these things happen. Your mother's handling this very well, I think. Me, I'm faking it. When she goes, I'm gonna be a basket case. But I don't care about that. She's here. I'm here. We're all here. That's kinda nice. I don't give a rat's ass what anyone thinks."

I laughed. "I always thought I was going to hate your guts when I finally met you. And now..."

"Now what? You wanna beat me up for taking your mother away?"

"No. Now I think you're an amazing person."

"That's only because of her. I love her. And so do you. We have that in common."

"I don't know."

"What don't you know?"

"About the love part. I've hated her for years. Hated her for making my life here so empty."

"It wasn't her fault."

"And then when Laura died I stopped hating her. I stopped having any feelings at all. I didn't care about anything."

"But now you're back. She's back."

"I'm glad my father can feel the way he does. I'm glad you can handle all the weirdness. But I'm not sure I want to be around to watch my mother make her exit out of my life again."

"But you're just getting to know her again."

"That's the problem. It was much easier to hate a woman I didn't know."

"Give it time," Frank said. "Give it time."

I tried to sleep, but I couldn't find the switch. When I tried to empty my mind, it overflowed with memories of Laura, with images of Jillian's face as I told the history of my downfall. The only comfort I had that night was the gentle but theatrical snoring of Frank. He didn't exactly keep me awake with the noise. It was a human, normal, comfortable sound that befriended me until the thin grey light of morning arrived and a lone sparrow outside the window began to speak the language of music.

There were trips to the hospital in Halifax after that, visits to doctors. I was chauffeur, a role I felt perfectly at home with. I let my father direct me. I was happy to be given orders and not decide anything myself. Medical records were sent down from Ontario. All the experts were polite but curt. They realized how much treatment my mother had already received; they studied X rays, CAT scans, blood tests, PSA levels. There was a lot of shaking of heads and apologies all around. "It's amazing she looks so healthy and vital," one doctor said to us even as she sat there in his presence.

Afterward, eating Dairy Queen sundaes in the car, my mother laughed and said, "They can't figure out what keeps me going. I've got a secret, but I'm not telling. Not yet."

After several more trips to Halifax, my father was halfheartedly convinced whatever would be, would be. He carried a great weight of sadness, I could tell, but he was always cheerful around us. We were the oddest of Canadian families, the four of us, but we truly did feel like a family. Frank insisted we stop the car often and buy ice cream or doughnuts or candy bars from the little convenience stores along Highway 7. We bought lobster and scallops and Atlantic salmon to cook for dinner, and we shopped together at the IGA where Laura once cashiered. We'd fill up two shopping carts, my father buying, Frank buying, my mother trying to be prudent by putting unnecessary items back.

"You gotta eat," Frank said. "We all gotta eat. Might as well eat like kings and queens."

"I agree," my father said, asking the lady behind the bakery counter for a three-level Black Forest chocolate cake.

True summer arrived on the Eastern Shore. There was news of the first tropical storm pushing north from the Caribbean. We watched on TV as it slammed into Puerto Rico and Bermuda, then stalled off our coast, the cooler northern waters sapping its strength. During the days, I'd hike out past Grandfather Rock toward Stoney Beach and the open sea to watch massive waves roll shoreward, big blue-green hills that pitched forward as they hit the shallows. Clean waves in an offshore wind. Surfing waves. Given a wetsuit and a surfboard, I would have paddled out and tried my California skills, my Pacific-learned craft, on the Atlantic walls of water. Instead, I sat halfway up the grassy embankment of a headland and mentally surfed wave after wave—paddling, standing, turning, tucking, dipping my head into the tunnel as it threw out a feisty blue-white lip of water, then carving a turn off the top and dropping into the trough, racing away along the long wall of the wave, dropping again and then up, launching skyward toward the gulls before kicking my board around to slide back down onto the clean, smooth face of the tropical energy left in the last great hurrah of the hurricane.

I avoided walking around Nickerson Harbour. There were trails through the woods to get me to the sea. I avoided the wharf. I would do this simple favour for Jillian. I would avoid her, avoid Wade. I considered myself a fool for opening up, for telling her about Laura. Too much, too soon. I had wanted desperately for Jillian to like me. I needed a woman in my life, and I had grown to know her just enough so that I felt that deep-down, aching tug on my heart. But it was all for naught.

The trips to Halifax diminished. The doctors had no news. Our kitchen was stockpiled with mega-vitamins, algae pills, capsules with extract from shark cartilage and yew trees. We had it all and we knew it wasn't going to do much good. Whatever was keeping my mother alive was something she hadn't admitted to doctors or family. I had ceased hating her. It was someone else who had deserted me, someone who couldn't possibly have been connected to this happy, gentle woman.

Nonetheless, I continued to hold a much more grievous grudge against myself. No matter how long I lived, or how much my life might change, I'd never forgive myself for allowing Laura to die. There was nothing I did in any given moment of any given day, happy or sad, consequential or trivial, that didn't connect in some way, in my memory, in my most private and personal core, with her loss. And yet, miraculously, I did survive. I could go on, wake up day after day, and continue to live my life. That was the great mystery to me. I couldn't begin to fathom my ability to continue living.

TWENTY-FOUR

I slept late the next morning. The "adults" woke up and admonished one another several times over to be quiet. Old people have a habit of whispering rather loudly, probably because of their own diminished hearing. It was all extremely diplomatic and polite for such a bizarre morning family reunion of wife, husband, and husband, but it went off without a hitch. Breakfast was a noisy affair with a lot of shushing, muffled coughing, phlegm clearing, and muted conversations that could have been heard into the next county.

Snuggled up in an old, musty-smelling sleeping bag I had pulled over my head, I did indeed feel like a little kid. I didn't actually feel like the real "me" but a half-imagined, idealized, long-lost kid who had never existed. And I was almost happy, secure in my surroundings, at peace even with my failure to get closer to Jillian. I had shoved all the anxiety, all the failure, the regret, the anger, and the guilt into some enormous far closet in the back of the household that was my brain, my memory.

"It's ten o'clock and he's still sleeping," I heard someone say after I dozed off again, luxuriating in the warm smell of pancakes slightly overdone.

"Let him rest," my mother said.

I decided it was time to return to a semblance of reality, so I peeked out from my cocoon, tried to see some evidence in my father's face that he knew my mother was dying. But he revealed none. He was smiling, Frank was smiling, everybody was smiling. And sunlight was streaming in through the windows. Before me was some outlandish Canadian version of the old *Ozzie and Harriet* TV show. I almost wondered if it was a long-delayed hallucinatory effect of some bad acid from so many years ago in Vancouver. But it was the real thing. And I liked the feeling of the moment very much. But I should have known then that something awful was about to happen.

After I got up, I ate too many pancakes drenched with maple syrup. Frank had brought us Laurentian Mountain maple syrup, a small vital tin of it that looked like something you would buy in a hardware store. It was intended to be a peace offering. And a good one it was. My father, mother, and Frank seemed to get immense enjoyment from watching me eat. When I was finished stuffing my face, I went for a walk. Without even thinking I headed to the harbour, ending up back at the wharf.

Paul's car was there. I didn't see any other fishermen. Then I spotted Paul standing at the end of the wharf, his back to me. I didn't see the shotgun until he turned sideways. The gun was aimed at the water; he was tracking something with the muzzle, shifting his weight awkwardly on his bad leg as he pivoted.

"Paul!" I screamed. "Please, no!"

Paul lowered the shotgun, turned, and looked at me as I ran toward him down the length of the wharf. The loose, heavy planking boomed ominously as I sprinted. Paul kept staring at me, then lifted the gun and pointed it in my direction. I stopped running, but I wasn't scared. I should have been. After all, Paul was crazy.

He lowered the gun, a big, fat smile on his face. *Just joking.* Of course. Mascarene, last of the great, dangerous pranksters. I continued to walk the rest of the way toward him. But, as I did, he turned on his good leg again, aimed the shotgun back into the water, and let go with two horrible explosions as he pulled the trigger.

The first spray of pellets pierced only water, but the second struck something solid as I screamed and dived at Paul's back. Hitting him hard, low on his spine, I knocked him off the wharf. We were out in the air, falling off the dock and coming down hard, me on top of him, into the cold water of the harbour. Underwater, I pushed away from him as he grabbed for my neck. I felt pain somewhere and wondered if I had been shot. When I surfaced and tried to kick myself away from Paul, I saw blood all around us in the water.

"I'm gonna kill you," Paul growled, and started to swim toward me frantically.

I did a halfhearted backstroke to keep my distance, looking Paul straight in the eye. It was a slow-motion, anger-driven aquatic ballet. Clothes weighed us down and we moved like fitful sleepers in a dream. I backpaddled into deeper water. I just wanted to keep some distance between us. I spun 180 degrees. Farther out I saw Cobain. Behind him was a red swath in the water. The seal was trying to stay on the surface, gasping for air.

I turned again to face Paul. He was floundering but still in pursuit. "Why?" I asked him as he got nearer.

"It's just a friggin' seal." He had a completely insane look. If he caught up, he'd try to kill me now; I had little doubt of that. And I still wasn't scared. I let him get close enough to reach for my neck again, then I brought my leg up from beneath me and kicked him hard in the jaw with my running shoe. The blow caught him off guard, and I waited.

Paul slipped under the water but quickly came up sputtering. He tried to come at me again, but he was having a hard time swimming. I backpaddled some more, keeping a close watch on his every move, certain he couldn't get to me and drag me down. A voice in the back of my head posed the obvious question, though: *What are you going to do if Paul starts to go down?* But I didn't have to answer. I watched as Paul started to panic. "Swim for shore, asshole," I told him.

That only angered him more. Paul would rather drown in an attempt to throttle me than save his own skin. But I turned away from him and made a slow advance toward Cobain. Paul screamed something unintelligible when he realized he didn't have the strength to catch me. Then he headed for shore, sluggishly, half swimming, half struggling.

When I came close to Cobain, he dived, trying to get away, but he surfaced quickly, gasping for air. "It's going to be okay, boy," I said, staring into his dark dog eyes. Blood was streaming out of the wound that I couldn't see, and the water was sickly red on the surface. He tried to dive again to get away from me but couldn't. I didn't know how to help. Even though he was a young seal, he was nearly as big as I was and probably weighed more than I did. This was his element, not mine. If he wanted to escape, he would.

I reached out to touch him, trying to break through the barrier between us, trying to get him to trust me so I could help. He blinked and his eyes remained shut for a long moment. I touched his head, patting him as if he were a dog. But he snapped at me, biting hard, and I felt the pain of his sharp teeth razoring into the palm of my left hand. I backpaddled again to get some distance. Cobain tried to dive but floated back to the surface, then stopped moving. I circled him and took another chance. I grabbed his tail with my right hand and began to tow him to shore. The seal seemed inert, completely lifeless now.

All I could do was swim ever so slowly, weighted down by my own wet clothes. Up ahead on the shoreline I saw Jillian and Wade. The nightmare was just beginning. Paul staggered out of the water near them and tore off his wet shirt. Wade started to run into the water, but Jillian pulled him back. Slowly but steadily, I swam with Cobain behind me. I was breathing hard, my hand hurting where he'd bitten me. I knew if he regained consciousness he'd bite me again. I didn't care, but I also dreaded my arrival on the shoreline. I didn't want Wade to see this. If I could have come up with another option, I would have gladly chosen it. Instead, I struggled shoreward.

Wade splashed back into the water and helped me drag Cobain up on the pebbled beach. I fell to my knees and sucked hard at the air until I could stop the world from spinning. Above me, Paul stood in the morning sunlight, bare-chested, looking down. He had me then, if he wanted to get even. He could have kicked me hard in the guts. He could have hammered me into the ground until I was senseless, and I couldn't have fought back. But he didn't. He just smiled, turned to Jillian, and said, "Taylor bought me the shotgun. It was a nice present while it lasted."

Jillian pretended not to hear. She and Wade were rolling Cobain onto his side, studying the wounds in the body of the beautiful creature that had once been free and swimming in the deep harbour. The seal's fur glistened in the sunlight. Blood had stopped pumping out of the wounds. Cobain's eyes were wide open. He wasn't breathing.

"Do something," Wade said.

"Is there a vet around here?" Jillian asked.

The closest vet was in Sheet Harbour, at least forty-five minutes away. I shook my head. I think I knew all too well the seal was dead. If he'd had the slightest chance of survival, he wouldn't have let me tow him to shore. He would have fought me to the end. He would have tried to kill me first.

"Do something, damn it!" Wade yelled.

I did what I could. I leaned over the seal, cupped my hands on his mouth, and blew air into him. Five times I tried this, knowing full well it wouldn't work. My lungs didn't have the power left to do any good. It was a fool's errand at best. I tried again to breathe air into Cobain, then gave up, falling back onto the beach and looking up at the blinding sun. As I lay there, I heard Paul start his car and drive off. I heard Jillian trying to console her son. I heard Wade crying as he held on to the back of the seal. Then I heard him say, "I hate this place. I hate all of you." And he ran.

"Wade!" his mother screamed. She ran after him, and I tried to get my bearings to stand up. I felt dizzy and my hand was hurting. I was left alone on the shoreline with Cobain. Jillian and Wade were gone.

Another truck was pulling up to the wharf—Vance Beaudreau and a couple of cronies. I didn't want them to have a chance to stand around and look at the dead seal. I didn't want any of them to touch Cobain, even if they decided they wanted to help bury him. Cobain wasn't a land animal. His attempt to make friends with even one small citizen of Nickerson Harbour had caused his death. Cobain was a sea creature, and at the very least deserved to return to the sea.

While the fishermen watched I dragged Cobain back off the beach and out into the water. I was up to my neck in the cold water again when I was sure the tug of the outgoing tide would escort Cobain back to sea. Before I let him go I rested my head on his soft, shiny fur and said, "I'm sorry, I'm sorry, I'm sorry." And then I released what was left of Cobain, letting him drift away from us.

Everybody at my house agreed it was a crying shame. "Should have locked that boy up and thrown away the key a long time ago," my father said of Paul Mascarene. "Nothing but bad news."

My mother encouraged me to take a shower, then said, "Have something more to eat. It'll warm you up."

I went looking for Jillian and Wade afterward, but they were nowhere around. Jillian's car was gone. I wanted to do something, but it seemed that every time I tried to help, things always got worse. Later that day I saw her return, followed by an RCMP car that pulled up in the driveway behind her. I immediately walked to her house and went in without knocking.

"Everything okay?" I asked.

I could tell from the look on Jillian's face that it wasn't.

"Who are you?" the Mountie asked.

"A friend. Taylor Colby."

He gave me a cold, hard look. He'd obviously heard about me—the bad stuff at least. "What are you doing here?"

"What happened to Wade?"

"Go home," Jillian said.

"Tell me what happened," I insisted.

Jillian turned to the cop. "According to Paul Mascarene, Taylor bought him the shotgun."

The Mountie stood up, a big man, younger than me but comfortably dominant in his role as an RCMP officer. "Mind if I ask you a few questions?"

"Shit" was all I could say to his face. I turned, intending to walk out of there.

"Wade's gone off somewhere," Jillian said before I could leave. "I'm really worried. I've never seen him so upset before."

"I'll take a walk out toward the ocean," I said. "I've got an idea of a couple of places he might have gone."

"Maybe you should stay out of this, Mr. Colby," the Mountie said.

"Thanks for the advice," I said, and left.

I headed to Grandfather Rock, past Scarcity Brook, and out to the edge of the harbour and the open sea at Stoney Beach. There was no trace of Wade. He was gone. Good and gone. I had a pretty good idea what his intentions were. He wanted the hell out of here. And I didn't blame him.

Twenty-Five

If a boy felt really bad, he ran home to his mother. If for one reason or another he thought his mother couldn't help him, he ran to his father. Even if that father was a thousand miles away in Philadelphia. Jillian must have known that, but I think she was afraid to say anything to the Mountie. That would have meant calling up the bastard lawyer at his weasel nest in the City of Brotherly Love and making things even more complicated.

The RCMP would send the word out to their cruisers to be on the lookout for a twelve-year-old boy, but the kid wasn't an idiot. He could probably spot a cop car a mile off and hide in the ditch or duck behind a tree if need be. People from up and down the Shore would think nothing of picking up a kid if he was hitchhiking and, say, drive him to the IGA or to Sheet Harbour or even Halifax. They wouldn't likely suspect he was running away, much less trying to make his way out of the country.

I drove all the way to Dartmouth once that afternoon and I was headed back, ready to make a second sweep, counting on the idea that he wouldn't get too far. If he had made it onto the 102, however, someone might pick him up and take him all the way to the

Trans-Cananda at Truro. Some other fool might take him farther if the kid had a good story about why he was hitching.

On my return trip to Nickerson Harbour, though, I found Wade standing outside the little shopping centre in Jeddore. He had a backpack on and was sitting on a concrete curb eating a Joe Louis and drinking Gatorade. I parked so he didn't see me coming, then sneaked up on the poor kid, scaring him out of his wits when I stepped into his view. "You keep eating those things and you're going to get fat," I said.

Wade looked as if he wanted to run, but he had his shoes off.

"Must've done one hell of a lot of walking," I said.

Wade threw his Joe Louis wrapper at the trash can but missed. "Leave me alone."

"Shoot, you think I was looking for you? I just came down here to do my laundry." I pointed at the steamy window of the laundromat.

"What did my mother say?"

"About what?"

"About me."

"I don't know what you mean. She thinks you're a nice boy. Smart. Good future. That's what she told me."

"She's figured I'm gone, right?"

"Yeah." I looked at the kid's feet; his socks had holes in them. "Must've done one hell of a piece of walking."

"I got a couple of rides, but they were all short."

"People round here don't usually drive too far unless they have to. Where you headed, anyway?"

"Home."

"Which way is that?"

Wade pulled out a map. He held it up for me to see. It was a road map of Atlantic Canada and it had a line traced from Halifax to Truro, Truro to Moncton, Moncton to St. Stephen, and across the border to Calais, Maine.

"I think hitchhiking's illegal."

"What are they gonna do, put me in jail? My father's a lawyer." Mr. Confidence speaking.

"Excuse me. I see your point. Then why don't you just call him up, have him come get you?"

Wade didn't exactly have an answer for that. "I wanna see if I can get there on my own. I'm tired of depending on people."

"I'm not sure you have much choice. But I'm with you on that. You can't depend on anybody but yourself."

"Yeah, right."

"I'm sorry about Cobain."

Wade opened his backpack and started to root through it. He was trying to pretend he didn't care, but his face betrayed what he was feeling. The kid was hurting bad.

"I'm really sorry. Paul Mascarene doesn't deserve to live."

"Why'd he have to kill Cobain?"

"I don't know."

"I thought you and me were gonna teach Cobain to stay away from the dock. I thought we'd talked about that."

"Yeah. Then things got complicated. Your mom wasn't sure she wanted me around you. I had all this weird stuff happening at my house. I really meant to do it with you, but, shit, I don't know."

"Like you said, you can't depend on anybody but yourself."

"I liked Cobain a lot," I said.

"I loved him. That creep shouldn't have killed him. I hate this place. I hate…everything." The statement was all-inclusive.

"I know the feeling."

Wade stood, swallowed what was left of the Gatorade, then heaved the bottle hard out onto the parking lot where it shattered into a million pieces.

I stopped myself from saying something adultlike. "Nice pitch," I said instead.

Wade adjusted the Phillies cap. "See ya. Please don't call my mom."

I let him get up and head out to the highway. He began walking west toward Halifax, and when he was nearly out of my sight, I saw him stick out his thumb.

Getting up, I went to my car. As I opened the door, a man in a white T-shirt rushed out of the laundromat. "Aren't you gonna clean up the glass your kid broke all over my parking lot?" He had been watching us and had a right to be indignant.

"Sorry. Can't right now."

The guy glared at me as I backed my Subaru out of the parking space and drove off. When I stopped alongside Wade, leaned over, and opened the passenger door, he looked at me. "Come on," I said. "I'm feeling nostalgic for the U.S. of A. I'll give you a ride."

Wade stalled. "You're gonna take me back to my mother."

"No. I'm going to take you to your father."

"No tricks?"

"No tricks. You want a ride or what?"

Wade got in and threw his pack in the back. I didn't turn around to Nickerson Harbour. Instead, I continued west, then connected with the 102 and headed north toward a rendezvous with the Trans-Canada, which would lead to another highway south to the United States. The car was running a little rough. It had needed exhaust work ever since I'd gotten it.

"This car's a piece of shit," Wade said.

"I like it."

"You should see what my old man drives."

"I'll bet."

I drove as far as a truckers' restaurant called the Big Stop just off the highway, not far from Stewiacke, a town whose claim to fame was that it was situated "halfway between the North Pole and the equator." At least that was what they used to advertise on the highway until a Dalhousie University geographer did a globe check and determined Stewiacke wasn't "exactly" halfway between anywhere of significance.

I ordered hamburgers and french fries. They had large, medium, and small of everything on the menu. I asked for large. The hamburgers were massive and the fries arrived in prodigious quantity. We stuffed ourselves. "Good food," I said, feeling bloated and gaseous from trying to keep up with Wade. Kids felt better when they had a chance to absorb abundant amounts of grease, however, and Wade appeared more relaxed.

"Not as good as McDonald's."

"McDonald's sucks," I said.

"What do you know?"

I didn't know much, but I knew American fast food sucked. However, I didn't need to debate it with a twelve-year-old who thought he knew everything. "I've got to at least call your mother."

"No."

"She'll think you're dead. Your body chopped up into parts and thrown in a dumpster somewhere. Mothers see these things in their heads clear as day."

"You said you wouldn't take me back to her."

"I said I'd take you to your father. I didn't say I wouldn't call."

"You tell her you're taking me to Philadelphia and she'll chase us."

"No, she won't. I'll explain."

"She'll call the cops."

"She already did that."

"Oh."

"I've got to call her. She's going nuts back there worrying about you."

"You won't turn me in?"

"No, stupid. I told you, I'm dying to return to the United States of Amnesia. Filthadelphia, here we come."

"Don't call her."

I left a twenty on the table and walked to the pay phone in the lobby. Truckers were jockeying their rigs outside in the parking lot. Men in cowboy hats were coming in through the front door with suntans and dark-mirrored glasses. It was West Texas, Nova Scotia. Or Las Vegas in the Maritimes. I was gambling on this phone call, I knew, but I thought I had a vague handle on what to do.

"Jillian, it's Taylor."

"Wade wasn't anywhere near the harbour, was he?"

"No. I looked. Nothing."

"Somebody said they saw him by the highway."

"Kids like to hang out around highways."

"Why am I talking to you? What do you want?"

"I want to help."

"Broken record."

I let out a sigh of frustration. "I'm with Wade."

"Is he okay?"

192

"The boy eats too much. He's going to get fat."

"Don't joke about this. Put him on."

"Not yet. I need to explain." Wade was walking out of the restaurant now, and that worried me. He was looking at all the eighteen-wheelers. I could see the plans hatching in his head. Sneak up into one of those truck sleepers and he might not be found for ten hours. Get the hell out of Nova Scotia. End up God knew where, but someplace no one would look for him. I wanted to hang up and run after him, but he suddenly turned and walked back through the glass door.

"I want to talk to her," he said.

"He wants to talk to you," I told Jillian.

"I heard."

"Mom?"

"You're okay, honey? Please come home."

Wade glanced out at the trucks. He put his face real close to the window, his head bowed against the plate glass. His voice was low and he was trying to keep me from hearing, but I leaned nearer. "I hate it in Nova Scotia. I'm going home to Dad."

"You come back here, Wade. We'll call him. We'll talk to him about the possibility."

"Bad idea," I whispered to Wade. He gave me a puzzled look.

"What are you doing with Taylor?" I heard Jillian ask.

"We just had lunch."

"Dinner," I corrected him.

"We ate. It was okay."

"Tell him to bring you home. Now."

I motioned for Wade to give me the receiver. He seemed happy to be cut off.

"Jillian, I'm going to drive the boy to see his father."

"What?"

"Take us two days to get there. I'm a good driver. He's safe. He'll have a chance to cool off, think about things. He's got to talk to his father if he wants to."

"Taylor, I can't believe you're saying this. I told you about his father."

I wanted to talk to her without Wade listening. I muffled the receiver, pulled a five out of my wallet, and handed it to Wade, then pointed to the video games over by the men's room. He grabbed the money and took it to the cashier to get change. I could now say what I had to. "Jillian, you have to trust me on this."

"I'm not sure I can trust you about anything, Taylor. How do I know all that awful stuff you've been through hasn't warped you in some horrible way?"

"I'm hurt, but not warped. Big distinction between the two. Besides, the way I see it, you don't have a choice. Your son is with me."

"What is this, blackmail?"

"No, damn it, it isn't. It's about trying to get something right. I started out trying to be Wade's friend and you pushed me away. I started to be your friend and you pushed me away. Hell, in one night I fell halfway down the well in love with you and then you told me to get out of your life. That hurt my feelings. Now I'm offering one shot at saving what you have going between you and your son. I think you should have a hard listen."

"You're going to save me and my son by *delivering* him to a reptile in Philadelphia?"

"Precisely. Wade wants escape from all the death and destruction of Nickerson Harbour. In his mind the streets of Philadelphia are filled with the kindest, gentlest people on the face of the earth. Let's face it, I was born in the land of yahoos that permitted Paul Mascarene to grow up and grow ugly without anyone even batting an eyelash."

"Don't change the subject. If Wade's father gets hold of that boy, I may never see him again."

"If Thomas is as much of a bastard as you say he is, you'll see Wade again."

"That's a big gamble."

"You were telling me the truth about him?"

"Yes."

"Then the only way Wade will be happy is if he sees it for himself. I'm just going to ensure he gets there safely."

"I could tell the Mounties you've kidnapped him," she said defiantly.

"Jesus, lady! Kidnapped!"

"I don't know what to do." She sounded more conciliatory.

"Then do nothing. Call off the Mounties. Call your husband or don't call him. Either way I'll take Wade down there and hang around for a few days. Maybe he'll change his mind and want to come back up north. Or maybe he'll have to stay around long enough for the reptile to show he's cold-blooded."

"What if Thomas tries to pull some legal manoeuvre?"

"Wade's a tough kid. If his father tries to do that against *his* will, he'll be out of there. I'll make sure his father knows that."

"What's Thomas going to make of you? He'll want to know who you are, how you got involved."

"I'm the neighbour, remember. Just a guy trying to help."

"Damn it, Taylor, why can't you stay out of my life?"

"Kind of like mould in the bottom of your refrigerator. You can get rid of it for a while, but it'll always grow back on you."

"Where are you, anyway?"

"On the road."

"You're sure this will work?"

"No."

"Then why are you doing this?"

"Wade feels stomped on, betrayed, kicked around, and hurt real bad. These are all symptoms I identify strongly with. If he's dragged back to Nickerson Harbour now, he'll take off again and we might not be so lucky. He has to come back to you of his own free will."

The kid was strolling back into the lobby. He held two empty hands in the air. Money all gone.

"I'm putting your son on the phone again," I said to Jillian. "Tell him not to be such a hard-ass while we're driving."

I handed Wade the receiver and headed out the door. The sunlight reflecting off the windshields of the big trucks made me squint. I didn't look back at Wade while he was on the phone. More drivers got out of their rigs and walked toward the door, a parade of large guts, big belt buckles, and sweat-stained T-shirts with slogans on them: MY HARLEY'S IN THE SHOP, BIG BOYS DON'T CRY, CHEVY RULES.

When Wade ambled out, he said, very adultlike, "I think she's okay now. I think she understands."

TWENTY-SIX

By the time we reached Moncton, we had figured each other out. Wade trusted me, I think. His trust seemed to be based exclusively on the fact that I let him control the radio. Things had started out poorly, however, as soon as he discovered the radio disgorged only static. I stopped the car along the highway and buried my head beneath the dash, lucked out, and found a loose wire, which I patched back into place. Then I told Wade the airwaves were his to control. We lost the Halifax and then the Truro stations, and Wade made gagging noises every time we picked up the CBC from a new transmitter.

"I love the CBC," I said.

"All they ever do is talk or play violins."

"There's nothing wrong with that." But I didn't push the point. I could live without the CBC. Country music wasn't tolerated, either, and AM radio was overpadded with oldies. Wade didn't know what to make of the French-speaking stations of New Brunswick. "It's like they don't know how to speak English" was his way of putting it.

"They're French. That's their language. Acadians live around here."

"Yeah, but don't they know we speak English in America?"

"This is Canada, knucklehead. We have two official languages on our Cheerios boxes here. Acadians have a right to speak what they want to speak."

"Yeah, right," he said. He either didn't believe me or he thought there was something wrong with anybody who didn't speak English. Wade was, alas, an American and had been indoctrinated in the Yankee way of thinking despite whatever liberalization his mother had attempted.

We pigged out regularly on junk food. We burned money on cans of Coke and Pepsi and Mountain Dew, and Wade called the shots when it came to Burger King, Wendy's, McDonald's or, out of dire necessity, settling for a generic mom-and-pop restaurant. There were meals and in-between meals. Jillian would have killed me, but I didn't know much about kids except to let them have what they wanted when it came to food.

Wade tuned in some contemporary music in Saint John and seemed content. The speakers burped and barked on the low notes and rattled on everything else. Wade preferred the volume loud no matter what the distortion level. It didn't seem to bother him.

As we were crossed the bridge over Saint John Harbour, Wade looked down at a small mountain of road salt that had been unloaded for winter use on the highways. "What's that?"

"Salt," I said.

"Oh, that's what they put in the ocean to make it salty?"

I gave him a wide-eyed look. "You're serious?"

He took off his cap and smacked me in the arm with it. "Got you."

When we got to the border crossing into the United States at Calais, Wade kept his mouth shut. All I had for ID was a California driver's licence. I explained about my mother and the cancer, and that seemed to appease the black woman who was trying unsuccessfully to look tough and professional.

I stopped at a bank machine and made it spew out a pile of American twenties.

"Is your mother really dying of cancer?" Wade asked.

"Yes."

"I don't know what I'd do if anything happened to my mother."

"Your mother's going to be around for a long time."

He sat quietly in the car for a long while after that. I almost expected him to ask me to turn around, but he didn't. For the next hundred miles, radio failed him. There was nothing but country music most of the way to Rockport.

We spent the night in a motel along the old U.S. 1 highway. It was an antiquated, run-down place made out of logs. Inside was a 1950s log-cabin motif right down to the antlers on the wall above the rotary-channel TV set.

"That's sick," Wade said, pointing at the antlers. And almost in the same breath, he asked, indicating the TV relic, "Where's the remote?"

"It's an old one. You used to have to get up and change the channel."

"You're kidding."

"No, I'm not."

"I thought that was, like, a hundred years ago that people had TVs without remotes."

"It just seems like a hundred years ago. When I was a kid, we didn't have a TV in the house. There were no stations you could pick up in Nickerson Harbour."

"Serious?"

"True."

Wade looked at me as if I'd told him I'd been born on Saturn. He called Jillian, and I called my father. Then we ordered out for pizza, and it arrived twenty minutes later. This seemed to assure Wade that we hadn't dropped off the map of civilization altogether.

"I thought for a while there that we had, like, gone back in time or something," he said. After all, we did only have a black-and-white TV. Wade had never seen one before.

"It's almost like the real thing, but different," Wade said.

The next morning Wade was sullen. I asked him what was wrong but received the old standby reply: "Nothing." I stopped asking him if he wanted to turn around and go back to Nickerson Harbour.

"They kill seals there, don't they?" was what shut me up. Barbarians. Savages. Paul Mascarene with a smile and a gun bought with my money.

The old, dilapidated Subaru ran amazingly well. By the time we hit the Tappan Zee Bridge, Wade was summarizing what he knew about the New England states. "Maine has a lot of trees and rocks and bad TV, and I saw a deer by the highway. New Hampshire was short." We'd only driven the thirty-mile turnpike that tethered Maine to Massachusetts. "Massachusetts is too hard to pronounce and the hamburgers tasted burnt. Connecticut has too many cars but good radio."

"They always say kids learn more from travelling than they do in school."

"Don't mention that word."

"What word?"

"You know."

"You didn't like school?"

"I hated my teachers."

"All of them?"

"Yes."

"Why?"

"Because they all hated me."

"Just you or all the kids?"

"All of them."

"Maybe that's just the way it *seemed*."

"All the good teachers quit."

"Why?"

"No one paid attention."

"That's why the ones who stayed 'hated' you?"

"It's a vicious circle," he summarized.

I became more than a little afraid that I was a prime player in some horribly sophisticated game of emotional and psychological manipulation as we drove down the Jersey Turnpike. "Decent radio at last," my companion said with a smile as we drove past Newark International Airport and a wasteland of refineries and chemical factories. Wade rolled down the window to sniff the air. "Smells like home."

"Sweet nostalgia," I admitted, "takes many olfactory forms."

We crossed over the Walt Whitman Bridge in Camden. It was a four-lane span named for a dead poet who had lived nearby. It reminded me of the only famous living poet I had ever met—Allen Ginsberg. I'd played guitar onstage at a big benefit in San Francisco that Ginsberg had organized and had admitted to him that I had never read much poetry. "If you read only one poet, read Whitman," Ginsberg had said. "He was the best." So I had read Whitman and loved the man's bold, vibrant enthusiasm for everything from spit to stars. As we passed through the toll booth in Camden, I looked at the remains of the little city Whitman had once loved so dearly: burned-out buildings, abandoned cars, garbage everywhere. If Whitman had dreamed the bright Technicolor vision of America, that dream had died and rotted like a corpse right here in his hometown.

The waters of the Delaware River below us on the bridge were coffee-coloured. The traffic all about us was angry and reminded me of California. Everyone was in a hurry. The most polite American citizens turned into crazed wolves behind the wheels of automobiles.

It was a Monday afternoon. I had the address of Thomas's law firm. The idea was to show the father in full lizard skin at work in his office. But first I'd try the easy way out.

"I wouldn't be all that upset," I said to Wade, "if you told me you changed your mind and wanted to go back to your mom."

Wade straightened his Phillies cap and rolled down the window again to breathe in the street smells. "They kill seals in Nickerson Harbour, right?"

Exasperated and unable to keep my mouth shut, I looked around us at a stoplight: empty warehouses, winos in doorways clutching brown paper bags with bottles inside, thugs of all ages from seven to seventy in black leather jackets. You could smell the anger and fear in the hot, humid air that was summertime Philadelphia. It was a less-than-tantalizing mix of burnt tires, urine, the aroma of fresh soft pretzels on sale from street vendors, and diesel exhaust. "What don't they kill in Philadelphia?" I countered.

I didn't like being back in the United States. I had never intended to come back here again. Nothing but success and heartache had come out of my life in the United States, living the American way. You made it big, raked in a lot of dough, then lived unhappily ever after. It was a simple, handy formula that fitted almost everyone I ever knew. Everybody else who wasn't stricken with success probably ended up on the street like the sorry souls outside our car windows. At another red light an old guy started polishing my window with a dirty handkerchief. When the light turned green, he didn't hold out his hand, but he looked at me imploringly. I reached in my shirt pocket and handed him a ten. He smiled, nodded, and I applied the gas. Halfway up the block I decided I envied that guy. I had this vision that he probably wasn't carrying around half the hurt in his head I harboured or, if he was, he had a bottle of booze somewhere that was medicine enough to erase it from his memory upon demand.

Ten minutes later we were there. "This is it," I said.

"This isn't where Dad lives."

"I know. He's working. I can't just leave you off at an apartment where no one's home."

"Why not?"

"I promised Jillian I'd take you to your father."

"Well, let's do it later. I don't want to go in there."

"It's where he works. You must have been here before."

"Never."

"Oh. Well, don't worry. He's probably dying to see you. Your mother called. He's expecting us. He just doesn't know when."

"I don't want to go in there."

"I can't leave you on the street."

"Yes, you can. I can handle myself on the street."

"I bet you can't. I know for a fact Nickerson Harbour has made you soft. Hanging around all those trees and birds, you lose your edge. I've read about this sort of thing. People here could take one look at you and see you're an easy target. Take my word for it, you'd be in big trouble. Let's go in."

The office was on the twelfth floor. The waiting room was all mahogany and ugly ultramodern furniture. The woman who was the receptionist had been manufactured with brittle ceramics and cosmetics. She was beautiful and antiseptic, the kind of woman that might be purchased but never embraced.

"We're here to see Thomas Santino."

"You have an appointment, Mr....uh?"

"Colby. Taylor Colby. No appointment, but he's expecting us. This is Mr. Santino's son, Wade."

The receptionist looked at Wade as if she'd never seen a twelve-year-old boy.

"Hi," Wade said.

"Hello." The voice was computer-generated. "Have a seat, both of you. Mr. Santino is with a client."

She didn't buzz his office. Rules were rules.

Wade thumbed through the latest issue of *Forbes*. I studied the ads in *Gentleman's Quarterly*. The furniture was designed to be uncomfortable. After twenty minutes of squirming to get comfortable, the receptionist asked if I wanted coffee.

"No thanks."

"Water?"

"Sure." It tasted as if she had scooped it out of a toilet bowl. Wade stuck out his tongue. I did likewise. It didn't take long to lose your taste for city water, especially if it came from a place like the Delaware River.

Finally the big polished wooden door opened and a man walked out. I looked at Wade. It wasn't his father; it was whatever criminal Thomas was currently keeping out of jail. I sized the guy up: rapist, murderer, or Mafia boss? Drug kingpin, I finally decided, and watched him wink at the ceramic receptionist as he silently oozed out through the door.

When Thomas appeared, he looked like the man I would have hired to play the part of a sleazy lawyer if I were casting for a movie of the week. He looked much younger than I had expected, or at least he looked fit and lean. His eyes were penetrating. He studied his son only briefly, then scrutinized me with the eyes of a man who had deemed me the enemy long before I opened my mouth.

"I'm sorry," he said to me. "I would have cut the meeting short, but that was a very important client and we had arrived at a critical point in our discussions." The man was carved from ice. But then he melted, turning to his son and hugging him.

"Wade. God, I've missed you, kid. Everything okay?"

"Not bad."

"Let's all go into my office. Coffee, Mr. Taylor?"

"No thanks." The door closed behind us.

Wade and I sat in two soft leather chairs with chrome armrests. Thomas sat forward in his executive chair, his elbows on his desk, his hands folded in front of him, a small cathedral of fingers pointing heavenward. "You don't know how good it is to have you back, Wade."

TWENTY-SEVEN

"Can I stay in my old room?" Wade asked his father.

"Sorry. I'm living in a new place. I gave up the lease on our old house when your mother and you moved out."

"Oh."

"Don't worry. I've got a room for you. It's bigger, much bigger. I was thinking we should get a TV for it."

"With surround-sound?"

"That's exactly what I had in mind. Surround-sound. It's yours."

The buyout attempt was entirely expected, although my confidence in my plan to resettle Wade in Nova Scotia was shaken to its roots. I cleared my throat. "You've talked with Jillian, right?" I asked Thomas.

"Yes, she called."

"You understand this is intended to be a sort of trial arrangement."

"I understand that Jillian sent my son back home here to Philadelphia."

"I think it's up to Wade." I already knew I couldn't compete with a big new TV that had surround-sound. I also knew Wade would get anything he asked for. But I wanted Wade to hear me say this.

"Fine," Thomas said. "Wade, what do you want to do? I assume you didn't drive all the way down here to say hi and then leave?"

"No."

"Do you want to move in with me?" Thomas wasn't looking very fatherly. He was making a power play. It was courtroom pressuring of a witness. He might not have meant it to come out like this, but it was in his blood. He was born of the thick-skinned, hard-assed clan of humans who had to win, whatever the case, whatever the cost. I had quickly become a mere pawn in someone else's high-stakes game to hold on to a son. All I could count on was Wade's own human instincts about people. I couldn't come out and say it, but I prayed silently that he would figure out for himself that Thomas and Paul Mascarene were cut from the same cloth.

"Yeah," Wade said. "I want to stay with you for now. Then we'll see."

His father raised both hands. "There you go. The boy knows what he wants to do."

I looked at Wade and glanced at the floor. Even though *this* was what we had driven down here for, he still felt as if he was betraying me, betraying his mother.

"Wade, could you wait outside with Cecily for a minute? I want to talk to this man before he leaves. Thanks."

Wade got up dutifully and walked out the door to kill time with the secretary. I wondered if Cecily had ever had a real conversation with a kid his age before. The door closed.

Thomas was silent at first, waiting for me to say something stupid. "He's a good kid" was all I offered.

The lawyer lurched across the desk and pointed a finger at me as if it were a weapon. He had probably been a bully all his life, short and simple. He wasn't a big man, just one of those males who had to have his way. "I want you to stay out of this," he announced, venom leaking from every pore.

"Jillian explained about what happened, right?"

"What? The thing about the dumb seal?"

"Wade took it pretty hard."

"He'll get over it." I pictured Thomas as someone who liked to throw rocks and kill frogs when he was a kid, but then he had probably never seen any frogs growing up. City kid. Tough kid.

"Yeah, he will. I like Wade. He's bright. He has a sense of humour. I want to see him grow up without getting his head screwed up too much."

"Thanks for the concern, but I think this is where you exit. I know *who* you are, Mr. Colby, but for the life of me I can't figure out *why* you got involved."

"Kid needed a drive. I had time on my hands. I said okay." I wanted to play down my role. I didn't want to give divorce courts even a sliver of information to work with.

"It's good he's away from his mother. She's very unstable."

"Jillian's a fine woman," I said, breaking my vow of silence. "You were a fool to let her go."

He leaned back away from me. He'd done his homework. He did know who I was. "Look who's talking," he said, "a guy who sits back and watches while his wife does enough coke to kill a horse. I'm surprised no one ever pressed charges against you for manslaughter." He was smiling. This was his game. His acumen for cruelty was more than excellent. I was mute. All I could see was the image of Laura lying on the floor. The paintings on the walls in the morning light. "Stay away from my son," he added. Then he stood, changed his demeanour entirely, spoke politely as if we had just finished a business transaction. He threw two hundred-dollars bills on the desk. "I owe you for giving him the transportation. Put that toward the gas and meals."

I didn't take the money. I got up and walked out of the office, closing the door behind me. In the waiting room Wade sat sullen and silent. Cecily was busy on the phone. "I'm leaving now, Wade," I told him.

He looked frightened. "I don't know what to do."

"I know. I don't know what to say. Just go with your father. See how it goes. I'm going to hang around Philly and do some sight-seeing. Maybe buy a new guitar." I wanted to be sure he could get in touch with me. I could only think of one hotel. I'd stayed there when I was in town as part of a cross-country tour. "I'll be at the downtown Sheraton. It's in the phone book. Call me there and give me your number when you settle in."

"I will."

"And if you want to go back to Nova Scotia, just let me know. Any time. You'll know if it's the right thing to do or not."

"Thanks for everything."

"Enjoy the surround-sound," I said, walking out of the office and wishing I'd never have to deal with a lawyer again.

Later, Wade called and left me his number. He said things were going great. His father was giving him all kinds of neat stuff and taking him to the zoo and Phillies games at Veterans Stadium. I called Jillian to tell her to be patient.

"I never should have let him go," she said.

"You didn't have a choice," I answered. "Thomas is everything you said he was."

"But he can be so nice when he wants to be."

"Only if he thinks it'll get him what he wants. Men are such assholes."

"I think you understand the essence of feminism," she said. "Have you been reading Betty Friedan?"

I, too, went to the zoo, but I felt sorry for all the animals. I walked through the Art Museum and the Rodin Museum. I ate long, lonely meals in small cafés on Chestnut Street. I saw the crack in the Liberty Bell and strolled through Independence Hall. I sat in bookstores on Market Street and spent an afternoon in Eighth Street Music trying out guitars. Once the sales guy had figured out who I was, he told me to hang out and try everything in the store. I came close to that. In the end I bought an electric/acoustic Martin and a hard-shell case. The sales guy asked me what my next gig was going to be, and I said I was still working on a really long-term project called "Survival."

"Is it like fusion or something?"

"Celtic," I said. "Mostly Celtic, but with a little bit of everything thrown in. It's very eclectic."

The hotel was comfortable but sterile. Metropolitan life seemed alien to me. Philadelphia was hot and sweaty, and I passed my days moving in and out of air-conditioned buildings. I wanted to be back in Nova Scotia. Every time I called my father I was told everything was okay.

Wade didn't call again for three days. But on the fourth he left a message on my hotel voice mail. "I feel funny. Something isn't right. I can't explain it and it doesn't make any sense. I say I want a new computer and it arrives. It has everything. I say I want to go to Disney World and two hours later he shows me the plane tickets. It doesn't feel right."

I had just finished listening to the voice mail when I received a call from Jillian.

"I should have never let you talk me into this," she yelled at me.

"Explain."

"A courier brought legal documents just now. Thomas wants custody of Wade." She was crying. "He's a bastard. He was a terrible father, and now he's going to make everything look as if it was my fault. I can't possibly win against him. I was afraid of this."

"Does Wade know about it?"

"No. Thomas says I'm not supposed to talk to him until we meet in court."

"That's absurd."

"Thomas is claiming I abandoned Wade."

"I'm not surprised."

"Not surprised! Damn it, Taylor, my life was crashing down around me and I listened to you. I have no idea why. Because of you, I'll have to fight Thomas tooth and nail, and he's going to win. I know he is. He never loses. The truth won't matter."

"It's up to Wade," I said, not certain I knew what I was talking about. "Once he knows what his father's doing, he'll have to take a side."

"No."

"What do you mean, no?"

"I don't want him to take a side. I don't want him messed up any more than he is. Thomas can manipulate him just like he manipulated me. I can't compete with that. If Wade's pushed to decide, he'll get hurt."

"Wade's tough. He has to be involved."

"No. Don't talk to him. Just leave us alone. You've already done enough damage!" She hung up.

I set the receiver down and lay on my bed. A familiar numbing wave of dull dread and hopelessness washed over me. It was the same feeling that had debilitated me for months after Laura's death. Everything I touched turned to shit. I felt a potent, terrible hatred of myself surface. It had been there deep within me ever since my mother left back when I was a kid. I had buried it over and over, but the belief kept surfacing that when things went wrong it was my fault. The dead eider duck. My mother's departure. Laura. Jillian drove home the point that I was once again responsible for pain and suffering. It didn't matter if my intentions were good or bad. I had come into this life with some awful sort of karma that insisted I would bring hardship to those I loved.

As I stood, I felt an ambitious anger fill the hollowness in my bones. I hated myself. My new eight-hundred-dollar Martin guitar was lying on the floor. I picked it up and smashed it hard on the corner post of my bed. The post punctured the back of the guitar with a bone-jarring, horrific sound. Then I went out for a long walk. I was drawn to the trees at Rittenhouse Square and lingered beneath them, envying their beauty and great green calm ability to survive in the maddening heart of the city. Next I walked along the turgid brown Delaware River. I studied the current as it fed fresh, silt-laden, polluted water out to sea. It was hard to believe that this river and the sea beyond were in any way connected with the rich blue Atlantic to the north.

Once again my mind locked onto the Great Escape routine. I had come this far from Nova Scotia. Perhaps I could keep on moving. There was money to burn. At least I had that ticket to freedom. Money had always come easily for me, but it had rarely brought much pleasure or happiness. I played music for the sake of music. Financial reward was accidental. I had a bank card and three credit cards. As I walked away from the river, I forged a half-assed plan to kiss off Philadelphia, forget about Nickerson Harbour yet again, and catch a flight for somewhere. Japan. Thailand. Bali. Anywhere foreign, radically different and free.

But my feet kept walking and eventually took me back to my hotel room. Sleep was all I cared about. The ability to sleep was one of the several strong positive traits I had inherited from my father. Sleep was my favourite of all drugs, and I would now indulge to excess.

Back in my room, I felt a twinge of regret when I saw my beautiful guitar impaled on the nineteenth-century bedpost. I lifted it as if it were a dead child and said, "Sorry. I'm so sorry." It was a familiar chant, the recurring sad song of my life. I strummed a manic A minor seventh chord and placed the instrument gently back into its hard-shell case. That was when I noticed a light was flashing on my phone. I punched the button to retrieve the message.

"Taylor," I heard my father's strained voice begin, "I wish I didn't have to tell you like this, but we took your mother to the hospital in Sheet Harbour. I'm there now. She's not doing so good. I'm not gonna be at home, so it won't do much good calling there." I heard him break down at that point, and I felt the walls of my room close in on me. "She says she wants to talk to you. I think she wants you there real bad, but she won't admit it. You know how she is. She says if you can't come, if you have more important things, well, it's okay but, Jeez, boy, I don't know. Do what you have to. Take care, son." He paused again. "I hope you're hearing all this. I don't like talking to a damn machine." It was at that point that he was cut off.

I wanted to talk to someone. Anyone. I didn't know what to do. All I could think of was to run away from it all. My destination had changed. Some place cold. Not hot. Alaska. Norway. North to where it was cold and clean and private. I sat in the stony silence and listened to the hum of air-conditioning. My mother was doing it to me again. Punishing me as Laura had punished me. Here she was back in Nova Scotia and I had run away to be someplace else.

I picked up the receiver and dialled the residence of Thomas Santino. Wade answered.

"Wade, I have to go back to Nova Scotia now."

"You're leaving me here?"

"I guess so. I have to go home. My mother's in the hospital. She's dying, Wade. I'm sorry, but I can't stay here any longer."

Wade didn't say anything. I could hear the sound of the television, the explosive violence of an action movie in surround-sound.

"Wade?"

"Yeah?"

"I really messed things up between you and your mother. She loves you, you know."

"I know."

"But your father…he's okay, too."

"I don't think I want to live here."

"You might not have any choice."

"What do you mean?"

I tried my best to soft-pedal the legal issues, but it came out sounding fuzzy and confusing.

"You mean my father's trying to prove my mother's no good?"

"I think so."

"Take me with you to Nova Scotia. I want to go back."

"I don't think I can. Everything's a lot more complicated now. If I try to take you back, who knows? Maybe somebody will accuse me of kidnapping."

"Take me back, please. I can't stay here."

"Why?"

"She needs me. I should be there. I should love everything about being here, but I don't. I've been trying to convince myself I've got it made. But it doesn't feel right. I have to go."

TWENTY-EIGHT

Wade was waiting for me on the street outside a beautiful eighteenth-century restored home in a part of the city known as Society Hill. While the inside of the place was probably choked to the rafters with the latest contemporary everything, the exterior appeared serenely historic. As I pulled up to stop for Wade, I looked at the house and realized that if I had made an enemy out of Thomas Santino by taking his son away from him, I had indeed made a formidable adversary of a man with a lot of clout and a great deal of money.

Opening the car door, Wade got in. All he had with him was one backpack. "You're not bringing the TV?" I asked. He had an extremely nervous look on his face, as if his father might arrive at any minute and catch him in his exodus.

"It wouldn't fit in the bag," he said, looking straight ahead at the windshield. "Can we go now?" He set the backpack on the rear seat with my guitar case. I didn't know why, but I was taking the smashed guitar back to Nova Scotia with me.

Pulling off slowly, I half expected to see a police car in the rearview mirror. "I forgot to set the burglar alarm," Wade suddenly said. "I'm supposed to do that whenever I leave the house."

"Guess you'll have to break that rule this time."

"Guess so. But he'll be mad."

"Oh, he'll be mad all right."

We got onto I-95 and booted it to the airport. I pulled up outside USAir departures and stopped in the taxi zone, where we got out and unloaded our luggage. A lone vendor was hawking pretzels in brown paper bags from a shopping cart. "Three for a buck," he said, shoving them toward us. They were fresh enough so that the smell still lingered. It was intoxicating—yeast and dough and salt. "I got mustard if you want."

"You know how to drive?" I asked him.

"Used to," the guy said.

"Still have a licence?"

"Yep. Why do you want to know?"

"See that car there?"

He nodded. "I've seen better."

"It runs good. I'll trade it to you for a bag of those pretzels."

"No shit?"

"None."

He was smiling but shaking his head at the same time. "Stolen, right?"

"Nope. It's cool."

"I don't get it."

"You don't have to. Maybe you can use it."

"I want to get out of this city. Go somewhere else."

"Now you have wheels. The registration's in the glove compartment." I wrote down my phone number on a scrap of paper and handed it to him. "Call me in a couple of days and I'll take care of the transfer." I handed him the keys and took the bag of soft pretzels out of his hand. "It might need a quart of oil," I said as I walked off into the airport terminal with Wade.

Wade had been pretty quiet, but he ate two of the three pretzels on the plane. "You should have got some mustard. I usually put mustard on my pretzels," he said.

We were at Logan Airport in Boston in less than two hours. After a wait of an hour and forty-five minutes, Air Canada was lifting us off the runway for Nova Scotia. It was late afternoon, and the sun was behind us to the west as we gained altitude over Boston's harbour, which was broad and blue with islands of rock and sand. There was a prison, too, sitting below us on one of the islands, and you could see the inmates walking around on the grounds inside the stone walls and barbed wire. Cape Cod curled like a beckoning finger into the sea and, beyond that, we were out over the Atlantic Ocean. Ships were heading toward Boston, and soon there was nothing but the open sea below. The jet veered north and east. Somewhere ahead my mother was lying in a hospital bed. There was something I had to say to her before she left me for the final time. Something very important. I closed my eyes. *Hang on. Please hang on…* I compressed my eyelids and squeezed back the tears that were welling up.

In less than an hour we were approaching Halifax International. "We might have a problem," I told Wade in a hushed voice as the flight attendant passed by to check our seat belts. "Your father might have overreacted and called the police."

"The police? What for?"

"Well, there are these legal complications, and no one knows the law better than your daddy. I'm afraid we're going to have to lie."

"What do I have to say?"

"You ever lie before?"

Wade smiled.

"Never mind. I'll lie. You just keep your mouth shut unless you need to back me up."

"Fine. So at least let me in on our story ahead of time."

Reluctantly I told him. "Okay. You're my son. I don't think they'll question that. We're okay if they haven't been alerted about your being missing. Your father might think we're driving." I suddenly worried about the pretzel vendor. Would he get stopped by Pennsylvania State troopers on the turnpike as he made his break from the city? No. Thomas wouldn't know the licence-plate number or the car description.

"What time does he come home from work?"

"At first it was five-thirty, then six. Yesterday he came home at nine."

"I think we're okay. I doubt anybody will be looking for us yet."

"Are we going to get in trouble?"

"Big-time," I said.

Wade smiled. "I don't care. As long as I get back to my mom."

I closed my eyes and heaved a sigh. Poor Jillian might have one hell of a legal battle ahead of her. But if she was willing to let me help, I'd foot the bill to hire one of the most hardheaded Bluenose lawyers on Bedford Row in Halifax.

As we descended through a thick layer of clouds over the Annapolis Valley, Nova Scotia, spread out green and elegant and beautiful below. Beneath us was farmland, cradled by the North and South Mountains in rich spruce splendour. As we continued downward, the sun was setting and it shone below the level of the clouds that were now above us. It cast a coppery light that illuminated everything with a spectacular glow. *Coming home. Coming home.*

"We've got to work on our story," I said in a muffled tone as the flight attendant came by again. "Just in case." I pulled out my wallet and extracted my California driver's licence. As I showed it to Wade, I realized the man in the photo looked much younger than me. Staring at the image, I was sure it must be someone else. "Ever been to California?"

"No. But I watch a lot of TV."

"Good. It's just like TV out there. Some families have their own laugh tracks going in their homes all the time. Family conversation stops every twelve minutes for commercials."

"You live in Beverly Hills?"

"No. But I'm not far from there. Hollywood area. But remember, *we*, not me."

"Got it, Dad."

A chill went up my spine as he said the word, but I tried not to show it. I heard the landing gear come down and snap into place.

"We have a pool?"

"No. Well…heck, yeah, why not?"

"You and me go to the beach where there's lots of girls in bikinis and stuff?"

"All the time."

"I think I like living in California," he said.

"Okay, okay. Don't get carried away. Just keep your mouth shut and agree with whatever I say. Remember why we're doing this."

Wade turned from me and looked out the window. We could see the Atlantic again as the plane banked and prepared to land. "You must feel pretty bad about your mom and all."

"Yeah. Pretty important I get to talk to her before…you know."

Wade didn't look back at me. "I want to go to the hospital with you."

"Why?"

"I don't know. I just do."

When we were finally off the plane and in the terminal, the Canadian customs officer asked to see inside the guitar case. "It had a little accident," I said.

"Will you be leaving it in the country?"

"I don't know."

"Estimated value?"

I shrugged. "A guitar with a big hole in the back is probably not worth much."

"Go ahead," he said.

The line at immigration was blessedly short. I handed the officer my flight card filled out with father and son, Taylor and Wade. Passport? I showed him my driver's licence.

"Any ID for your son?"

I looked at Wade and was ready to explain that he'd forgotten it, but Wade interjected. "All I had was my school ID, but it went into the pool with me once when we were goofing around. One of my friends pushed me in. Got messed up."

The inspector laughed. "Rough life."

"Tell me about it," Wade said.

"Purpose of visit?" The man looked back at me sternly. I couldn't give him eye contact, and he was aware of my paranoia. I had to say something before Wade shot his mouth off again. Pretty easy to get something wrong if you kept jabbering.

"I'm coming to see my mother," I said. "She's dying."

He looked down and away, stamped my flight entry card, and handed back my driver's licence. "I'm sorry. Go on."

The light was fading quickly as we got into a rental car and drove south and then east into the night. Wade scanned for stations on the radio, then looked at me and turned it off. "I keep thinking about Cobain," he said.

"I know."

"Do you think he felt any pain when he died?"

Some old movie had delivered a package of lines to me that I was supposed to deliver, but I didn't believe them. "I think he felt pain, yes. Animals feel pain just like people. I think that when you die all the hurting stops." I didn't mean for the words to come out quite that bluntly. Even in the dim light from the dashboard, Wade could see the troubled look on my face.

"I shouldn't have asked that. It just kept going around and around in my head. I couldn't stop thinking about it. I tried to talk to my father about it, but he said he didn't think wild animals felt any pain."

"I think anything that's alive can feel pain. It's part of living."

"It's one of those things that's not fair, right?"

"Maybe it is, maybe it isn't. Maybe we need to feel pain. I don't mean like what Cobain suffered. That should have never happened. But the rest of us, we need some pain, need it to see things clearly."

"I hate seeing anything suffer."

"So do I, Wade."

***

At Eastern Shore Memorial Hospital I was led to my mother's room. As we entered, Frank smiled at me and at Wade, then touched me on the shoulder. "It's good you came. She needs to talk to you."

"She's dying, Taylor," my father said. "She's leaving us again." He pulled me to him and I heard his ragged breathing in my ear. "Tell her you love her."

My mother was conscious and raised her arm to let me know she saw me. She said nothing but waved me toward her.

Frank and my father moved toward the door. My father gently ushered Wade out of the room, and I was alone with her. I pulled up a chair and sat close to the bed, leaned over and watched as she took off the clear, cupped oxygen mask and let it fall onto the bed. "I knew you'd come," she said.

I didn't know what to say. I ran my hand along the soft skin of her cheek and felt how hot she was.

"I love you, Taylor. I wanted to be the best mother in the world, but I couldn't stay there with you and your father."

"Frank told me about what happened when you went to Ontario. I know."

"It's no excuse. I just wasn't strong like your father. That's why I had to get away. And I was so selfish. I should have been stronger. I should have been a good mother."

"You should have told us you had problems. I don't think Dad knew. I didn't know. We both would have helped you."

"I guess I know that now. But back then all I could think about was getting away. I was trying to save myself any way I could. I cared about you both, but I was afraid that if I stayed, I'd lose my mind and drag you both down with me."

I moved my hand up and held it on her forehead. "That feels nice and cool," she said. "For a long while I thought I did the right thing. I heard that you and your father were doing okay. Then I heard about your music. It all sounded so wonderful."

"Why didn't you write a letter or call? You could have stayed in touch."

"I felt too guilty. I was sure that if I came back into your lives I'd make things worse. I didn't think anyone would understand about Frank. Better you didn't know. It hurt me deep down to stay away, but it seemed like the right thing to do."

As I looked down at my mother, I saw fear in her eyes. "Are you in pain?"

"Some."

"Shall I call the nurse?"

"No. Just stay here with me. We need to talk."

She swallowed hard and blinked. I glanced away from her and stared at the cold linoleum floor, totally shocked by what I was feeling. I was so angry that I wanted to scream. Now that I was here, now that it was approaching midnight in Nova Scotia where, outside, it was cool and empty and black, I was alone in a hospital room with my mother, finally prepared to make my peace with her, ready to embrace her, to love her and tell her so but, instead, I wanted to scream at her.

She reached out to touch my face, but her hand slipped back down. She seemed exhausted. "I hurt both of you bad. I know that. I can't change it. I would if I could." Her face contorted for a brief instant. The cancer was wreaking its havoc in her. She sucked in her breath and seemed to have a hard time exhaling. She tried not to show it, but I was sure she was in severe physical pain.

"I need you to forgive me, Taylor."

I looked into my mother's eyes, watched the tears roll down her cheek. I stroked her face gently as she watched me. She knew I was having as much of an internal struggle as her own final fight to stay alive. I tried to find it within me. I tried to find those simple words, the language to say it, but the syllables couldn't find their way to my mouth.

She tried to keep her eyes open, but her eyelids fell. Her breathing stopped. I felt a horrible panic rise inside me. I went to the door and called for a doctor. Frank and my father rushed back into the room. Wade followed. The doctor arrived and told Wade to leave. He slipped outside as the doctor checked her pulse, placed a hand respirator over her mouth, and began to pump air into her lungs. Frank and my father hovered tensely. A crash cart arrived and an intern prepared two paddles. The doctor looked straight at me. "The cancer has done a lot of damage. She's been on a heavy dosage of painkillers. Even if we bring her back, I don't think she can last much longer, but I can try if you want me to."

"If you try to revive her, does that mean she'll suffer more pain?" I asked.

"I don't know."

I looked at my father, who had his head bowed over her. He glanced up at me, then spoke. "She asked that we do whatever we could so she could hold on until you came. That's all she wanted. We need to let her go now. That was her wish."

The doctor stopped compressing the resuscitator. He motioned the intern away, out of the room.

As I stared in disbelief at my father and at Frank, I couldn't believe I had failed to say those few words. I was overcome by an ache so powerful that I felt nothing short of total paralysis. I was angry at myself now for not saying what should have been said, even if it was a lie. Why couldn't I say it? Why couldn't I forgive her?

Now that she was gone, I felt an intense loneliness and realized I had never learned to understand my mother, never learned to love her, despite the damage she had caused. Worst of all, I had never forgiven her. Just as I couldn't forgive myself for Laura's death.

I walked out of that room and found Wade looking at me. "She's gone."

"Did you say goodbye?" he asked, a simple childish question, a logical one.

"I tried," I said.

In my mind I pretended I had a duty that was more important than staying with my grieving father. I pushed all of my own pain, regret, and anger into a secret place in my mind, then rolled a rock in front of that dark cave. It was a skill I had learned as a child and, even now, it served me well. I wouldn't forgive, I wouldn't continue to chastise myself for my inaction, and I wouldn't even allow myself to grieve at that moment.

"You're not crying," Wade said. "You should be crying."

"I can't," I said.

TWENTY-NINE

I waited with Wade until my father was ready to go. When he strode out of the hospital room, I put my arm around him and walked him to my rental car. Frank followed. I knew he was hurting as bad as my father, but I didn't quite know how to offer comfort to both men.

Wade didn't turn on the radio. He suddenly seemed much wiser and older than his years. If the death of his seawater friend had sent him running off blindly in adolescent escape, the death of my mother had taught him a kind of mature grace. But no one spoke a word on the drive back to our little fishing village.

We pulled into the driveway of the home where I had grown up, the headlights flashing on the boat sitting in the cradle in the front yard, the now-faded FOR SALE sign on it. I pulled up near the back door and stopped the car. "I'll walk home," Wade said.

"I'd like to walk with you if you don't mind," I told him.

"Sure."

We got out of the car and waited until my father had opened the back door and turned on the inside light. Both he and Frank moved as if they were underwater. It was a sad, slow-motion mime of the agony of loss, of the depressing, overbearing punishment of surviving. From outside in the darkness we looked through the window as if watching a television screen from a distance. This night had us tuned to the Death Channel. My father went across the kitchen, took down a metal teapot from a shelf, walked back, and filled it at the sink. Zombie-like, he made his way to the stove and placed it on a familiar spot. All the while Frank stood by, bent over, hands clasped near his face almost as if in prayer while he regarded my father. He had become stone.

Wade had learned patience in the past two hours. It was probably a skill he didn't even know he was capable of. Here he was, standing in the silent darkness with me, seeing me drown in the visual sorrow before us in the kitchen light.

"I don't know what to say to them," I told Wade.

"Words don't always work, anyway."

It was a profound thought. Truth. "I didn't know what to say to my mother, either. Do you think she understood I was trying to forgive her? That I really did love her?"

"Mothers understand things."

We walked back down the driveway and up the gravel road to the house Jillian was renting, then went through the gate and up onto the small porch. The door was unlocked. I knew I probably wasn't wanted here, but I needed desperately to talk to Jillian. I knew my duty was to be with my father, but I wanted to be with Jillian for selfish reasons. I needed the comfort of a woman. And even though I doubted she would even talk to me, I was here, anyway.

Wade walked in first. I hung back and let the screen door slap shut. Janis was startled and barked loudly. "I'm home," Wade said.

Jillian rushed into the room and hugged her son. "I thought I'd lost you."

The dog barked again, at me this time. Her failing vision allowed her to see there was a stranger standing outside the door. She sniffed the air warily and let out a second mournful howl. Jillian looked up at me through the screen. Wade whispered something to her. She ran her hand through Wade's hair in a gentle, consoling way, then let go of him. "Come in, Taylor."

I tugged open the flimsy door and bent over first to let Janis sniff my fingers. She wagged her tail. Good omen. I petted her gently on the head. "I don't know what to do," I said.

"I hated Philadelphia, Mom," Wade said. "I didn't like the way Dad talked about you. Everything was so weird there. I had to come back. Taylor had to lie to get me into Canada."

"I'm good at covering up the truth," I said.

"I'm sorry about your mother," Jillian said. "If you weren't trying to help us, you'd have been here, able to spend more time with her."

"That was my decision."

"I'm just glad you brought Wade back. When Thomas finds out, he'll probably have the CIA here."

"You really know how to pick your men," I said, then turned to Wade. "No offence."

"My father's good at his job and he knows how to shop for electronic stuff. And he's okay if he wants to be."

"Everything's going to be real difficult, isn't it, once we get going on this legal war?" Jillian asked me.

"Yeah. But I can help out with the finances. And we're in Canada. I don't think he can just have his way."

"It should be up to me where I want to live," Wade said. "And I want to stay here. I know that now. I'm gonna get ready for bed. I'm really tired." Wade hugged his mother again, then left us alone in the room.

Jillian glanced at me before looking away, puzzled. "I don't know what to think about you, Taylor."

"I'm bad news. You stay clear. Your instincts are good."

"Then why are you still standing there?"

"I don't want to go home and be around the past. I'm also afraid I might start blaming my father for not going after my mother when she left for Ontario. I keep blaming myself for a lot of things, but I've got all this anger inside and I want to blame someone else. I put it all onto her for all these years. Now she comes back and turns out not to be the enemy. I don't know who it is."

"Maybe there is no enemy."

"No," I said. "I can feel it in my bones. Somebody or something is punishing me and I deserve it. But I want to fight back anyway." Inside, I was a Molotov cocktail of hurt and guilt and anger, ready to explode. I wanted desperately to get close to Jillian at that moment and yet I was saying all the wrong things. I could tell she looked a little frightened. For good reason. She understood the rage of men.

"I'm scaring you, aren't I? Maybe I should go."

"Stay," she said. "Stay as long as you like."

Despite her misgivings, Jillian had allowed herself to be vulnerable. She felt something for me. Maybe it was only pity, but it was akin to compassion. It was an unselfish, uncompromising welcome. And it allowed me to let loose the floodgates. I sank to the floor, sat there, and rubbed my hand on the back of the old dog. I scratched Janis behind the ears and petted her mangy flanks until she put her head on my knee and looked up at me with those endearing opaque, cataract-laden eyes. I cried as I had never cried before, and the hot, salty tears fell onto the dog who didn't mind at all.

Jillian sat on the floor beside me and stroked my neck as if I, too, were an old homely house pet. After a while we got up and sat at the kitchen table in a small pool of light.

I wasn't prepared for what Jillian said next. "I think I'll have the courage to fight Thomas if you'll stick by me."

"Me? I'll be a millstone around your neck. He'll say I kidnapped your son. He'll say we're having an affair. He'll use me against you in every way he can."

"I don't care."

"It's probably not a good move."

Jillian brushed her hair out of her eyes. I realized it had grown since she'd moved here. She was changing ever so slightly in some barely definable way. I was grateful for her comfort tonight, allowing me to break down like that without judging me. But what she was saying confused me.

"I've been pushing people away for a few years now. I'm going to change that. I liked you from the start, but I didn't trust you, so I pushed you away. That was my style. Armed and dangerous at all times against villains, do-gooders, and emotional intruders. Now that I have Wade back, I realize I can't keep living like that. I want you around as part of our lives."

"Jillian, I'm not ready."

"Shssh. You're not listening. I didn't say I wanted to marry you. I'm not even sure what kind of relationship I want with you. I just want us to have some time together and see. I won't push you away again."

"I don't know."

"You keep saying that."

I studied the pattern of the oak table surface. Jillian was building bridges and all I could think of was tearing them down. It didn't make sense.

"Look," she continued, "you taught me a big lesson. You took a big chance by getting involved with me and Wade. You got involved up to your neck and you didn't seem to care if we kicked you in the teeth. You, Taylor Colby, were the first person to intrude into our lives since we left the States. And that was a good thing. I can see that now. You taught me that if I'm going to live, if I'm going to do more than survive, I'm going to have to take a few chances. I feel stronger again for the first time in a long while. You did that for me."

She leaned across the table and pulled me toward her, then kissed me. I wanted to give in to the moment, to luxuriate in the feminine softness of her lips. She was saying she was willing to let herself fall in love with me. But I wasn't nearly as brave as she made me out to be. In my world love required pain. It was a vindictive equation that I didn't want to relive.

As Jillian pulled away from me, I could see she was aware of my reluctance. "I guess I haven't really kissed anybody for a long time," I said.

"It'll come back with practice." Jillian smiled softly, reassuringly, and I knew then that I wanted to fall in love with her. I just wasn't sure I was capable of it.

That was when I noticed an eerie glow coming from the south window of her kitchen. I got up and looked out toward my father's house. Flames were shooting high into the sky. "Oh, my God!"

I raced out the door and heard it flap shut behind me as I ran as hard as I could down the dark street on this horrible night. By the time I cleared the final stand of spruce trees and got a clear view, I saw an intense, raging pyre. The *Helen VI* had been torched, and there was a great tower of flame piercing like a knife into the night sky. Neighbours were starting to come out of their houses and run toward us as I circled the flames, searching for my father. He stood fixated and mute with a can of gasoline in his hand, looking dreamily into the fire that made him glow as if with an inner light. A single river of tears ran down his cheek. Frank was at his side and spoke first. "I told him this wasn't necessary."

"Dad?"

He glanced at me. "No. It was necessary. It's over now. It's all over. The hopes and possibilities. That's all through."

Somebody yelled, "Call for help!"

"No!" I screamed back into the darkness. They'd never get here in time to do any good. And, besides, we wanted to watch her burn—my father and I. To hell with what anybody thought. We were going to be the crazy Colbys from here on out if we damn well wanted to be. Crazy as a bag full of hammers, as we used to say.

My father had poured the gasoline and lit the match to a beautiful spanking new thirty-foot Cape Islander boat, a grand seagoing vessel that no one wanted, that would never fish, never slap bow against harbour wave, never head out to sea or return after a good day on the water. He had lit a match to several hundred hours of his own skilled labour. The tears still stained his face, but he was smiling.

"Listen to her sing," he said. And we listened to the crackle and hiss, the great consuming concussion of the boat burning its pine and spruce boards to ash. The glass windows popped, and splinters of glass fell onto the burning boards with the sound of icicles broken from winter eaves troughs. My father and I both stared into the heart of the blaze and found it satisfying, pure, luxurious. The heat was like sunburn upon our faces, and I understood well my father's need to do this nihilistic act. There was something spiritual in a fire, something magnetic in the visual power of a flame.

My father was the most unlikely of arsonists, a man who lovingly created from wood, never wasted a plank or a scrap, never performed an impractical deed in his life. A man who held in check his emotions while his family fell apart. I knew why he burned the boat and I respected his right to curse the atrocities of our life in this brilliant, silent way. I looked deep into the cabin of the boat, engulfed as it was, and thought I could see men—the crew that would never take her to sea. I think my father saw them, as well. There, in the roaring heart of the flame, were shadows and form, compressed energy and time, alternate worlds of what might have been or should have been or what would never be. The fire consumed in fanatical avarice and allowed a few brief moments of spectacular glory and even hope on a dreamy dark night. And then it was gone.

I saw Jillian and Wade standing with the other neighbours and they, too, stared into the flame. She went quickly, the *Helen VI*. Grey-black ash drifted into the night sky, and the boldness of the visionary flame blotted out the Milky Way, diminishing the needle points of light for a while until the fire began to die and the stars were given back the keys to the evening sky.

A fire truck finally did arrive, but Frank spoke with the men aboard and they hovered at a distance, polite enough not to intrude upon the grief of father and son. We all stood silently and let the flames subside on their own. There was no wind to spread the danger. Soon all that was left was a deep red glow of embers, a charred carcass, a warped metal drive shaft with a prop, and the red-hot molten engine block looking like a fierce red devil.

As I walked my father back into the house, I heard the firemen start up the truck and pour water on what remained in our yard. Afterward, they left without a word. Everyone headed home. The night grew quiet again, and I could hear a loon calling from the harbour. My father remained silent in his troubles. I said nothing.

"That was a sad thing," Frank said to me after my father had gone to his room alone. "I don't understand why he would do a thing like that, but I know we're all going to miss her. She was one of a kind. A wonderful woman."

"Did she talk about me much, Frank, while you two were together?"

"All the time. She told me stories about you as a little boy. She told me stories about what she imagined your life was like in California. She kept meaning to find a way to patch things up between you, but she was so afraid she'd do the wrong thing and make everything worse. I didn't know how to help. Maybe I should have encouraged her. But the truth is, I was always afraid of losing her, too. I told her to stop worrying about the past and live her life. But maybe I was being selfish. I'm sorry if I was helping to keep you apart, I know that now." Frank seemed more bent over than ever. The weight of the grief was a physical reality in his case. He looked ancient, tired, all energy drained from him.

"It's okay. You were a good husband."

"Did she say that to you?"

"She said that and I know it was true. Good night." I turned off the overhead light and left Frank sitting on the edge of the sofa in his pajamas, bent over, a mere ghost of a man.

I slid between the sheets in my old bed, in my old bedroom. As I drifted slowly toward unconsciousness, I was a boy again, a very tired little boy who had spent a summer day with Laura poking along the edges of the harbour—hiking, swimming, lingering, living. I was a boy who watched a flying heron and became that heron as it flew. I was a boy who swam, twinned with a girl charged with the spirit of the sea. We swam beneath the surface of the sun-and-cloud-dappled harbour through long arms of kelp and scanned the bottom of a kingdom of seaweed, sea urchins, long-legged crabs, and even starfish.

As I slipped off to sleep, I dreamed we had no need to surface but could stay down there for as long as we wished. We could linger in the sweet silent clear world of the sea, bright with life, vibrant with discovery at every instant. It was Laura I was swimming with and she was my guide, always a few feet ahead, me always grinning and swimming and trying to catch up but never tiring, never wanting to go back up for air as we swam deeper and farther from shore into waters that felt warm and friendly. It was as if she were leading me to a place far off, an exotic, distant kingdom, an underwater world that was safe and beautiful. A child's paradise where time stood still and all things were possible.

THIRTY

My mother had asked to be cremated, and so it was. There would be no official funeral in a church or a funeral home. The death of my mother mysteriously brought on full-fledged summer—a truly hot, cloudless string of summer days—to Nickerson Harbour on the forgotten Eastern Shore of Nova Scotia. Here on the north Atlantic coast we were blessed with the rivalry of the Gulf Stream clashing with the cold arctic flow of waters incessantly pouring down from farther north. As the ice caps melted in the relentless warming of the globe, the scientists said, the waters around Nova Scotia actually got colder year by year as the polar waters surged southward.

But the death of my mother was more potent than global warming and the rivers within the ocean that air-conditioned these shores. Her death had seemingly made the winds cease and the land heat up. Plants wilted, the gravel road was as dusty dry as a West Texas town, and gardens began to desiccate during the long summer days of sunlight.

Back when I was young, it always seemed as if something terrible accompanied the rare days of hot weather. Guns would go off or someone would lose a finger to a hungry chain saw while cutting firewood in his backyard. German shepherd dogs got into bloody territorial fights with each other and owners would get bitten badly as they pulled them apart. Grass fires were set by boys playing with matches. Cars crashed into power poles. It was as if people on the Eastern Shore didn't know how to handle heat. We were a people of fog and coldness and, while we didn't always love it, we adapted poorly to the weather that was the summer staple of most of the continent.

I prayed for rain the morning I woke to say my final goodbye to my mother. But the heavens wouldn't cooperate. Instead, the sun poured into my room. I awoke early and walked to the kitchen table. The urn containing her ashes sat on the table in the sunlight. The grief, the hurt and pain, of a child, had evolved slowly day by day into something else that became the fabric of life, but the regret of the boy who had missed his only opportunity for true reunion with his mother was a disease as potent as a lingering cancer. I had failed her this one simple request. Now she was ash.

An hour later my father and I were lifting a brand spanking new dory out of the shed and setting it in the back of the pickup. The three of us drove to the harbour that morning. Frank sat in the middle, the two Colby men on either side. No announcement had been made, no phone calls placed to anyone, but when we arrived at the wharf, nine o'clock that Thursday on a hot, dry summer morning, almost everyone from the village was there on the wharf or along the shorelines.

Breathing heavily and sweating at the brow, my father backed the boat down to the stony shoreline and set the parking brake. The water was like glass. The surface seemed solid. I half expected to be able to walk on it. As Frank held the urn, we gingerly lifted the new dory and set it in the shallows. No one spoke, a gull shrieked, a loon called far off.

My father fitted one oar into the oarlock and then a second. There had always been something magic and exquisite about a new dory, especially one being lowered into these waters for the first time. It was a consecration. A small seagoing vessel, shaped by human hands, was a thing of wonder: solid, immaculate, precise, and balanced.

I motioned for Frank to get into the front of the boat, but he shook his head and handed me the remains of my mother. "I've already said goodbye to her. Now it's your turn."

My father stepped in and seated himself in the centre of the boat, facing backward. He gripped the oars and allowed them to pierce the shallow water. I sat in the stern, facing my father as Frank, with some difficulty, pushed us from the shore and out into the harbour.

I watched the muscles in my father's arms tense as he pulled us out into the harbour. I watched his grim face, a man set upon a task. He wouldn't look me in the eye, but past me as a rower would, eyes fixed on a stationary point ashore that allowed him to row in a straight line with his back toward his future. We slid quietly past the people on the wharf. Jim Dan held his wife, Sheila. He nodded, cocking his head slightly sideways to me, an almost imperceptible but poignant statement invented by Cape Bretoners and brought to the mainland, an understated declaration of empathy with anyone who had been made a fool of or wronged or suffered in trivial or consequential ways. I'd seen it a thousand times before used by fishermen and miners and other country people around the province. "I know what it's like," it said. But to me it meant that Jim Dan had allowed me back into the human race. He wouldn't hold me responsible for the death of his daughter anymore.

Vance Beaudreau was there, and Kyley and Lydia, the old woman who had once given comfort to Laura and me on the farther shore. She must have been ninety or more. Old Milt Boyle was present, too, as was Max Snell. There were men whose names I'd forgotten, women who had once been young and were now old. Everyone had simply known we would do this. We had never once mentioned it to anyone. They just knew. Where and when and why. And they came out to pay their respects, thirty or so Nickerson Harbour souls who were kin to grief.

As we drifted past the end of the wharf, there stood Jillian and Wade, set off from the rest of the observers. Wade waved and I smiled at him. Then, as I looked up at his mother, I was suddenly stricken by her beauty. In the morning sun she looked like an angel.

All of the hard edges I had seen in her had been worn away, softened. I tried hard to stay focused on her face, but the sunlight was in my eyes. I saw her forming words with her mouth, but I couldn't hear them or lip-read their meaning.

And then we were past the end of the wharf, out in the deep, clear waters, rocks and kelp below, a gentle current, a nearly full tide that had just accomplished its daily chore of satisfying the tug of earth and moon. The basin had filled to the brim and had begun to pour itself back out into the sea. This task had been repeated over and over for a million years without complaint. And upon the back of the tide we drifted, my father stirring the waters with his oars, his breathing heavy in the still morning air.

We were well away from the wharf, and far enough from the watchers on the shore that we could talk without audience. No one would hear anything we said. I closed my eyes and felt the soothing sensation of simply floating in my father's boat. He feathered the oars, but it didn't take much to keep us in one spot.

"God, I'm going to miss her," my father said.

"Me, too," I said. "Although I'm not sure I ever really knew who she was."

"I knew who she was. I should have planned things differently, so they would have worked out. I blame myself for not being able to keep her happy."

"It wasn't that."

"So much I didn't understand, Taylor. I guess I didn't try hard enough."

"Things turned out the way they had to, I guess. I'm glad she came back to us."

"I want to be able to say that, too, but I'm not sure I can right now. It hurt the first time pretty bad. Now we go through it all over again."

"I know," I said. "And it hurts worse than the first time."

"She loved you, Taylor. She always did."

"She had a funny way of showing it."

"She came back here because she didn't want to die without being forgiven for what she did. I told her I still loved her. I'd forgive her for anything."

I sat mute.

"She needed to hear it from you, too, son. That's why I'm so glad you came right back from Philadelphia."

"I got back as soon as I heard."

"I think she held on just to wait for you. She was in pain but said it didn't matter. After a while I don't think the painkiller stuff was working."

"She didn't seem like she was drugged. She seemed very alert right to the end."

My father continued to stir the waters, examining me now as I peered into the depths. I didn't realize it at first, but I was hugging the urn tightly to my chest. "You did say it, didn't you? You told her you'd forgive her?" my father asked me.

I didn't want to have to answer, but it was a small boat. There was no place to hide. "No," I said, "I couldn't."

Horace Colby lowered his head, closed his eyes, and shook his head. "Jesus, Taylor, she wasn't asking for much."

I hugged the urn tighter.

"Do it now," he said.

"It doesn't matter now."

"It does, damn it. It matters." He was almost shouting at me, his neck thrust forward, his eyes burning holes into me.

"She's dead. It's too late."

"It's not too late," he said. "What? You think you just die and that's the end of a thing, the end of a human being? It's not that simple. Something continues. I don't exactly know what it is. But it's still there. It's still real." He let go of an oar and reached forward to touch me. I was shaking. "We were never what you call a model family, but inside each of us we were still together. And we still are. Helen's gonna be with me for the rest of my days."

A small window opened up to let light into my internal darkness. My father, a man who was rarely good with words, had just said something that cut through the iron curtain of my grief, confusion, and despair. My mother had returned, and although I had only briefly begun to get to know her again, I had grown to realize she wasn't the witch I had made her out to be. I had stopped hating her at least. She had freed me of that. I had almost begun to blame my father for letting her slip away, but she had weaned me of that evil thought, as well. In the deep, dark pit that was my own consciousness, there were so many demons that I hadn't fully recognized when one vacated the premises.

My mother had returned to Nickerson Harbour to relieve me of one curse and all she wanted me to do was mouth the words. And I hadn't.

"Do it now. It'll still mean something. She'll know."

The current had subtly begun to increase. My father had stopped holding us in one place and allowed us to drift seaward gently beneath the bold morning sun. I looked up and around. Everything seemed impossibly beautiful. For this one brief shining moment upon the harbour in my father's boat, I had been reunited with father and mother in a way I had believed inconceivable.

I lifted the lid from the urn and sifted the ashes with great care out onto the cool, dark waters. "I forgive you," I said. "I want you to always be with me. Please?"

My father watched me as my eyes welled up and my vision blurred. I wiped a sleeve across my face and, when I looked up, a heron had lifted from the shallows along the shore at Scarcity Brook. It flew directly above us, its wings carving the most beautiful percussive sound I had ever heard.

I set the urn gently into the bottom of the boat and heard the song of my father's oars dipping without splashing into the harbour water. "It's so peaceful out here," he said. "Do you remember we used to come out like this on a summer morning, the three of us?"

"Yes," I said. "I do." And it wasn't only the memory of a single summer morning in a dory that came back to me, but a flood of a thousand childhood moments. Happy moments. Good times with a loving mother and father. And I knew this was my mother's final gift to me. Having forgiven her, I had finally brought her back into my life.

THIRTY-ONE

We drifted in the sunlight for several minutes on the calm waters of the harbour. The empty urn sat on the wooden floor of the dory. My father had frozen into a hunched statue, and I dared not attempt to find meaning in the expression on his face. Without moving from my seat I gently took the oars out of his hands and leaned far forward so I could row. He looked into my eyes then, and I saw the face of someone helpless and confused. It was as if he didn't know who I was or where he was. It was the exact same look I had seen in the mirror of my California home after Laura left me. I had observed it only once and then smashed the glass from every mirror in the place.

I angled in toward shore and found a languid back current. It took very little effort to coax the boat along the rocky coast lined with tall, dignified trees. Hanging from the branches of the spruce trees and the few brazen maples was the delicate, jewel-like grey-green fungus we called old man's beard.

Close to the water's edge I could see plants that were so familiar to me as a child: glasswort and orach, both edible and delicious, salty to the taste. The taste of wildness, the taste of life and summer and childhood. The taste of Laura in my mouth. I could also see beach peas growing through the sandy and rock-strewn shoreline, and sea rocket and sea oats with tiny sparrows clinging to the shafts, bending the plants to the ground.

A fish jumped near us and caught a low-flying insect. A lone otter slid from the bank and silently swam toward us before dipping his head and diving beneath. Every living thing around us was profound and holy. I had grown up in this world of solemn beauty and for years now hadn't really registered how much I missed these simple pleasures of wild beauty. I envied the boy who had grown up as a wanderer along these shores, envied him for his innocence, for his companionship, for his pureness of spirit, and for his ability to absorb everything of the coastal life through his eyes and his ears and his skin. He had absorbed it through his pores, as well, until it had become who he was. We were drifting back toward the wharf, back toward community, civilization, back to a world we had to return to, the life ashore.

My mother had somehow given me these few graceful moments. It was her parting gift, but I didn't believe it was her final gift to me.

I leaned forward again and touched my father's knees with the oar handles. He didn't look up at me, but his hands moved, almost of their own accord, gently grasping each oar as I released control of the boat to him. He took a deep, cleansing breath and began to row. It seemed to be much harder for him now to tug the boat along and to keep it straight and steady. My father was a much older man on the return voyage than he had been on the way out.

Jillian and Wade were still standing at the end of the wharf when we returned. Everyone else had remained on the wharf or along the shoreline while we were afloat. They stood in silent vigil. These were my people, I tried to convince myself. They knew this place as I knew it. But it didn't ring true. There was still a hollowness to it. I knew they were kind, some of them, and I was grateful for their compassion in attending the unannounced funeral. But I was certain I was different from them. Even big Jim Dan still cradling his wife in his arms would never fully understand who I was and what I carried within me. I could never say to him all the things I wanted to about the love I had for his daughter.

I heard the car first, then I saw it. Paul Mascarene was pulling up near the end of the wharf. He looked straight at me, and I studied him as he opened the car door, awkwardly stepped out, and leaned against the fender. A single, empty beer bottle rolled off the car seat and down the stones toward the harbour. I was sure he had arrived, late as he was, purely for the entertainment value.

My father's oar strokes seemed more difficult as we passed beneath the people of Nickerson Harbour and beached the dory. Frank was there on the shore to drag the boat up onto the sand, then steadied it as we got out. He helped my father out of the boat, and I wondered what everyone made of this: two old men who had been married to the same Nickerson Harbour woman. Something to talk about for years. There was a story there. A curiosity. My father, always strong, tall, and not so bad-looking, rugged, they'd say, and a man of great character and integrity, the best of the best of boat builders on this shore, a craftsmen who earned more than his keep. But also a poor sod who'd lost one of the most sought-after women of this town to a shoe salesmen from Scarborough. Who knew what Frank had been as a young man, but he had certainly never been a looker. Here he was, a stub of a male, round-bellied paunch, bald, with a large nose and skin sagging from his face. How could she have left one for the other? How they would talk about this.

Frank and my father headed on to the truck. I waved them away. I needed to hang back. My father drove off slowly as people filed past me and I smiled. Jim Dan touched me on the shoulder and gave me the Cape Breton nod again. *Tough one. Life does that to you. Nothing for it but to hang in there. Wait for the next disaster.* Laura's mother tried to look at me but quickly hid her face in her handkerchief.

I could feel Paul Mascarene behind where I stood. He hadn't moved from his post beside his car. Jillian and Wade were the last in the solemn procession off the wharf. Wade was picking up rocks and casting an evil look at Paul. But his mother had an arm around him.

"C'mon, I'll walk you home," Jillian said to me.

"Not yet. You go."

"Are you all right?"

"I'm okay. I'll come over later. I just want to stay here for a while."

Jillian gave me a hug and kissed me on the cheek. Wade looked a little uncomfortable, but he gave me a thumbs-up as he walked away.

Everyone had left except for Paul. I stood silently on the stones, feeling the true heat of the day mounting and stealing the energy from me. I closed my eyes and turned my face up to the sun. It felt like California. It wasn't the cool, sweet Nova Scotia sun that caressed your face. It was an alien hot, heavy-handed southern sun that wanted to scorch, burn, blister, and suck everything out of you like a solar thief.

I heard Paul's footsteps approach. Then he was standing right beside me, but I hadn't opened my eyes and he hadn't spoken. A gull shrieked somewhere far off. I felt the first soothing inflection of sea wind on my face. When I opened my eyes, Nickerson Harbour was still there.

"Never seen anything like it," Paul said matter-of-factly. "When my grandmother died, we had this real boring ceremony in a church. They tried to make me wear a suit and tie. Some old tiresome guy said a bunch of boring shit and then we lowered her into the ground and dumped dirt in the hole. Not you guys. Not the Colbys. No, you do things your own way."

I turned and looked at Paul. "That's the only way we know how to do anything." I couldn't honestly tell if he was trying to be polite, if he thought he was consoling me, or if he was trying to start another fight, still picking at some emotional scab of his own, still feeling cheated out of something in life, something he believed I had savoured while he had been denied.

Paul sniffed the air as a dog would or a fox, checking for prey or predator. "When I read about you in that music magazine, I kept thinking it wasn't fair. I was a better guitar player. I could sing. I never heard you sing a song worth shit. How come you get the big bucks and the lifestyle of the rich and famous and I stay here?"

I laughed. "You're kidding me, right? You think I have it so great?"

"Yeah. You *had* it. You just screwed it up."

"No lie to that. Hey, man, I'd have gladly changed places with you. You should have called me on the phone. I could have told

Laura you were going to do my gigs, take my sessions. Hey, let's move back to Nickerson Harbour. I would have convinced her. And she would have still been alive."

Paul seemed annoyed that I wasn't taking him seriously. "Taylor, old buddy, ever think you been living your whole freaking life in a dream world? Did you ever just wake up and see what the hell was going on around you? Man, you were always so blind."

I decided not to give him the courtesy of agreeing with him. He was pushing toward something I didn't want to hear. I shook my head and started to walk off.

"Like your perfect little romance with Laura," he taunted.

I stopped and turned. "You know, I don't need this. I don't want to talk about Laura with you. Leave me alone, okay?"

"No, I won't. Maybe I'm doing you a favour if I just kind of let you in on something you never knew. Maybe it'll be a little cold water in the face. Wake you up, make you a stronger man."

"What the hell are you talking about?"

"I'm talking about Laura. She was more adventurous than you could see. I'll bet she never told you."

"Told me what?" Ice filled my veins.

"About those times when she'd stay here while you were out on the road with your pissy little band, off to Truro or Moncton or wherever. What do you think she was doing back here? Helping her mom with the laundry? Hell, no, she'd come by to see the Savages playing at the hall in Sheet Harbour. We'd have a few drinks after. Toke a little and fool around. Hey, we even got completely carried away once or twice...well, you know."

I displayed nothing. Beads of sweat evaporated on my neck. I felt the crystallization of salt on the skin, a barely perceptible prickling like the most minute of pins being placed in just the right nerve endings. Acupuncture of the heart.

Paul laughed. "I guess you already knew about that, right? No big deal. No hard feelings? It wasn't anything, anyway. Just good times. That's all any of us wanted back then, right, bro? Music, drink, get a little buzz, have some fun? We missed you guys when you left. Both of you. Too bad about Laura. Guess she didn't know when to stop."

My feet moved and I walked. The reasoning part of my brain told me Paul had been jealous of me for years. This was his idea of fun: getting back at Taylor. *Get him good when he's down. Kick him in the balls and grind 'em good into the ground. Make up anything, anything at all, and toss it in his face.* Paul was from a world with no rules, only action. When the fun ran out, you got revenge on whoever you could for whatever you'd been cheated out of. Old Savages never died; they just got old and cruel. Paul consumed and then threw away. He knew nothing of recycling. He knew nothing of love.

As I walked toward my home, the houses along the road appeared unreal and unfamiliar. The rational part of my brain insisted I had been delivered the news that Laura had been unfaithful, but who was the messenger? Paul Mascarene, who had no principles. He'd lie. He'd say anything. Why should I believe him?

Simply *because* he had no principles. I knew he would have taken advantage of Laura if he could. And I also had to admit that some of what he was suggesting was true. I had always thought of Laura as perfect. I couldn't ever see her flaws and that was why I had let her die. I didn't like to think of Laura as an adventurer, the same Laura who had lured me out onto the ice. I convinced myself Paul was telling the truth. He had told me this to hurt me, to spit on me, to get back at me for my so-called success. But I believed him. And if what he had said was true, what else was there I didn't know about Laura?

What if the truth was this: I had never really known who Laura was? I had loved her, cherished her, taken her away from here, committed my soul to her, and yet there were secrets of her life she had never shared with me. Secrets I had never suspected. Secrets like the escalating drug use that had ultimately killed her. The earth quaked for me just then—much worse than the night it had toppled my California neighbour's house into the canyon. I staggered on. The ground opened, I was swallowed, and I plummeted down, down. But I continued. My feet found their own way to the back steps of my house and I walked in the door.

My father slept for nearly twenty-four hours, and even when he awoke he seemed tired. Frank asked me to drive him to the airport. "I gotta go back now. I got almost nothing to go back to, but I gotta go, anyway."

In the little cafeteria at Halifax International, I bought Frank a coffee. We didn't say much to each other. It had already been said. Just before he went through security Frank leaned over and looked at my feet. "It was size ten, right?"

"Nine and a half."

"Wear the ten. They make the sizes smaller now. I don't know why it is, but you'll find a lot of nine and a halfs don't fit right anymore. You ever do much running?"

All my life, I wanted to say. That was all I ever did was run from things, but I didn't want to lay that one on Frank right now. "Not much. Sometimes, though, I would if I was really restless. In the mornings in the canyon down the road. You had to watch every step because the place was crawling with lizards."

"I'm gonna send you some running shoes. Make you feel like you have wings for feet. I'm gonna go back to the store part-time. I don't care what they pay me. I don't know much, but I know shoes. Footwear. What the heck else am I gonna do?"

"Go to Florida maybe?"

"Sure, like the rest. Go there, sit around, and get old. Not for me. Give me a long, cold winter in Toronto any day. I got a few friends. They think I'm lost down here in the wilds of Nova Scotia. Maybe I can get your father to come up for a visit."

"That'll be the day."

"You never know."

And then Frank was ready to say goodbye. I watched this small, round man with a large soul fumbling to put his keys and his change in the plastic container to go through the X-ray machine. Once past the metal detector gate, he turned, waved to me, smiled an elfin smile, and walked on. Family, I kept thinking. Frank and my father. That was what was left of what I could call my family. I was sad to see him go. I had needed someone to talk to about Laura again. While we were sipping the acidic coffee, I had almost broached the subject with Frank, but we had talked about footwear instead.

It was a long, solitary drive down the Eastern Shore. Back in Nickerson Harbour, my father rattled around in his kitchen, making a big pot of soup or stew or something in between. "Twelve vegetables and three kinds of fish and it still doesn't taste like anything," he said. "I don't know how she did it."

I sat at the kitchen table and did nothing at all. My father looked at me and realized I had put up a barrier again. Words couldn't reach me. He gave up on the soup, left the pot on the oil stove, and went to lie down on the sofa. He would fall asleep again. This was a safe place he could return to when he knew nowhere else to turn.

As for me, sitting at the kitchen table, I had arrived at the very precipice of my dead-end freeway again. I had raced through the darkness, skidded to a stop here at the edge of emptiness, and now stared off into a space that smelled of boiling beans and onions, turnips and garden greens, mackerel, hake, and haddock. So little had changed in my home that I could look around me through the eyes of Taylor Colby at any age I wanted to choose. I could peel the layers off one by one until I was small and helpless and secure.

My father woke an hour later and saw me sitting like that. He got up, walked into my bedroom, and took out the guitar case I had brought north from Philadelphia. "I'd really like it if you'd play something for me."

An A minor chord. A never-ending arpeggio would be appropriate, finger-picked and finely repeated, over and over into infinity.

He opened the case, lifted the guitar, and saw the shattered back. "Holy smokes! It's in bad shape. What happened?"

"Pennsylvania bedpost. A bad moment."

My father puzzled over the shattered wood on the back. "We can fix it."

"It's okay."

"No. I want to fix it."

My father had never worked with musical instruments. "It's not like boats. I don't know much about it, but I think you need special tools, special woods."

"I know about wood. I got tools. I'll improvise. Jeezus, I'd like to hear you play this thing. Hungry yet?"

"I'm hungry," I said. "Let's eat."

THIRTY-TWO

Much of life had remained a mystery to my father. But he did understand wood. I watched in amazement as he used a small, sharp chisel and a razor blade utility knife to remove the back of my smashed guitar with surgeon-like precision. Gently he carved through the wooden support struts and lifted the back off and handed it to me. "I guess the Colby men do have a bit of a temper, after all," he said.

Setting the guitar aside, he went to a far corner of the shop and brought back a shipping crate of some sort. "Mahogany," he said. "It washed in years ago. See how the sides are thin but stiff? I knew I was saving this for something."

He dismantled the crate like a fishermen gutting a cod, removed the rectangular board, and held it up to the light. Flat, smooth, nothing warped. "Once was a tree in the Philippines, is my bet. Imagine wasting good wood like this just to crate something up."

I handed him back the damaged guitar, and he laid it flat on the mahogany and traced the outline. Instead of using a saw, he grabbed a short, stubby, very sharp knife and carved the outline once, then twice, and then a third time. A new guitar back was born.

COLD CLEAR MORNING

My father worked swiftly but carefully, sanding, fitting, refitting, replacing the struts, gluing with carpenter's glue, setting the clamps in place, finicking over a rough edge that didn't look exactly right to him. Maybe Horace Colby, in a previous life, had been a master craftsman of musical instruments in fourteenth-century Italy. Or maybe he was just a man who had been around wood all his life, a man who could design, fashion, or fix a farmhouse, a schooner, or a precision-made acoustic guitar. I saw a pride in the way he worked and knew it was akin to what I felt when I played music, when I performed or worked in a studio and things were going well. It was something we had in our heads, something that came out of us and helped define who we were: Colby men, men with a skill at something.

He said very little while he worked, but he knew I was watching and he enjoyed the appreciative audience. I was again reminded of my own performances. Sometimes, on the road, I cared little for the approval of an audience of ten thousand cheering fans in a stadium or in a concert hall. Other times I felt the thrill of the audience served up by a small group of musicians who understood what I was doing as I caressed the strings of the guitar. But the most important audience of all had always been Laura. Alone with her I had often played acoustic guitar, and invariably the music wasn't of our own time. When we were intimate, alone together, feeling very peaceful, I'd play an old Cape Breton air, a Celtic lament, an Irish ballad, a classical piece of music. At those moments the sound of the strings vibrating in the air in our home in L.A. or our dingy apartment in Vancouver or Portland or wherever it happened to be was something that joined our souls together in some perfect way that went beyond even the intimacies of sex and lovemaking.

The repaired guitar was taken into the house overnight, where it was warmer, for the glues to dry. Padded C clamps held it all in place, reminding me of a human victim of a car accident, say, Paul Mascarene trussed up in mechanical devices to hold his bones in place until they healed. The guitar, braced and clamped, sat on the kitchen table as the sun went down on Nickerson Harbour that night and I fell asleep with California in my head. Unfinished music, unfinished conversations, unfinished everything. As I slept, I dreamed of walking those dry California hills and continually coming across snakes. I dreamed of lizards on the path and desert cactus in bloom on hot, dusty days. I dreamed of Wade and Jillian in a dory parked in the middle of Hollywood Boulevard with traffic flowing around it. I saw the madmen of the streets shouting things at them and tourists turning away from the Chinese Theater to watch as Wade and Jillian drifted off in the tide of traffic toward Pasadena.

I didn't know why I was in California in my dream because I was certain I had no desire to be there. Then, as I dreamed on, I was back in Nickerson Harbour looking at the blessed clear waters flowing out of Scarcity Brook. I glanced up and away and saw mist and the familiar harbour but suddenly realized I wasn't looking at the harbour at all; it was one of Laura's paintings, one of her great misty murals that covered the wall of our "music room" back in California. I turned and saw another wall, another mural, another view of the harbour in different lighting. In my dream I turned again and again and waited for her to appear. I waited for Laura to be there when I turned east or west, north or south. I truly expected to see her, but she wasn't there. I was alone again in that awful place and I felt empty.

Then I heard the sound of a poorly tuned guitar—dissonant notes played one at a time, like a child thumbing an adult instrument he knew nothing about. I opened my eyes.

It was morning. My father was standing alongside my bed, grasping the repaired guitar. He held it in front of him and tried to strum it now, like a bad imitation of a cowboy singer, and smiled broadly.

I lifted myself up. "Let me guess. Hank Snow, right?"

"How'd you know that?"

My father didn't know much about music. He had been a country music fan, and I'd always made fun of him for having such lowly tastes. But Hank Snow had grown up in Nova Scotia. He was a huge success in the American music industry and, by the time Nashville and the record industry had cleaned him up, he didn't have the slightest smell of cod tongues or mackerel oil that would have suggested his origins. Back in Nova Scotia, Hank had always remained a native son, but for the rest of the world he was about as American as you could get, right down to doing a Roy Rogers by stuffing his favourite horse when it died and keeping it in his living room as a reminder.

"You put all the strings back on in the right places," I said, taking the guitar my father was holding out to me, "but I'm not sure you have the tuning down yet."

"I always had a tin ear," he said.

I looked at the back of the guitar. Unfinished wood. But the fit was immaculate. I ran my hand across the smooth, dull mahogany that had once been part of a tree in the tropics and had now been absorbed into this fine musical instrument. I gave the guitar a quick tune-up and felt the sound stir something within me.

"Go on, play something," he said, sounding like a little kid, impatient.

I refused to play anything sad. He wouldn't get anything close to a Scottish dirge from me this morning. I closed my eyes and let my fingers find the strings. I let them decide. Slowly, delicately, they danced through lines of music simple and uplifting. They traced an arpeggio melody from a C chord, then a G, followed by my best friend in all the world, the A minor, then its cousin an E minor, an F that made my hair stand on end, a return to all our musical origins— the C, an F, and a final exalted G. I played it a second time and a third and, with my mind set on heavenly musical cruise control, added a flourish and a variance each time.

It was the simplest of classical tunes, a kind of anthem to spirit and yet a mere exercise in the mechanics of music. It was my rendition of what had originally been "Pachelbel's Canon," although surely he had borrowed those chords from some angel or at least a spy in heaven. My father was transported by the music as far away as I was. As I played the same chords over and over, I remembered the first time I had played this music for Laura. We had been in my father's boat shed and had just made love in the loft. It was a sacred place for us there, and sex had introduced itself into our lives in the most natural and gentlest of ways. We made love, moving gracefully and naturally from kiss to caress to nakedness and physical union, pure unabashed ecstasy, and there had never been pressure or guilt or remorse or any form of coercion.

We had been supremely lucky in ways that few young lovers could have imagined. While it was never discussed, I knew my father was aware we were out there doing what came naturally. I was certain even Jim Dan and Sheila McGillivray knew. The truth was that probably the whole village knew. But we had never heard a negative word, a warning, an admonition, or even a word of caution. In retrospect we often wondered, she and I, how we had learned to live so completely in a world of our own making as if we were outside space and time.

And it had been a summer night. There were stars in the open window. I pointed to Orion and his belt. She traced a finger across the glass, showing me the cosmic bridge of the Milky Way. She loved to hear me play the guitar, and I had a surprise for her.

I had been playing music—guitar music, rock music, and folk— for six years or more. Although it seemed so thoroughly absurd, the truth was I had no idea there was any connection whatsoever between popular contemporary music and classical music. I had heard little classical music in my life but appreciated some of it from a distance—film music, the odd popular arrangement of something by Peter Tchaikovsky or Wolfgang Amadeus Mozart.

But that very day I had walked into my father's shop while he was at lunch and the radio was tuned to the CBC. I heard a piece of music I had never encountered before. I didn't breathe for well over a minute and a half. I stood before a half-finished dory and, as I listened, I discovered it was beautiful and so bloody simple in its basic parts. The "canon" was a repeated sequence of a mere handful of chords. "C, G, A minor, E minor, F, C, F, G," I said out loud. I listened in awe to the entire piece and then heard the Halifax announcer, Jim Bennet, come on the air and state, as if it was no big deal at all, that he had just played "'Pachelbel's Canon,' as performed by the London Philharmonic." I ran straight into the house for my guitar and played those chords. Over and over and over. And that night, after making love with Laura, I invoked the spirit of Pachelbel to celebrate who we were.

I would always be grateful to the CBC for the awakening. Ever afterwards I listened to classical music—Brahms, Mozart, Rimsky-Korsakov,

Haydn, Vivaldi—and I discovered that music was music. It didn't matter what label was put upon it. I learned from every composer, every orchestra. I listened and I reinvented my own music every time I learned a new combination of notes or chords or harmonies.

In the following years, when things went badly for us, I'd play "Pachelbel's Canon" on whatever guitar was handy. Laura, a much finer singer than she ever gave herself credit for, learned to trace the melody with her voice in the darkest nights of our travels. And wherever we found Pachelbel, we found home.

I watched my father prepare breakfast for me—a very large meal, cholesterol-laden, home-cooked, and delicious—as I played for him at the kitchen table. The guitar had a remarkable sound, unlike anything I had ever bought in a store, and I knew it was in the wood, but it had also been imbued with something special that had come from the heart of the craftsman who was my father.

My fingers found many chords and tunes but kept coming back to a folksy pop song I had co-written with a now-dead singer who had risen to heights of public glory in a meteoric rise before burning himself out completely and then disappearing without a trace. The music had been mine, but the lyric was his: "California, love requires repair." Love. Love. Love. How often we songwriters flirted with that word. An encyclopedia could be written on the use and the meaning of love in the popular song. The mere repetition of the word had ultimately sapped it of meaning and power. People *loved* their cars or their VCRs or their guitars more often than they loved someone special to them.

I had long since refused to allow my co-songwriters even to use the word unless it had real meaning, which meant it virtually never appeared after the California song. In the L.A. music scene I had become known as the "Love Cop," and it was a standing joke. But in the music scene out there I had always been an oddball. In a land that cultivated eccentricity, that wasn't a hard rep to live with.

I could say in all human honesty I had loved Laura with all my heart. I still loved my father, for who he had been and who he now was. In the end, the very end, I had even learned to love my mother for who she was. In fits and starts I had observed myself fall in love with Jillian. But it was here that the love cop in me was issuing warrants for my arrest. I was still deeply, painfully, inextricably in love with Laura. I hadn't even begun to let her go. I had been running from her ever since she had died, but I couldn't stop loving that woman.

And now I had a big problem. I had woven myself into the personal lives of Jillian and her son. Wanting to don the garb of good Samaritan and make amends for all the ills brought on the world by the male race, I had wanted to help. And I had been rewarded, after being buffeted away on several occasions, with warmth and compassion from Jillian, a genuine friendship from Wade. But I wasn't prepared to go a step farther. It scared the hell out of me.

THIRTY-THREE

I walked through the morning village, smelled the salt-wet harbour, the damp, rotting kelp and eelgrass wafting up from the shoreline. The sky was clear above, but a low-lying mist hunkered over the tiny town where I had grown up. Everything was dew-soaked. The cedar-shingled walls of houses bloomed with great patches of green and yellow-orange lichen. Spiderwebs, usually invisible but made credible by the weight of the morning wetness, hung from the tall grasses and sea oats. Wild irises bloomed in every dooryard. Not a house in Nickerson Harbour had a yard without a ribald, gangling, head-high bunker of pink wild roses, each bush trying to outdo the next with an explosion of flowers.

Late-blooming lupines—red, blue, white, pink—begged attention from the side yards and ditches. It was a scene that suggested we lived in a tropical world. There was no such thing as winter.

The gate still creaked as I opened it and walked the gravel path up to Jillian's door. I smelled coffee through the open window as I tapped gently with my knuckle on the loose glass pane in the door. Janis Ian barked.

Wade opened the door and smiled. "I was just going for a hike.

You wanna come with me?" he asked, spinning his Phillies cap on his head so that it was backward.

"Can I catch up with you later? I want to talk to your mom."

"Sure. I'm gonna walk out toward the brook."

"Meet you at the rock."

"Got it."

Wade breezed past me and sauntered down the road to the harbour. Janis barked once more, then sniffed my pant leg, wagged her tail, looked up at me with those sad opaque dark eyes, and rolled onto her back. I leaned down and scratched her chest and belly, then patted her behind the ears.

"Wade's happy to be here now," Jillian said. "Thanks to you."

"You hear from Thomas?"

"I heard from Thomas's lawyer."

"A lawyer has to hire another lawyer to do his dirty work?"

Jillian laughed. Whatever was going on, she had a pretty good attitude about it. "Hey, you think a heart specialist is going to do double-bypass surgery on his own heart? Have a little respect for my husband's profession."

"I don't get it. You don't seem upset."

"I've decided I'm going to stop being afraid. You taught me that."

"I did?"

"Yes. You stuck your neck out. I felt as if I've been spending my whole life around people who have been holding back. Afraid to be kind, afraid to get involved. Afraid they might get sued or afraid they might say the wrong thing. Afraid to invest anything emotionally for fear they might get hurt. You were different."

"I have the merit badge for being different. I've got it somewhere in a box under my bed."

"I'd like to see it sometime."

"The merit badge?"

"No. The bed."

I think I almost blushed. "Are you flirting with me in front of your dog?"

She poured me a cup of hot black coffee, and the steam rose in the sunlight above the oak table. "I'm a hard-assed feminist, remember?

I have a doctorate to prove it. Feminists don't flirt."

"Of course, Professor."

I bent over my coffee and tried to absorb the caffeine through my pores. This was all going the wrong way. This wasn't what I had come here for, and it was going to be that much harder to say what I had to say.

"How's your father doing?"

"Okay, I think." I told her about fixing the guitar.

"Father and son. Male bonding."

"We used C-clamps and carpenter's glue. Works every time." If only I could have kept the conversation on that level—the ruse of word games, the Eastern Shore language drill of taking very serious subjects and making understated, quirky offhand remarks.

"But there's something else, right?"

"Yep." I gave my great sigh, the one that said: *Here goes, can't play the games anymore.* "I think I really did forgive my mother. Finally, out on the open the water with my father. He taught me how. I don't know how he did it, but he did and so did she."

Jillian was staring straight at me—dreamy, serious, intent, and caring.

"I guess I thought that once I learned that trick everything else would fall into place. I thought I'd be somehow free of this pain I've been carrying in my chest like a barnacle-encrusted anchor that's been dragging me down all my life. But it hasn't worked that way."

"Laura?"

"Yeah. Laura. I'm finding out there might be all kinds of things about her—more than just the drugs—that I never knew about. I'm afraid if I stop blaming me I'm going to start blaming her. And if I do that, I'm going to be more screwed up than I am now."

"You should let it go. It's all in the past."

I slurped a little coffee that had gone lukewarm. "Good thing you decided to teach about novels instead of psychology."

"I want to help."

I shook my head. "I'm afraid I'll drag you down. You and Wade have enough problems without me."

"I don't see it that way." Jillian reached out and took my hands.

I could feel her determination, her strength, in the way she held them so tightly. "Look, mister, you were the one who came into our lives unannounced. You couldn't take a hint."

"I was always taught you have to help a lady in distress. Didn't know that chivalry had died in the fifteenth century."

"Well, maybe it didn't. Maybe it still works in this century. Hope it survives into the next. Now just take off your armour for a minute and listen."

"Go ahead." I let go of Jillian's hands, folded my arms, and leaned back. I felt like a little boy being lectured.

"Wade thinks you're some kind of hero."

"The boy's not nearly as bright as I thought."

"He's smart all right. And he's got people smarts. He was the one who clued me in. He told *me* to take off my armour. I did and I'm not sorry. You know why, damn it?"

"No, why?"

"Because I discovered I was starting to fall in love with you."

"Please don't do that."

"Shut up and listen. I was starting to fall in love with you and it helped to heal me."

"What are you talking about? I wasn't trying to heal anybody. I can't even heal myself."

"I know. That's the irony. I was a wounded woman and I couldn't heal. I was only getting worse. Closing myself off, afraid of men, afraid of the world. I had run away. And then you came along."

"Me? Well, I think you made a big mistake. *I* made a big mistake."

"No. You didn't. Besides, it's too late."

"What do you mean by that?"

"Wade wants you in our lives. I want you in our lives. We need you."

"Oh, my God," I said, leaning back and pulling my hands down over my face. "I screwed up again. Big-time."

"Cut it out, Taylor. You've got problems. We've got problems big enough to choke an elephant. But we have a chance."

"I'm sorry, Jillian. I've got to go back."

"No, you don't. You're home. Stay here."

I shook my head. "I really do have to go back. I want to fall in love with you, but something keeps stopping me. It's Laura."

"Laura would want you to get on with your life."

"Probably. But I can't. Years ago I ran away from here to find some magical new life with her. We found it and it killed her. I went numb for a few years and then I ran back home, but I've got to go back out there and sort this out. I'm not even *close* to being over her. I'm not healed. Maybe I'll never be right."

Jillian pushed away from the table and looked at me hard. "We'll go with you."

"No. That would be wrong. Thomas will have a hard time getting Wade away from you if you stay in Canada. If you go to California, you'll have no chance at all. Thomas will have L.A. lawyers and private investigators crawling all over the place. You wouldn't stand a chance. Besides, I can't drag you down with me."

Jillian pounded a fist on the table. "Damn you, Taylor. I don't want to lose you."

"What is there to lose?"

"Everything."

"You're better off without me. Everything I touch turns to dust."

"No. You're just afraid, aren't you?"

"Yes, I'm afraid of almost everything. Most of all I'm afraid of you. Afraid of hurting you and Wade, but also afraid of my getting hurt again. What if you change your mind about me after a week or a month? Then what?"

"I'm not going to change my mind."

"How do you know?"

"I know."

"I don't think I can take that risk. Look, I haven't gotten involved with any woman since Laura killed herself. I'm not doing well, but at least I've protected myself from more pain from someone new."

"You have to take a chance. That's what you taught me, Taylor. You took a chance on us. You taught me to take a chance on you."

"I guess I can dish it out, but I can't take it myself."

I stood up. I felt awful. I wanted to stay and live out this fantasy she had going, but there was too much that was unresolved for me. I had to go back to that room where the paintings still hung on the walls.

"Go back to California," Jillian said, looking out the window. "But we'll still be here. I won't give up on you."

I felt a chill go through me. It was one of the most profound things anyone had ever said to me. It was an utter statement of unconditional love. It was exactly the way I had felt about Laura all those years. I had been blind-sided by Paul Mascarene's revelation, but I had never stopped loving Laura even then. I said nothing more.

As I started to leave, she came to me, buried her face in my chest, and put her arms around me tightly. "I love you," she said, although the words were muffled in my shirt. I wanted to echo her, but something stopped me. I couldn't say those same words because the healer couldn't even begin to heal himself.

I found Wade sitting on Grandfather Rock, tossing small pebbles into the water. As I walked toward him, I felt like a criminal. I had misled his mother into thinking I was capable of something I couldn't do. I had duped Wade into thinking I was his friend, maybe his only friend in this weird, insular little harbour town of fishing families with no fish to catch. And now I was going to skip out of his life.

"I miss Cobain," he said, wading ashore. "I keep expecting him to pop up any second, but he doesn't."

"Want to walk all the way out to the mouth of the harbour?"

"Sure. What's there?"

I shrugged. "The sea, waves, sand. Nothing much."

"Let's go."

We walked on the backs of rocks from stone to stone along the low-tide shore, and Wade never slipped once. We stopped now and again to pick up a stranded starfish that had made a bad choice of a place to wait out high tide. The wiser ones were safe and wet in deep crevices between boulders, but less-cautious starfish were huddled between dry stones with no salt water where they had begun to shrivel and die. We stopped often and picked up the improvident ones and placed them gently near their cousins in the deeper pools, then watched as the tiny filaments along their legs wiggled and fretted and their arms curled back into life. That day, I was sure, we robbed the gulls of many fine meals they expected from the ruined lives of starfish.

Wade enjoyed the task immensely. It had its own rhythm, and there was a story or a question for each starfish to whom we gave salvation. "Why do some have five arms and some only four or three?"

"I don't know, " I said.

"What happens to the ones high up along the shore when we're not here to put them back in the water?"

"Some survive. Afterward, their starfish mothers probably say to them, 'Never do that again!' "

"I bet some of them learn for themselves."

"A few. But the mothers still get in the word."

When we reached the mouth of the harbour, we walked silently past the little sandy spit on the harbour edge where we had beached the dory the day Wade had nearly drowned. We continued around the farthest point of land and gazed toward the waves breaking on Roaring Bull shoal. Then we began to clamber beyond the mottled rocks of Stoney Beach and along the wide, sandy shoreline that faced the open sea. The mist had burned off earlier in the morning and now the sky was a brilliant blue. As I gazed out at the waves, I thought of my mother's ashes mingled with the sea, scattered by tides, currents, and winds. I could still see the shadow of the heron in my mind as it had passed over my father and me on that morning.

The wind blew off the land and sculpted the face of the waves. About fifty yards offshore, immaculate, tubing, head-high waves broke hard on the sandbar, peeling perfectly right to left into deeper waters.

"I wonder if anyone has ever tried surfing this place," I said.

Wade laughed. "Too cold. No one would want to be out there."

"I would. If I had a board and a wetsuit... With no crowds, no pollution, this would be a fantastic place to surf."

"It would?"

"Ever try it?"

"No. I saw some guys doing it on the Jersey Shore, but we were only down there for a day."

"You should see the waves in California." I had a crystalline image in my head of surfing with Larry near Malibu or at that "secret spot" up the coast past Santa Barbara. But as I looked at the waves in front of me, I realized they were as good as anything I'd ever surfed in California. "You should try it sometime."

Wade looked a little embarrassed. "I don't think I trust the sea anymore. You can figure out why. I'm not ever going in the ocean again."

"Fear's a good thing, but only in small doses. Like those starfish back there. If they live, they learn a lesson, but it doesn't mean they have to spend the rest of their lives in deep water, does it?"

"No big deal. I can live without swimming in the ocean."

"Look at those waves, Wade. Know what it would feel like to be standing up, cruising across the face of that great wall of water?"

Wade squinted and put his hand over his eyes so he could focus on the amazingly cylindrical waves peeling off the sandbar. "I could never do that."

"That's what I said the first time my buddy Larry took me surfing in California. And I fell off the board a hundred, no, two hundred times until I got it right. I got whacked around by waves hitting me on the head, waves tipping me off my board, then banging me in the ribs with it. I did everything wrong over and over and then, one day, it suddenly clicked. Just when I thought I'd never get the hang of it."

"But this isn't California."

"No," I said. "Water's colder. But wetsuits keep you warm."

"I don't think I could do it."

"You could. I'm sure of it."

Watching the hollow waves building, rising, walling up, then throwing out over the sandbar and smashing into a fine display of billowing white foam, I suddenly realized I was leading Wade the wrong way. I wanted to tell him I was leaving. I wanted to say we would continue to be friends but I would be gone. I wouldn't forget him, but I wouldn't be around. And here I was creating false hope about surfing icy Nova Scotian waves. This was all wrong.

"Those waves are beautiful," he admitted.

"I'm glad you got to see the ocean like this. It's not always heartless and cruel. Maybe if I come back I can teach you to surf."

"I knew you'd leave," he said, admitting no surprise.

"I'm sorry. You're a good friend."

"Why do you have to go back out there?"

"No easy answers. Unfinished business. It's like I was in the middle of playing this long, sad song and I just walked out of the studio in the middle of a verse. No more words. Notes hanging in the air, waiting for the tune to go somewhere. I left a lot of people hanging. They don't even know what happened to me. If my house hasn't slid down the mountain into my neighbour's pool, it's probably been stripped of anything that's not padlocked, but I still have to go back and stare it down."

"You coming back here to Nickerson Harbour?"

"I don't know. I'd like to."

We walked in silence all the way back to the wharf. The tide had reversed itself and risen, so we had to go along the forest trail set back from the edge of the harbour. We came across a porcupine who failed to see us. He sat right in the path, and we gave him a wide berth as we moved around him. In the trees no birds sang. A few black flies attacked us, and bees travelled from one wildflower to the next in the clearings. The forest floor was a great, green, thick, lush carpet of moss, inviting and restful to the eye and the soul. I wanted very much to explain further to Wade, but I knew I would only make things worse.

Before we emerged from the forest back at the wharf, I had already begun to feel homesick for this very place, this forest, these shores, the people of the village. Heartbreakingly homesick for my father, for Jillian, and for this kid who had made himself my best friend. I missed this place terribly already and I hadn't even left yet.

THIRTY-FOUR

California, like a failed test on the meaning of life. California, like a fast flash of gunpowder on the sidewalk. California, like a warbled laugh track twisted in the temperamental time slot just before doom. California, like a hot/cold bullet of mercury in the bloodstream of temperature. California, oh, California, your hot asphalt runway kissing the wheels of Air Canada with a chirp like some demented northern bird. California, I have to settle this with you.

I never took buses, but I decided to take one this time, me and my home-repaired guitar inside its hard-shell case. I transferred a couple of times, got lost, got confused, but ended up in tourist hell on Hollywood Boulevard with nothing in my hand but a guitar and a whole lot of hurt. I was surrounded by the whole family of fools who were my cousins in calamity, people who would never be able to make a life of *is* out of *once was.* Somebody tried to sell me a map to the homes of the stars, but there were none of those left in this part of town except for the polished brass plugs on the sidewalk, each one shaped like a Nickerson Harbour starfish, frozen into the concrete.

Shaking my head at the tourists and the losers, I wondered how

I had ever come to live in a town like this. Of course, when I lived here, I never spent time on this boulevard. I was above all that commercial crap, above everything, safe in the dry desert hills where I played my guitar, loved my wife, made music and love in all the rooms of the house, made money even out of my love and my music, then sat back like a blind demented king and let it all crumble away.

The air was hot, sweltering. An old guy in a heavy coat and no teeth tugged at my sleeve, tried to sell me a framed print of Jesus Christ in the Garden of Gethsemane. The frame was battered and the glass had been busted out. He'd found it in the trash. I reached for my wallet. All I had was Canadian money. I offered him forty bucks Canadian, and he smiled, took it, and handed me Jesus. I glanced at the sorry son of God and felt a twinge of empathy, then handed it back to my new friend. "Keep the money," I said. "Sell it again to someone else. I just needed a hit."

The old guy smiled, genuinely lost, but took Jesus back and parked Gethsemane under his arm. I pointed to the money I had given him and then to the bank across the street. Maybe he could cash it in for American green.

I walked on, uphill to the north, block after block, up and away from the madness but not the heat. I sweated and dripped as I stumbled through the residential neighbourhoods. The guard dogs barked one after the other, and the signs on the majority of lawns warned of criminal prosecution if I dared to take a step onto the property unannounced. I hiked higher and higher into burglar-alarm heaven. Behind many doors I knew that home owners were armed and dangerous. Everyone in the nether world of money and dreams was forced to spend a good part of their income and time trying to hold on to what they had accumulated.

My house, the one I didn't own but leased, was still there. The bushes and flowers in the yard looked dead. Everything died here without nurturing, without watering. It was a long, difficult walk from the road to the front door. I found an old spare key in my wallet, one I'd never used before. It had been Laura's idea. Some night, she said, we'd come home late and blitzed from a party, and we would have lost our keys. Then she would remind me of the spare.

I lifted the key from where it had moulded itself into the leather of my wallet. Then I discovered I didn't need a key. The door was open. The dead bolt had been bashed through the door frame. I walked in and took a deep, agonizing breath. The place was a mess: stuff knocked all over by the house thieves. Not everything had been stolen. Musical gear, electronic stuff—they were predictably gone. TV blessedly gone. Microwaves, food processors, coffee grinders—all gone. Somebody had stolen Laura's clothes but left most of mine behind. I was almost glad that a lot of the unessentials of my life had been removed free of charge. I wouldn't have to pay anyone to haul them away. Stripped down—that would be a better lifestyle. Get monastic, lead a basic existence. No women, no wine. Shaved head and a couple of meaningful words. One way to go.

I went out to the back deck, not wanting to go into the room where I had found Laura. Sitting in the horrible hot summer L.A. sunlight, I let it suck the essence out of me, let it burn its cancers into my face, let it make me sweat toxins through my pores. I was here. Now what?

I closed my eyes and envisioned those great tectonic plates beneath me pushing against each other, silently shoving one half of the earth up against another, getting ready to grind and jam and to hell with whatever fool wanted to plant his home atop the fault.

The injured look on my father's face still haunted me when I couldn't answer his question: why was I coming back to this awful place? I had originally moved here to fill my life with meaningful work, meaningful music. I wanted everything and, as a result, ended up with nothing. I was emptied by this place and would have been better off if I had been left homeless like the guy on the street. Instead, what was left of me was sitting on lawn furniture.

I honestly didn't know why I had come back. It was as if my sub-conscious had already worked out a grand scheme, a thematic purpose to the action, but I hadn't trusted my conscious mind enough to read the blueprint. I wondered, as I roasted in the sunlight, if I had come here to die. The thought didn't scare me in the slightest, but I couldn't see myself having the gumption, the nerve, the intensity of purpose it would require.

Jillian, of course, was right: I couldn't heal myself. And I wouldn't forgive myself, either. However imperfect Laura was, she was forgiven. Whatever she did, I was sure, was never done to hurt me. It was done because of my own inadequacies. My love wasn't strong enough to save her life. I knew for a fact that if I had enacted an escape plan, if I had shunned musical success, she would still be alive. Inevitably that night came back to haunt me.

When the ambulance arrived and the emergency crew saw me holding a woman, I was asked to let go and stand back. But I couldn't do it. They had to pull my arms from around Laura. But then, a quick assessment told them she was long gone. They said nothing to me. But as they prepared to take Laura from my home, they phoned the police.

Death didn't startle the men in uniform who arrived. It was their trade. They took me to police headquarters. I was questioned, harassed even, in a formal yet insidious way, but it was all very routine. Even as I answered their questions, I felt the true me huddled far away from the scene, deep inside myself in a safe, numb, lifeless place. When it was established I was nowhere around when Laura overdosed and died, they seemed satisfied. But it would have been more satisfying had they charged me with negligence causing death. Or outright murder. Instead, I was dropped off back at that house. I was sentenced to live without Laura.

The sun had had its way with me. I retreated indoors. As I walked through the house, I noticed now that things were tossed about on the floors, but the house hadn't really been trashed. Furniture was jumbled about but nothing had really been broken. I lifted my guitar from its case. It was my only crutch, the only ally I could muster for my journey. I walked on into the one room I had so far avoided— the music room, the place where Laura had died. I sat in the centre on the floor. The looters hadn't taken the art—too big, too easy to identify, impossible to fence. I had been visited by professional thieves working their trade, I surmised, not vandals. The paintings, thank God, were unmolested.

I had only one desire: to bring her back. I wanted as much illusion as I could conjure. I got up and went to the closet in our bedroom.

Near the bottom of a pile of old record albums was a box of cassettes. I found the one marked "Joni, Judy, Joan." Beneath the box was an old beat-up cassette player the thieves had ignored. I took both to the music room and plugged in the player, rewound the tape, and listened to us singing together: "Four Strong Winds," "The Circle Game," "Mist on the Sea." I played along on the guitar my father had repaired. Closing my eyes, we became a trio. Laura then. Me then. Me now.

Between songs I listened to Laura and me laughing and talking on the tape. We were young then; we were utterly alive. Our music together had been nothing less than a holy ceremony.

The tunes were etched in my brain, the ones we borrowed, the ones we had written together—those lyrical, naive ballads about beauty and sadness, about love and loss. I think we were just guessing back then. I think we intuitively knew the deepest meaning of those words, but we weren't singing about our own lives. Now, however, it was as if the lyrics about despair and longing had become concrete objects. And now I became the sole survivor of our songs, the sole owner of those terrifying gifts. As my fingers danced over the chords, I believed our music back then had somehow constructed a template of what I was to become.

The tape ended and I turned it over. The other side was raw electric power chords, drums, dissonant guitar. Ambitious, angry noise. Tracks recorded live with the band from Portland. Loud, intense, but empty. I stopped the cassette player, then remembered taping this crap over top the unedited, nonprofessional "practice sessions" Laura and I had recorded. And I cursed myself yet again.

Outside, a bird was singing. Looking out the window, I spotted a yellow-and-black canary on the sill, a twin to the goldfinches I saw only in the summers in Nova Scotia.

I put my guitar down gently beside me on the rug. Here in this room I had cradled Laura in my arms for the last time. I couldn't let that thought drift far from me.

I hadn't yet looked directly at the four paintings on the walls, but I knew now they had something to do with my return. Soon after Laura's death I had searched through every nook and cranny of the house, believing that somewhere Laura had left me a note, a letter, a final message. I found nothing. She hadn't planned her death and there was no suicide note, no other private epistle that would satisfy me in some impossible way. But as I listened to the voice of the canary, I realized the message was here before me in the paintings.

The images had baffled our houseguests. The art seemed unfocused, abstract, certainly not realistic or representational. But I knew each painting to be a scene of Nickerson Harbour. I could look into the pale blue-white maze of the winter painting and see the two of us out on the ice. I knew precisely where to focus my eyes to see me leading Laura by the hand across a frozen plane of snow, while saltwater waves lapped against the ice nearby.

I saw the next scene of spring—greys and greens and soft edges to old buildings weathered into holistic reunion with the living things of the world. There were ghostlike images of people, but none of them were distinct. Most houseguests who had seen this one thought it had an eerie sensation, but I had always felt comforted by the serenity of the fog, the overlay of misty air, taking hard edges off all reality. Summer was the green of new shoots from spruce boughs and a backyard with fragments of old boats mouldering in the yard. Spiderwebs with morning dew and a sun made ragged and scintillating by the tops of trees, dark, dark, and vigorously grasping at the sky with cathedral-like spires.

My breathing had steadied and the tightness in my chest diminished. The fist that had been squeezing my heart relented slightly as I turned to face the fourth painting. It had been the last one Laura had created before she had seemingly lost interest in art.

It was a work so understated, so simple and serene and uncluttered, as to make a viewer believe it was the work of a child. Nothing but a tableau of the harbour water's surface. Almost no definition at all. I had always viewed this painting from the same place, sitting in the centre of the room. Now I got up and walked toward the window, then turned to face the painting. I could see thin lines of mist rising from the water now and I could see the surface of the harbour. Not a ripple. I thought for a second I could see *through* the water to the very bottom of the harbour, and then a powerful, disorienting sensation came over me.

I had misjudged the painting entirely. I wasn't looking down at the harbour. I wasn't looking at the water at all. I was looking up at the sky. I was lying on my back in the grasses near Scarcity Brook at the edge of the harbour on a morning in early fall. The sky was cold and clear with wisps of clouds and no wind. I was lying on my back in the grass with my arm around Laura. It was the fall of our fourteenth year. The morning was so exquisite we both told our parents we didn't want to go to school. There was no protest. They understood.

We lay like that for over an hour. Bird sounds, tiny wavelets slapping the shore, the lilt of the brook alongside us. We lay on our backs looking up, far into the sky. That was all we did. It was one of the most wondrous experiences of my life. As I lay beside Laura, I felt myself being drawn into that sky, and together we became free, weightless, indifferent to everything in the world. We were drawn into that sky and wanted never to return to earth.

That was what the painting was about. Laura and me. Time suspended. We lay there looking at the heavens for all eternity. We never spoke. We drifted on together into that sky. She had never told me this was what the painting was about. That was the final message I had been hoping to find. It had been waiting for me here in California. I looked away from the painting now and heard the echo of her voice in my head. Laura at fourteen, saying, "Most people are never this lucky. One perfect day. One perfect time together. Maybe that's enough."

I remembered kissing her and walking back to the wharf after the wind came up and the clouds began to pull in from the northeast. I remembered us both getting an F on an English test we were supposed to have taken. I remembered looking at each other and not having to say it didn't matter at all. I remembered going back to socalled normal life after that while believing we had been changed forever by our time of intimate silence with sea and sky. Probably because it was all so inexpressible, we had never really talked again about it or tried to share it with family or friends. It just *was*.

Walking outside, I peered up into the yellowing haze of the afternoon. I looked off toward the canyon and wondered when it had last rained here. I admitted to myself I didn't mind fog, didn't mind Maritime drizzle. I was plenty tough enough to endure days, even weeks, of Nova Scotian rain. It had been necessary to come back to California, however, to believe fully that there was a place on this planet where I belonged.

I found an airplane boarding pass in my pocket and picked up a pencil that had been left weathering on the deck. I began to make a list. There were things I needed to do. A hell of a lot of things I'd been putting off. I would be on the phone for the rest of the afternoon. The thieves had left one wall-mounted phone in the house. I wanted to talk to all the studios, all the players whose lives I'd walked out of. I expected they had learned to get on without me, that the music industry rolled relentlessly on, hungry for product— good or terrible—to feed the thirsty ears of the public. I was anxious to find out which one of my music associates understood what I had gone through. Which ones cared.

First, I would call Larry. I knew he had been worrying about me. I felt bad that I'd left him high and dry. I would apologize and then talk to him about surfing. I wanted to tell him about the waves I'd seen in Nova Scotia.

I probably needed to pay a few bills, collect my mail from the post office, talk to the landlord. Explain to everyone that it was like waking up after a really long sleep. The ultimate jet-lag recovery. Like flying to China twice in the same day. Only much worse.

How to begin to explain to them? It was like this. When I left California, I had nothing. Now I had something to work with. A painting. A patch of nearly translucent sky. A cold clear morning in October. A personal geography and a few people who really mattered.

Summer in Southern California wouldn't be over until December. Even then warm days lingered through winter. It was reassuring to know that on a shoreline far away, north and east of here, a continent away, the waters were still cold and clean. The sea would conjure up chill winds and plentiful waves. Grey mornings would give way to lucid, still evenings and, just before the water in the ponds began to skim over with ice, just before the first teasing white test of winter snow, there would come a quiet day of sunshine and empty blue sky.

Almost no one would be fully aware of the asylum of that special day, the exquisite beauty in that morning that would forever be tinged with sadness. But the sadness wouldn't diminish what was etched in the sky and in the sea and in the empty spaces between one person and the next. On that farther shore someone would try to articulate what he was feeling and fail to get the words right. But he would keep on trying to formulate the meaning of it as long as there was an audience, no matter how small, who cared enough to stop and listen.

MORE NEW FICTION FROM BEACH HOLME

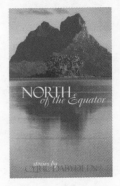

North of the Equator
by Cyril Dabydeen
SHORT FICTION $18.95 CDN $14.95 US ISBN: 0-88878-423-6

Cyril Dabydeen's new collection of stories, *North of the Equator*, looks at the polarities of tropical and temperate places. Acclaimed novelist Sam Selvon (*The Lonely Londoners*) says, "Dabydeen is in the vanguard of contemporary short-story writers, shuttling with equal and consummate skill from rural Guyana to metropolitan Canada." Dabydeen's characters live in limbo, stretched between two worlds: one, an adopted home in Canada; the other, a birthplace in the islands scattered across the equator.

Hail Mary Corner
by Brian Payton
NOVEL $18.95 CDN $14.95 US ISBN: 0-88878-422-8

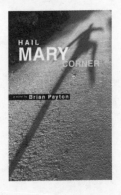

High on a cliff overlooking a pulp mill town in British Columbia, sixteen-year-old Bill MacAvoy and his friends lead cloistered lives when other boys their age run free. It may be the fall of 1982, but inside the walls of their Benedictine seminary they inhabit a medieval society steeped in ritual and discipline—a world where black-robed monks move like shadows between doubt and faith.

Tending the Remnant Damage
by Sheila Peters
SHORT FICTION $18.95 CDN $14.95 US ISBN: 0-88878-417-1

Sheila Peters creates people who often feel out of sync with the spiritual, emotional, and physical environments they find themselves in. Two old people on a farm try to comprehend the inevitable fate befalling them, all the while contemplating the strange goings-on of neighbours. A young woman on the lam from Texas finds herself beached in the Queen Charlottes on her way to Alaska. Their universe is our universe, but with a twist that makes it refreshingly new and decidedly different.

BEACH HOLME PUBLISHING ◆ WWW.BEACHHOLME.BC.CA